EXPLORERS OF THE BLACK BOX

SUSAN ALLPORT

Explorers
of the
Black Box

The Search for the Cellular Basis of Memory

W · W · NORTON & COMPANY · *NEW YORK* · *LONDON*

*The text of this book is composed in Times Roman, with display type set in Typositor
Friz Quadrata. Composition and manufacturing by the Maple-Vail Book Manufacturing Group. Book design by Marjorie J. Flock.*

FIRST EDITION

BURGESS
QP
406
.A63
1986

Library of Congress Cataloging in Publication Data
Allport, Susan.
    Explorers of the black box.

    Includes index.
    1. Memory—Physiological aspects.   2. Neurons.
3. Neurophysiology.   I. Title.
QP406.A63   1986   152.1'2   86–8502

ISBN 0-393-02322-2

W. W. Norton & Company, Inc., 500 Fifth Avenue, New York, N.Y. 10110
W. W. Norton & Company Ltd., 37 Great Russell Street, London WC1B 3NU

1 2 3 4 5 6 7 8 9 0

To David

I sometimes marvel how truth progresses, so difficult is it for one man to convince another, unless his mind is
vacant.

— *Charles Darwin, letter to Alfred Russel Wallace*

I went the other evening to the Zoological Society,
where the speakers were snarling at each other in a manner
anything but like that of gentlemen.

— *Charles Darwin, letter to John Henslow*

Contents

Acknowledgments

I AM VERY GRATEFUL TO the many scientists who gave so generously of their time in helping me write this book. I list them here in alphabetical order: Tom Abrams, Juan Acosta-Urquidi, Daniel Alkon, Lucena Barth, Jim Bower, Jack Byrne, Tom Carew, Vincent Castellucci, Ian Cook, Doug Coulter, Terry Crow, Jack Davis, Kerry Delaney, John Disterhoft, Joseph Farley, Robin Forman, Alan Gelperin, Bob Hawkins, June Harrigan, Graham Hoyle, Jon Jacklet, Irving Kupfermann, Alan Kuzurian, Izja Lederhendler, Rodolpho Llinás, Ken Lukowiak, Joe Neary, Philip Nelson, Paul O'Lague, Chip Quinn, Meryl and Florence Rose, Chris Sahley, Manabu Sakakibara, James Schwartz, Felix Strumwasser, Mutsuyuki Sugimori, Ladislav Tauc, Richard Thompson, Terry Walters, and Andrew Weiner.

I am also grateful to Jamie Schreeve and John Valois of the Marine Biological Laboratory for their many arrangements on my behalf; to Eduardo Macagno and Ronald Hoy, who allowed me to sit in on their course at MBL; to Rimon Faye for the experience of one of his invertebrate collecting trips; and to Ed Donahue for his patient answers to my many questions about NIH. This book has benefited enormously from the unfailing interest and astute suggestions of my editor, Mary Cunnane, and from the close reading of Renee Schwartz. I'd like to thank Mary Carpenter, Sarah Cross, Katy and Kiri Sokoloff, and Mary Ann Smith, who read and commended on the manuscript in various stages of its completion, and Jack Byrne, Daniel Alkon, Harold Pinsker, and Chris Sahley for their comments on selected chapters. This project would have been impossible without the generous and loving assistance of Margaret Rose, of my mother, Jane Allport, and of many other members of my family.

EXPLORERS OF THE BLACK BOX

Prologue

ONE OF THE CENTRAL questions in the study of nervous systems today is how the small number of "brain genes" in an animal's DNA contrive to make a brain, to produce millions or billions of nerve cells connected to one another in a very precise fashion. There can't be a gene for every cell in a nervous system—let alone for every twist of a dendrite or synapse—so the question is how so much diversity and specificity can arise out of so little.

At least part of the answer to this question must lie in the properties of growth cones, specialized structures at the tip of a nerve cell's axon that allow an axon to grow, to sample its environment, and to seek out other nerve cells with which to interact. These growth cones are expanded regions on an axon. They have special, undulating membranes that extend themselves into highly mobile, fingerlike extensions that explore and even taste the environment. They ingest material from the outside and send it up to the cell body of the neuron to be analyzed. When the results come back, the growth cone might be told, "Move ten degrees to the right," or "Do not interact with any axons in this vicinity." Growth cones are also the sites where most of the new material is added to a growing axon, and when an axon branches, it almost always does so by the formation of a new growth cone.

In 1963, a young psychiatrist named Eric Kandel, it can now be said, started a new growth cone along the axon representing the study of the brain when he had the insight to realize that an animal with a very simple nervous system could be used in experiments to address previously unapproachable questions about the cellular basis of such higher brain functions as learning and memory—to explore, as it were, the black box of the mind. Since then, that growth cone has continued to enlarge, to reach out and synapse with other disciplines—molecular biology, biochemistry, neuroanatomy, and psychology—and to absorb from its environment information about the protein channels, second-messenger systems, and so on. Nobody knows exactly where it will go from here, but just as the study of one growth cone on one nerve cell can tell you a lot about how an entire brain is made, the study of one growing field of neurobiology can tell you a lot about the nature of science, much about nerve cells, and at least a little bit about the content of the brains of the scientists who study brains.

ONE

The Sea Hare and the Scientist

A CONVENTION OF neuroscientists is in many ways much like any other convention. There is perhaps a greater percentage of men, certainly more beards, and probably more casual dress—more blue jeans and shorts and fewer suits. But since neuroscientists—those scientists who study the brains of earthworms, humans, and everything in between—take great pleasure in uninterrupted shoptalk, the hall in which a meeting of brain scientists is held, like any room full of people who spend their days pursuing a common goal and engaged in similiar activities, is filled with the very loud, almost mechanical-in-its-constancy hum of many people talking at once.

Like any other group of professionals, neuroscientists have their own jargon. Their conversations are so full of technical terms and familiar words—spikes, fire, drive—to which they have assigned strange new meanings that it's easy to lose sight of the fact that they are about brains—about those tangles of billions of nerve cells that are the seat of all imagining, all emotions, all behavior, all curiosity about the nature of brains. Most of us have spent some time wondering how our brain works. Brain scientists spend their entire lives pondering it, looking for a way even to begin asking the question, How does the brain generate mind? The brain, after all, is so complex an organ and can be approached from so many different directions using so many different techniques and experimental animals that studying it is a little like entering a blizzard, the Casbah, a dense forest. It's easy enough to find a way in—an interesting phenomenon to study—but also very easy to get lost. Many intelligent men and women have gotten lost; they've spent a lifetime accumulating data and constructing theories that may have seemed extremely important in their time but that were soon forgotten, disproved or reinterpreted, swept into the pile of discarded hypotheses and data founded on erroneous assumptions—a pile that in the history of neuroscience is particularly large.

Brain scientists, a Canadian researcher once told me, are like the proverbial group of blind men trying to describe the elephant. The difference between the scientists and the blind men is that the scientists have so much more—entire careers and reputations, decades of their lives—invested in their particular view of the elephant, in their idea of which of the myriad phenomena of the brain they should study and how they should go about it. With few exceptions, the types of experiments neuroscientists perform demand what one has called an "impossible measure of patience." Every step of an experiment has an extremely high rate of failure; whatever story emerges from a laboratory does so very, very slowly.

"As long as the brain is a mystery," Ramón y Cajal, the great Spanish neuroanatomist, wrote at the turn of the century, "the universe, the reflection of the brain, will also be a mystery." Eighty years later, remarkable advances in brain research have yielded treatments and diagnostic techniques for a number of the brain's diseases, as well as a fairly good understanding of how a few of the structures of the brain are wired together, how a nerve cell transmits an electrical impulse, and how sensory information is first processed. The brain as a whole, though, is still fundamentally a mystery. Some neurobiologists hope that it will always remain one and that science (despite their own efforts to the contrary) will not cross what is often called the last frontier of understanding. But if an understanding of the brain contines to elude scientists, it will not be for want of trying.

The magnitude of the current attempt to understand the brain is nowhere more evident than at the annual meetings of the Society for Neuroscience, an organization with over 10,000 members from many different disciplines who share an interest in nerve cells and brains. At the 1984 meeting, held at the convention center in Anaheim, California, over 7,210 participants gathered to deliver or listen to more than 4,710 different presentations over a period of five days. Just the abstracts from the meetings formed two volumes about the size of the Manhattan telephone directory. On any given morning or afternoon, a convention goer has to choose from among over 40 sessions taking place simultaneously, each of which includes 12 to 26 short presentations. At any single moment, a physicist might describe the membrane biophysics of a particular type of nerve cell, while elsewhere a psychologist discusses the specific memory defect in a patient with alcoholism-related amnesia, a biochemist tells of the properties of a newly discovered neurotransmitter, a physiological psychologist talks about how information coming in through an animal's chemosensory receptors is processed by the brain, a pharmacologist presents data on the binding properties of an inhibitor of synaptic transmission, an invertebrate neurophysiologist explains the neural circuit that controls swimming in the leech, a developmental neurobiologist describes factors that enhance nerve cell growth, an anatomist reports on the migration patterns of neurons in the visual cortex during the embryonic development of rats, and so on and so on, multiplied many times over for five days.

It is, in fact, too much for a single brain, even the brain of a neuroscientist, to take in, and after just one day there is much talk among those present of being burned out or saturated. More and more time is spent in informal conversation in the halls. There, scientists exchange more details about their work and talk about results they don't yet feel sufficiently confident about to publish or present in a talk. Many of these private exchanges contain the stuff of next year's meeting and the one after that; others are concerned with jobs, tenure proceedings, positions that may be opening up, laboratory space and new labs under construction, department politics, new departments and directorships, grants and grantsmanship, government and nongovernment funding sources, whose work is respected, whose isn't.

"———— has always impressed me with deep thinking," one neuroscientist replies when a colleague asks whom he would recommend to head a new neuroscience group at Johns Hopkins University.

"Yes, but he's probably being spoiled at Rockefeller University with all those computers. Why would he want to come to Hopkins?"

"Then you might think of ————."

"He only models the brain," says the Johns Hopkins professor. "He doesn't actually do experiments, so people don't take him seriously."

Scientists who are just starting out in the competitive world of science are very concerned about the declining funds for basic research and about making a name for themselves.

"I suffer from a lack of attention," a Princeton professor

tells two friends. "It's a trade-off. I like working with this new technique, but it's so new that no one else is using it."

"You'll be all right. You just need a good story to go with the work," one of the friends replies.

"Don't worry. As soon as you have some data, you'll get the attention," adds the other.

Because the 1984 meeting took place only a week after Secretary of Defense Caspar Weinberger suddenly banned the use of cats and dogs in research funded by the Department of Defense, many scientists were also talking about the threat that antivivisectionists pose to basic research. Some were afraid that the National Institute of Health, which funds 40 percent of the biomedical research and nearly two-thirds of basic university science in this country, would be the next to follow the animal-rights activists' suit.

"If we don't do something, we're going to lose everything," comments one scientist.

"We've been so sure that what we're doing is right that we haven't taken the time to convince the public."

"What would be really inhumane would be to ban basic research," runs one refrain.

Some joke that they are glad to know what kind of organism the Reagan administration did care about. A Vietnam veteran and paraplegic, who studies spinal-cord regeneration in cats, comes forward at a meeting on the use of animals in research to say, "Neuroscientists look self-serving when they talk about the benefits of animal research, but cripples don't. Basic research has a product to sell, and the public should be made aware of it."

There are many ironies in the increasingly heated debate over the use of live, anesthetized animals in research. Not the least among them is that scientists, a predominantly atheistic or agnostic group, are here drawing on the Judeo-Christian tradition, which holds that animals were put on the earth specifically for the use of man. Another is that no animal-rights activist in this country has failed to benefit from animal research, since it is the basis of more than 90 percent of all the new medical knowledge of the past century.

For neuroscientists, an especially difficult irony is that at the same time they are using animal brains to find out about human brains, they are finding out more and more about animals: their perceptive capabilities, their abilities to learn and adapt, the intricacies of their systems of communication. The erroneous but clear ideas as to which animals have minds, consciousness, and souls that guided the research of previous centuries no longer exist. Those issues are very much up in the air. So is the question of whether they should have any effect on animal research. Some neurobiologists view the question of animal rights as intimately tied up with that of consciousness; others argue that basic research is ethical, no matter what the mental capabilities and sensibilities of the animals, because it benefits mankind.

All one can say for sure, looking around at the amazing quantity of research presented at the neuroscience meetings, is that some will benefit mankind and some won't. The reason for this is not just that some scientists work on animals to find out about animals, about the tens of thousands of species we share this world with, while others work on animals with the direct aim of finding out more about humans. Rather, it's that research is a hit-and-miss endeavor. Some of it will contribute to the fund of useful scientific knowledge, but much of it will soon be forgotten or reinterpreted. Two sociologists of science, Jonathan and Stephen Cole, designed a study to see if the advance of science depends on the work of a few talented scientists or on the contributions of the rank and file. Their conclusion was that since most of the scientific papers published each year are cited only once or not at all, science would lose little or nothing if the vast majority had never been written. I asked Stephen Cole if he thought there was any reason why this study, which examined research in physics, might not apply to biology. He thought not. "I am convinced," he told me, "that the great bulk of publications in biology is trivial, meaningless; it doesn't add anything to anyone's knowledge."

When I expressed incredulity to a Texas physiologist over the number of presentations at the neuroscience meetings, he related the story of a Harvard professor who ended one of his courses with the bad news that half of what he had just taught his students would turn out to be erroneous or useless information. The very difficult part for the students, scientists, funding agencies, and the public alike, is that time provides the only sure way of telling the good half from the bad.

"Truth is the daughter, not of authority, but time," Francis Bacon remarked. Scientists know this, but it's a hard dictum to live by. A piece of scientific work can be disregarded either because it was no good or because other scientists never knew about it. So at the same time that history teaches scientists that much of what they do will be revised, reinterpreted, or forgotten, they must vigorously promote their work at professional meetings and bring it to the attention of their colleagues. The science writers Nicholas Wade and William Broad have explained the process in terms of Adam Smith's theory of how private greed can advance the public good. "Each scientist in the research forum tries to win acceptance for his own ideas or recipes: on balance, over time, the better recipe for dealing with nature generally prevails, so that the stock of useful knowledge grows steadily greater," they write in *Betrayers of the Truth,* their study of fraud in science. "The more vigorously that scientists pursue their own personal goals, the more efficiently does truth emerge from the competing claims."

Laypersons expect less rhetoric and more reasoned, objective behavior from scientists. Most tend to view science as the collective and rational vision of scientists; in doing so, they fail to see that scientists' choice of problems and their way of structuring experiments and interpreting data is every bit as personal as an artist's choice of subject matter, color, and brushstroke. And just as an artist tends to encounter diverging assessments of his work, so a scientist has to deal with opinions of his research that may range from "brilliant" to "trivial." This is not really so surprising, since a scientist, like an artist, must give an external structure to something that is largely invisible, but it runs counter to most commonly held notions of science. Jonathan and Stephen Cole designed another study to see if the peer-review system of the National Science Foundation was an old-boy network: they found no evidence that it was. What surprised them was that they also found very little consensus among the reviewers as to what research should be funded and what should not. The reviewers disagreed, the Coles concluded, because there was no general agreement as to what good science in their field is or should be.

You don't have to be in a group of scientists very long to realize that science, like most human endeavors, is highly stratified, that it has its lesser lights and its brightly shining stars. It also doesn't take very long to discover the stars— those scientists thought by a large number of their peers to be doing significant, original work. At the neuroscience meetings, young graduate students can be heard discussing the merits of some scientist's work in almost reverential tones; conference rooms fill up for the presentations of certain scientists, then empty shortly afterward; only a very select group of scientists are asked to chair symposia and give keynote speeches.

By the time the Columbia University investigator Eric Kandel stepped out onto the stage of the Anaheim auditorium to deliver one of the keynote speeches of the 1984 meeting before some seven thousand neuroscientists, he had already been honored once that evening. One of his students, Richard Scheller, had been given the Society for Neuroscience Young Investigator Award, one of the most prestigious awards in neurobiology (and one that Kandel himself had won), and Scheller's short acceptance speech was an emotional tribute of gratitude to his mentor. Kandel, an unprepossessing-looking figure in a wrinkled khaki suit, came out a little later and began, as he often does, with a rhetorical question, as simply delivered and difficult for a layperson to grasp as it was loaded with implications and meanings for the neurobiologist. "How does one move from the study of molecules and how they determine the differentiation of cells to the complex behavior of primates?" Kandel asked. Before a different audience, this energetic researcher who is well known for his ability to make his research on the brain accessible to nonscientists, might have begun, "What are the specific molecules that the brain uses to remember, to produce a mood, an emotion, an idea—the mind?" But to this audience of his peers, Kandel spoke in more-scientific terms.

"You can't go directly from the study of molecules to the study of behavior," he continued in his well-modulated voice with its thick Brooklyn accent. "You must look at nerve cells and their connections in between." As he talked, one of his hands began describing large circles in the air to a rhythm that mirrored the cadences of his speech. And while doing this, he paced from one end of the stage to the other, and back again.

To followers of Eric Kandel's twenty-five-year-old study of the physical basis of learning and memory, this speech held no big surprises. Like most of the presentations at a neuroscience meeting, it added only one or two small pieces to a large puzzle that might take years or decades to put together. For Kandel, the puzzle is a particularly fundamental and difficult one: How do we learn? How do the cells and circuits of the brain change to accommodate and store the new information that we get from experience, and how is that information retrieved and read out? Kandel is addressing these very complex questions in a simple experimental animal—a large, shell-less sea snail called *Aplysia* and known also, because of its long, thick tentacles, resembling a rabbit's ears and flabby posterior, as the sea hare. In no way can the sea hare be called a quick learner or an animal with a good memory, but Kandel has chosen it as his experimental animal because of the advantages of its nervous system, the fact that it is built, as one neurobiologist puts it, "like an old Philco radio, with simple circuits and large, easily identifiable parts."

In the two and a half decades that Kandel has been probing the nerve cells of *Aplysia*, his work has produced some provocative and important findings about the nature of learning and, beyond that, about the physical basis of mind—findings for which many of Kandel's colleagues have already conceded him a Nobel Prize. It has also resulted in the creation of a small, highly competitive field of research made up of five or six principal researchers who have adopted Kandel's "simple systems" approach, which uses a simple animal like the snail to explore the complex brain functions of learning and memory. Though Kandel's work is the most widely recognized by far, most of these other investigators believe that their own experimental approach—and not Kandel's—will turn up the most valid and universal truths about how brains learn and remember.

When I first set out to write about this group of researchers, a group I saw as a growing tip—or growth cone—of neuroscience that lay at the crossroads of psychology and biology, I, like the Coles, expected to find a certain consensus about the strengths and weaknesses of a scientist's experiments. I began, therefore, with the idea that the best way to get a thoughtful, balanced appraisal of one researcher's work was to ask the other researchers in the field. In fact, what I usually got by this method was so devastating an attack on the assumptions, techniques, and interpretations of the scientist in question that it sometimes seemed that he or she was perpetuating a hoax on funding agencies, the scientific community, and the world at large. This was not true, of course. I had expected scientists to be largely in agreement but found out instead that science progresses through disagreement and that this disagreement can often be greatest between scientists whose work seems to be the most similar. I had also expected that scientists could be objective about their work and that of others, but I soon came to realize that objectivity and rationality—those long-accepted traits of the scientific mind—were seen better in the way scientists design experiments and collect data than in their views on the research of their contemporaries. I can hardly remember now why this should have been surprising. It would be far stranger still if, by the time a neuroscientist has committed himself to a certain approach and experimental animal for the ten, twenty, or thirty years that it takes to make significant headway, he didn't have a certain lack of objectivity, a blindspot to the advantages of alternative approaches.

My first encounter with many of the neurobiologists in this field was at the Marine Biological Laboratory, a research facility in the small, seaside village of Woods Hole, Massachusetts. Sometimes referred to as the nation's unofficial (and unfunded) national biological laboratory, the Marine Biological Laboratory, or MBL, is the summer research home of some 450 scientists occupying investigational niches as abundant and varied as the aquatic habitats of the area's rocky pools, mud flats, lagoons, bays, and open waters. It is also the year-round institution of almost 200 others. For much of the last fifty years, it has been at the center of neurobiological research in this country and perhaps the world, and during the summer, scores of neurobiologists drop in for a day or a week to lecture, to use the library, or to catch up with old friends.

Having worked one summer as a technician and bottle washer in one of MBL's labs, I returned to Woods Hole ten years later as a science writer, drawn by what I remembered of its unusual atmosphere. I found that it hadn't changed very much. Woods Hole could never be mistaken for one of the many other summer resorts that dot Cape Cod. That the bells in the Catholic church's bell tower are named Mendel and Pasteur, after the fathers of genetics and of bacteriology, is a subtle distinguishing feature. So is the house whose street number is the $\sqrt{\pi}$. But it's the scientists themselves who give Woods Hole its unmistakable air. Whether waiting for the drawbridge that bisects the town to be lowered or for a bowl of chowder in a local restaurant, they are in constant conversation. Their scientific jargon—"ATP," "calcium spikes," "symbiotic bacteria"—always fills the air, mingling at the beach with the lapping of the waves or in a restaurant with the smells of coffee and fried clams. And it's not just their conversations but also their behavior that distinguishes them from nonscientists. In this town full of observers of nature, everyone makes eye contact with everyone else. It doesn't matter whether you are passing on foot—in the hall, on the beach, or on one of the small roads that wind through Woods Hole's warren of cottages and beach houses—or even in cars. It's a bit disconcerting at first, but before long you begin to feel that you're part of some greater intelligence, that this is a place where knowledge is being accumulated and communicated.

Eric Kandel has a year-round laboratory at Woods Hole. So does Daniel Alkon, a scientist who is ten years younger than Kandel and who sees himself as Kandel's most serious competitor in the race to solve the problem of learning and memory. Both men have spent over two decades looking at learning in their chosen snails, and both have by now uncovered biological processes, or mechanisms, that explain how the snails they are studying learn and remember—at least for a short time. One of the questions they face today is which of the mechanisms used by snails is used by humans as well.

It's possible that both mechanisms are (psychologists suspect that there are different types of learning, doubtless relying on different physiological mechanisms); it's also possible that neither mechanism applies to humans. The work of Kandel and Alkon could be of fundamental importance for persons with memory and other mental problems; it could also be irrelevant to humans and another scientific cul-de-sac. It was at MBL, a place that has served as a training ground where a certain scientific ethic has been instilled in generations of new biologists, that I came to see that this so-called race between Alkon and Kandel was as much about the nature of science and scientists as about learning and memory, as much about the way that competing scientists behave toward each other and promote their research as about molecules and conditioning paradigms.

By incredible insight, energetic investigation, and a knack for making the complex seem simple, Kandel, one of the four highest-ranking professors at Columbia University and the senior investigator for the Howard Hughes Institute of Molecular Neurobiology and Behavior, has managed to create and make acceptable his approach to the study of the brain, turning it into what is now a scientific empire funded for more than six million dollars a year. This is the story of how his approach evolved, of the complex interplay of data and personality that is behind this one growing tip. In pursuing this story, I unwittingly became involved in what had previously been a well-muted priority dispute—a dispute between two labs over which had been the first to discover an important new phenomenon of nerve cells—and this involvement led me to see that science operates on almost as many levels as the brain.

Eric Richard Kandel, the son of Viennese parents who emigrated to the United States in 1939, a year before Hitler's invasion of their city, didn't start out with any intention of becoming a neurobiologist. Ten years old when he arrived in this country, Kandel was raised in the Flatbush section of Brooklyn, an area that in the 1940s and 1950s was predominantly white, middle-class, and Jewish. He went to the local high school, Erasmus Hall, ranked then as one of the ten best schools in the country; from there he moved on to Harvard in 1948.

At Harvard, Kandel, a handsome youth with brown hair and lively brown eyes, majored in history and literature. His classmates remember him as having been serious, diligent, and purposeful. He had a special interest in German literature and thought of becoming a writer. His extracurricular activities included sports and membership in several social-service and moderate to slightly left-wing political organizations. Then, close to graduation, Kandel suddenly decided he wanted to become a psychoanalyst. Today, he jokingly attributes this switch to the subconscious workings of his Viennese birthplace. But according to Jimmy Schwartz, one of Kandel's closest friends and a longtime research associate, it had much more to do with the influence of the father of Kandel's girlfriend of the time, who was himself a psychoanalyst.

By the fall of 1952, Kandel had taken the basic science

courses required for medical school and was ready to enter the New York University College of Medicine, popular with would-be psychiatrists because of its association with the psychiatric wards of Bellevue Hospital. At the time, writes the essayist Lewis Thomas, chairman of the pathology department at NYU when Kandel was there, Bellevue "was a unique place for learning how to provide the best of all possible medical care for the sickest of patients under the worst of conditions." Because Bellevue was a city hospital and obliged to take in every patient who arrived at its door, its psychiatric wards were a gold mine of learning situations for the student. It was also a place, as one of Kandel's classmates wrote in the class year-book, from which, "at the end of three weeks, we stopped trying to get our patients freed."

The four years of medical-school training are often a time of mild to radical shifts in interests for many students. Like Eric Kandel, a number of members of the class of 1956 began with an interest in Freud and the intention of going into psy-chiatry. Some stuck to their course, but others soon found the practice of psychoanalysis to be based on too much unproven theory and too little fact for their liking. Allen Silverstein, one of Kandel's classmates who started out in psychiatry but soon switched to neurology, remembers the exact incident that made him change his mind. "In my first year, as a prospective psy-choanalyst, I used to try to attend as many psychiatric grand rounds as I could," Silverstein recalls. "On one, a young woman who was suffering from grand mal epileptic seizures lay there incontinent and biting her lip. As one after another psychiatrist stood up to say that her seizures were an extragen-ital form of masturbation, I decided that this was definitely not for me."

Though psychoanalytic theory tended to be disparaged by many on the teaching staff at NYU, not all made changes like

Silverstein's. Others entered medical school to go into neuro-biological research but were, as Harvey Bezahler puts it, "turned off by the laboratory environment, by all those test tubes." "I discovered," says Bezahler, one of those who switched from an interest in the basic physiology of the brain to psychiatry, "that I was more intrigued by the life history of people than in the blood level analysis of how things work. Thank God there is room in medicine for both."

Kandel's interests also underwent a change, but of still a different kind. Unlike Allen Silverstein, Kandel, whom one classmate described as "one of the bright ones, one of the ones who never had any trouble with the material," never really gave up psychoanalysis. He finished his psychiatric training and actually practiced psychiatry for a time at the Massachusetts Mental Health Center in Boston; to this day, psychoanalytic theory remains for him the only framework that is large enough to contain the full complexity of what it means to be human. During medical school and his psychiatric residency, however, Kandel became more and more interested in the basic mechanisms of the brain, in what was responsible for the behaviors observed by psychiatrists. He became what he calls a "hard-noser," one of those psychiatric residents who, although "attracted to the humane and existential aspects of the analytic perspective, thought that the psychoanalytic view of the mind was slightly vague, difficult to verify (or discredit) and therefore limited in its powers."

"The hard-nosed yearned for more substantial knowledge," Kandel told a group of psychiatrists in 1979, "and were drawn to new ways of thought. In particular, many were drawn to biology. By contrast, the soft-nosed residents had little direct interest in the biology of the brain, which they thought had promised much to psychiatry but delivered little.

The soft-nosed saw the future of psychiatry not simply in the development of a better body of knowledge but in the development of better therapists.''

Although Kandel switched from psychiatry to basic research, he still thinks in terms of psychiatry and human mentality. In articles with such titles as ''Psychotherapy and the Single Synapse'' and ''From Metapsychology to Molecular Biology: Explorations into the Nature of Anxiety,'' he often outrages his biology-trained colleagues by extrapolating from his research on snails to humans. He has not regretted the switch, though, and wrote in his twenty-fifth-anniversary class report for Harvard, ''Having been trained in the humanities, where one learns early how depressing life can really be, I am delighted to have switched into biology, where a delusional optimism still abounds. I continue to explore the science in which I work almost like a child, with naive joy, curiosity and amazement. I sense myself particularly privileged to be in neurobiology, an area which—unlike my first love, psychoanalysis—has grown magnificently in the last twenty-five years.''

In his switch from psychiatry to basic neurophysiology, Kandel was perhaps influenced by the emphasis on basic research at NYU. Equally important must have been the changing climate surrounding brain research. Before the 1950s, the brain was virtually a terra incognita. Very little was known of either its structure or physiology. Then, in a relatively short time, scientists began to acquire several basic, but very powerful, tools that made exploration of the brain possible. Chief among these were a staining technique that permitted tracing the course and connections of nerve cells throughout the brain; the microelectrode, which made it possible to record the electrical activity of single neurons; and pharmacological agents with which researchers could begin to probe the chemical nature of brains. For the first time, it looked as if men really might be able to understand the mysterious workings of the body's highest and most complex organ.

But for Kandel, who started out with an interest in why human beings are what they are and do what they do and in the relation between their behavior and brain function, not in the basic cell biology of the neuron, the most exciting change was the fact that researchers' basic concepts of the brain were undergoing what philosophers of science like to call a paradigm shift. Not only were new techniques becoming available, but the actual framework of ideas in which scientists posed their questions about the brain and designed their experiments was changing. It was moving from a holistic view, according to which the brain operated as a whole in performing any of its higher functions—learning, perception, emotion, consciousness—to a more localized view, which held that specific areas of the brain carry out specific functions. This shift was making the brain far more accessible to a scientist's probing.

Not many years before Kandel entered medical school, the dominant view of brain function had been a holistic one; the man largely responsible for it was the Harvard University psychologist Karl Lashley. Lashley had spent a lifetime of research in what he described as "the search for the engram"—the engram being the memory trace, the site in the brain where the memory of a learned thing is stored. He went about his search by teaching rats to perform certain tasks—running a maze, for example—then cutting out, or ablating, various parts of the rat's brain in hopes of finding that spot whose removal would destroy the learned capability. But Lashley's ablation experiments failed. Rather than finding that particular areas of the cortex were responsible for particular learned behaviors, Lashley, who started out sympathetic to a localized view of the brain, discovered that what mattered was not which part of the brain he removed, but only how much. The memory for the learned task, it seemed, was not localized in specific cells and circuits of cells in specific areas; rather, it was somehow distributed throughout the brain. When an animal learned a specific task, it learned with all of its cerebral cortex. If Lashley went in and removed part of that cortex, the animal's performance would be diminished by an amount that depended only on how much was missing.

Lashley's holistic view of the brain made any attempts to understand the structural basis of higher functions seem futile. It was also extremely puzzling. Anatomists could not understand why the synaptic connections between cells in the brain were so precise and varied so little from one brain to the next if the way nerve cells were connected had nothing to do with how the brain functions. Nevertheless, an anticonnectivist, holistic view held sway during most of the thirties and forties, in part because of Lashley's reputation and prominence. The leading American neuropsychologist of his day, Lashley convinced many psychologists that future developments in cellular neurophysiology could contribute little to the study of learning or any other higher mental function.

Like much scientific work that has fallen by the wayside, Lashley's work has never been disproven. Instead, his data and the assumptions on which they are based have been reinterpreted, largely because of the operations on epileptic patients performed by the Canadian neurosurgeon Wilder Penfield in the late 1950s. Penfield didn't set out to study memory; he started out doing corrective surgery for epilepsy, the object of which was to remove the damaged tissue in the brain that triggered the patients' seizures. The problem was to find out just where this tissue was located. Penfield's idea was to use the fact that epileptic fits in each patient are ushered in by a "mental aura," a curious warning sensation that the patient becomes aware of just before a seizure, to probe for that tissue. His technique was to open up the locally anesthetized skull of fully conscious patients and then to move across the brain with a stimulating electrode and deliver a weak electrical shock to various areas. The procedure sounds painful, but it actually did not hurt the patients at all, since the tissue of the brain—the seat of all our perception of pain—is itself devoid of pain receptors.

Penfield was hoping to stimulate the site on the brain that produced the mental aura and whose destruction he believed would cure the epilepsy. His technique was often successful; it also unearthed a highly intriguing and novel phenomenon that radically altered notions about how the brain worked. When Penfield stimulated certain areas of the temporal cortex or lobe, that area of the brain which lies above the ears, patients began to recall in vivid detail certain events from their past. Stimulating one site on the temporal lobe might cause a patient to hear a certain melody; another, to recall a visit to a traveling circus or a moment in a garden listening to a mother calling her child. The stimulation of the same point elicited the same memory every time. Penfield, it seemed, had by accident found Lashley's engram, the site where a memory is stored. And as Penfield's work came to be accepted, Lashley's results were written off, being attributed to misguided notions about learning and to poor surgical technique. An animal's ability to learn its way around a maze, it is now said, is far too complex a task, involving too many different sensory (sight, smell, touch) and motor skills, to be used in studies of the localization of memory. If an animal loses one skill to the experimenter's knife, it still has others that enable it to get around the maze. Also, because Lashley's methods were not aseptic, infections in his animals might have increased the actual amount of brain tissue that was lost after any operation.

Jimmy Schwartz, who was three years behind Kandel at

NYU, remembers the Penfield experiments and their implications as being "one of the most inspiring things we learned about in medical school." For Kandel, with his unusual combination of interests in the full complexity of human behavior and in the fundamental mechanisms of the brain, Penfield's work meant that specific areas of the brain were involved in producing specific functions and that memory and other higher functions did have a locus, a storage site in the cells and circuits of a particular area of the brain. It meant that the psychologists and psychiatrists, beginning with the observed behavior of humans and animals, and the neurobiologists, starting with the structure and function of single nerve cells, might someday meet on common ground.

After graduating from medical school in 1956, Kandel spent a year as a psychiatric intern at Montefiore Hospital in New York. For the next three years, he was an associate in research at the National Institute of Mental Health's (NIMH) Laboratory of Neurophysiology in Bethesda, Maryland, during what was perhaps the most exciting period in the entire history of the National Institutes of Health (NIH).

In the late fifties, NIH was still seeing the results of the great post–World War II surge in technological developments; it was also beginning to enjoy an enormous growth in its appropriations. Under the direction of James Shannon, who insisted that the congressional mandate to conduct research on cancer, heart disease, and arthritis be interpreted broadly and who used funds to build a basic-research capability rather than targeting them for specific diseases, NIH's appropriations increased from $81,268,000 in 1955 to $1,412,983,000 in 1967. From 1956 to 1957 alone, the total of NIH's grant dollars rose by 250 percent, one of its largest increases ever. During the same period, NIMH, one of eleven NIH institutes, doubled its appropriations.

Philip Nelson, a researcher in the Laboratory of Neurophysiology at the same time as Kandel and now chief of NIH's Laboratory of Developmental Neurobiology, remembers, "It was a time when we felt few constraints upon us either in terms of resources or money." It was also, says Nelson, a time that exemplified what he likes best about science, "vigorous interactions with very smart people on difficult problems." The lab had a very active seminar series, and in it "opinions were rigorously scrutinized and worked over, but the atmosphere was fundamentally positive and constructive." "It was vigorous but benign," Nelson adds, "and that's not always the case. Too often you can have either a bland acceptance of ideas or a destructive, put-down atmosphere." He remembers Kandel as having been an optimistic and energetic experimenter and a very fine person. "Even when you were arguing most vehemently with him," says Nelson, "you had a very good feeling about him."

"Eric has always been an articulate, amiable person with high intellectual standards," notes Felix Strumwasser, a researcher at the Marine Biological Laboratory and another of Kandel's colleagues from that time. "He has also always been extremely ambitious."

Besides Strumwasser, Kandel, and Nelson, the Laboratory of Neurophysiology included a number of other investigators—Wade Marshall, Walter Freybang, Karl Frank, Alden Spencer, and Mike Fuortes, its director. They were all there to expand the scientific understanding of nerve cells, the basic units of brain function that had long been known to be capable of receiving and sending electrical signals. Exactly how nerve cells accomplished this, though, neurophysiologists had been asking for only about ten years, since the development of the microelectrode, a finely drawn glass tube that could be inserted into individual nerve cells, made it possible to address this question.

In the ten years since the first microelectrodes were put in nerve cells, these delicate instruments (the tip of one of these electrodes is about a five-hundredth the width of a strand of human hair) had told scientists a great deal about the mechanisms responsible for the electrical signals—or action potentials—that nerve cells send down the length of their tails, or axons. Most of what microelectrodes would have to show about neurons, though, remained to be shown, and one of the first tasks of any new arrival at the Laboratory of Neurophysiology was to learn the arcane art of making these instruments. They were by then both the neurophysiologist's chief tool and the bane of his existence.

"At NIH, a lot of time was spent struggling with microelectrodes," says Philip Nelson. "The basic problem was that the electrode had to have good electrical properties. Its tip had to be large enough to pass current [positively charged potassium ions], but tiny enough to get into a cell."

The first microelectrodes were made by hand, but by the time Kandel arrived in Bethesda, the Laboratory of Neurophysiology had a "puller," a small, simple machine consisting of a clamp that held a short length of glass capillary tubing, a heating coil that wrapped around the middle of the tubing, and a solenoid, another coil of wire that acts like a magnet when a current passes through it. The heating coil heated the glass, and at the same time the solenoid tugged at it. As the glass melted, the solenoid pulled the tubing into two pieces, each of which now had a long, fine, hollow tip. Undoubtedly, the machine marked a great improvement over the pulling of microelectrodes by hand over the flame of a bunsen burner, but the procedure was still notoriously temperamental. The critical element, it is now known, is the exact temperature of the glass at the time when the tip is pulled apart. This is determined by the position of the glass relative to the heating coil, and that is so sensitive and variable that, to this day, the machine hasn't been invented that can turn out a good microelectrode every time.

Once an investigator has one of these electrodes, he fills it with a good conducting solution (often potassium chloride) and connects it by means of a wire to the rest of the electrical apparatus used in recording and interpreting intracellular signals—signals from inside nerve cells. At NIH in the 1950s, before the miniaturization of electrical circuits, the apparatus for one recording setup was bulky enough to fill a large laboratory. Like today's version, it included amplifiers for amplifying the tiny signals sent by cells, voltmeters for measuring the voltage, or difference in electrical potential, between the inside and outside of nerve cells (this voltage difference changes in magnitude as a nerve cell receives or sends a signal, and the change very accurately reflects the innumerable submicroscopic events actually taking place across the nerve cell's membrane), and an oscilloscope for displaying the voltage difference as a function of time on a fluorescent screen. The microelectrode is inserted into a cell with the help of a microscope and a micromanipulator, a vicelike device that holds the electrode and guides it into position. It is only after an investigator begins the demanding process of getting the electrode inside the cell that he will find out whether his microelectrode is any good.

When Kandel was at NIH, investigators were using these instruments to look at many different questions regarding neurons. Philip Nelson was puzzled by how dendrites, the fingerlike processes at the receiving end of a nerve cell, take in signals and how the cell adds these signals up to decide whether or not it will fire an action potential. Kandel and Alden Spencer were interested in whether the nerve cells in the brain behaves in the same way as those in the spinal cord or periphery. Until that time, most of the studies on nerve cells had been carried out on cells in the spinal cord for the simple reason that those were the cells most accessible to a physiologists's probing. Kandel and Spencer were among the first to attempt to find out if the results from those studies also applied to the central cells in the brain when they opened up the skulls of cats and recorded from nerve cells in an area of the brain called the hippocampus, a small, curved structure in mammalian brains that was chosen by Kandel and Spencer because of its simple architecture and advantages for intracellular recording. Their studies represented some of the first detailed electrophysiological studies of neurons within the cortex of any animal and are still cited in the scientific literature.

During this time, the Laboratory of Neurophysiology was also the stage for an important act in a newly emerging concept of neurons as highly plastic cells, capable of changing their behavior on the basis of their previous experience—capable, as some would say, of remembering. In the years since the 1920s, when the English physiologist Edgar Adrian discovered that neurons transmit action potentials—all-or-nothing electrical signals that travel down the axon of a nerve cell without any loss of strength, much as a flame moves down the length of a fuse—scientists had come to adopt a somewhat simplistic view of nerve cells and their function. Neurons were thought of as switches; they either fired an action potential or they didn't. The nervous system was envisioned as a kind of telephone exchange in which you got the same house every time you dialed the same number. Later, with the growth of computer technology, the computer replaced the telephone exchange as the dominant analogy for the brain, but the view of nerve cells remained basically the same. They were now thought to be analogous to transistors, the on / off switches that are the basic units of computer function.

The first indication that this static view of neurons was a gross oversimplification came with the development of the microelectrode. Now able to place electrodes inside of cells, scientists soon found that action potentials were not the only kind of electrical signals that nerve cells could send. The electrodes also picked up other, short-lived electrical signals later called synaptic potentials. Unlike the all-or-nothing action potentials, these synaptic potentials varied greatly in amplitude or size and dissipated quickly over short distances. Their discovery led to the finding that nerve cells do not communicate with each other directly via action potentials but, rather, use an intervening chemical messenger called a neurotransmitter. When an action potential travels down an axon and into the synaptic terminals of a nerve cell, it causes this chemical messenger to be released. Individual molecules of neurotransmitter then travel across a narrow gap—the synaptic junction—to the dendrites of connecting cells. There they bind to special receptors in the dendrite membranes; in so doing, they open up channels in the membrane that allow small ions, either sodium and potassium or chloride, to enter the cell, thereby producing small local, ionic currents—synaptic potentials. The cell adds up these currents produced by the action of neurotransmitters; if its internal electrical state is changed past a certain threshold level, it fires an action potential. If the synaptic potentials don't add up to produce an action potential, they simply dissipate. A synaptic potential gives a nerve cell a small push toward producing an action potential. If enough pushes add up to make a shove, the cell responds.

The discovery of synaptic potentials radically altered the view of the neuron as an on / off switch. The picture got even more complicated when it was found that synaptic potentials came in two different flavors: excitatory and inhibitory. Some neurotransmitters produced synaptic potentials that pushed a cell toward an action potential, whereas others resulted in potentials that tended to inhibit action potentials.

The Laboratory of Neurophysiology at NIMH added to the growing awareness of the complexity of nerve cells when, in 1959, Karl Frank and Mike Fuortes reported another kind of inhibition that could occur between nerve cells, one resulting not in inhibitory synaptic potentials but in a reduction in the amount of neurotransmitter a cell released when it did fire an action potential. Fuortes called his new phenomenon presynaptic inhibition. Unlike action potentials, which last for only hundredths of a second, Fuortes's phenomenon lasted for at least seconds. Because presynaptic inhibition represented a relatively long-lasting change in the output of a nerve cell as a result of that cell's previous experience and because learning is often defined as a change in behavior as a result of experience, it looked like the kind of mechanism that might be useful to a brain if it was to learn and remember.

Eric Kandel was extremely excited by this emerging view of neurons as plastic, impressionable cells capable of changing the strength of their output as a result of their experience. He was one of those who began to relate this concept to questions about learning and memory, questions of key importance to the study of character development as well as to the study of how brains generate their higher faculties—and the mind. If nerve cells were plastic rather than static, then learning could occur not through the growth of new circuits and connections but through the modification of existing ones. Scientists had long suspected that this must be true since the alternative suggestion that learning is accompanied by new circuits would mean that brains grow in size during learning (an implication not supported by the similarity in the size of adult brains), but they had no evidence to support their case.

Kandel decided to look for an animal whose nervous system would allow him to study how nerve cells change when an animal learns. He therefore needed an animal in which he could identify the nerve cells that control a specific behavior, then analyze those cells before and after learning—a modification of that behavior—took place. Vertebrates were unsuitable for what Kandel had in mind because of the many thousands of very small and invisible neurons that are involved in any single behavior. Lobsters and crabs, popular animals with some neurobiologists at the time (and not only because of the gastronomic perks they offered), had nervous systems of more manageable proportions; moreover, it was known that they could be made to undergo classical conditioning, a process in which an animal learns to associate two stimuli or events. For Kandel, though, they were useless for the very basic reason that they died when they were opened up for analysis. Insects, such as cockroaches and locusts, also had nervous systems with relatively small numbers of cells, but those cells were small, invisible, and difficult to get at because of the insect's hard external covering.

Felix Strumwasser, who came to NIH from the laboratory of Theodore Bullock, a professor at the University of California, San Diego, one of the founding fathers of comparative neurobiology and the author of *The Structure and Function of the Invertebrate Nervous System*, a bible for neurobiologists looking for the ideal animal in which to study various aspects of nervous systems, remembers Kandel's search for just the right animal (or preparation) and passing on to him information about the different animals that were being studied in Bullock's lab. He also remembers the day Kandel was introduced to the sea hare.

The occasion was a lecture at NIH given by Angelique Arvanitaki, a visiting scientist from a seaside laboratory in

France. Tall, dark, and with a stiff manner about her, Arvanitaki spoke to the NIH researchers in halting English made almost incomprehensible by a thick Greek accent overlaid and altered by the French accent she had acquired during her many years in France. "But" says Strumwasser, "it wasn't what she said so much as her beautiful color pictures." They were of the sea hare's abdominal ganglion, a collection of some one thousand nerve cells that innervate and control the behavior of *Aplysia*'s internal organs. Particularly impressive, Strumwasser remembers, were the size of the cells (some were one millimeter in diameter, or the thickness of a pencil lead, very large to a neurophysiologist); the fact that you could take the ganglion out, put it in a dish, and probe it; and the pigmentation of the neurons. Unlike most animals' nerve cells, which are invisible against their background, *Aplysia*'s neurons are a bright orange-yellow and stand out clearly against the cloudy whiteness of the surrounding tissue. Several of the cells Arvanitaki could identify in animal after animal—some on the basis of their size and position alone; others because of their distinct electrophysiologic personalities. She pointed to one cell in the ganglion and called it a bursting cell; if she put her microelectrode inside of it, she could record rhythmic bursts of action potentials followed by periods of silence, bursts of action potentials, periods of silence. The same cell had the same characteristic in every *Aplysia* she had looked at.

Strumwasser, who had long been interested in finding a preparation in which he could study the basic mechanisms underlying circadian and seasonal rhythms (a problem for which *Aplysia* might be perfect if, for instance, one of its bursting cells showed a daily fluctuation in activity), left the lecture knowing that he would spend his life working on *Aplysia*. He has no doubt that Arvanitaki's pictures had a similar effect on

Kandel. "I know that Eric wasn't interested in working on invertebrates up to that point," Strumwasser told me. "Afterwards, as soon as he was finished with NIH and his teaching obligations, he found a laboratory where he could go and learn more about the sea hare."

TWO

Rethinking the Brain

MANY NEUROSCIENTISTS have favorite ways of expressing how they think the tissue of the brain relates to the mind, the sum total of all our feelings, thoughts, moods, perceptions, dreams, desires, and ideas. Some like to describe the brain—that three pounds or so of pinkish-gray, rubbery-to-the-touch mass that lies protected in the skull—as a computer and the mind as its software; others refer to the mind as an "emergent" or "ensemble" property of the brain, something that emerges from the simultaneous activity of billions of neurons. Much as the force of gravity comes into existence only in the presence of sufficient matter, so mind, many neuroscientists think, emerges only when nervous systems become sufficiently complex.

"Whatever the mind is, it is an ensemble property," Dr. Gerald Edelman, a Nobel laureate in physiology and medicine, has said. "That is to say it is a property of a collection of things, a very large collection of things, just as, for example, temperature is an ensemble property of molecules." Temperature has no meaning if you reduce the ensemble to a single molecule. Mind has no meaning if you talk about single nerve cells.

To Irving Kupfermann, a former student and longtime research associate of Eric Kandel's, the mind is a set of functions carried out by the brain. It is what the brain does, just as walking is what legs do. To ask where the walk of the legs is would just be confusing.

The idea that the mind is what the brain does, that all mental activity has its origin in the workings of the brain, may be the basis of modern neurobiological research, but it certainly was not the dominant view of the brain in earlier centuries. It was a long time before men were convinced that the brain had anything to do with mind, that it was, in fact, the organ of thinking. At one time or other, the mind, the seat of a person's individuality and soul, has been located in nearly every other tissue of the body. To the ancient Egyptians, the soul was in the bowels and heart; to the Sumerians and Assyrians, it was located in the liver. Hippocrates' experiences with epileptic patients taught him that the mind was in the brain, but his injunction ''Men ought to know that from nothing else but from the brain come joys, delights, laughter and sports, and sorrows, griefs, despondency and lamentations'' left centuries of philosophers unpersuaded.

Since the exertion of pressure on the exposed brains of soldiers who had been wounded in battle did not produce consciousness, Aristotle argued that the seat of the mind and soul was not the brain but the heart. The brain was too bloodless and cold, he reasoned; its function must be to cool the blood. Thus the idea of the heart as the organ of feeling and thought flourished for over a thousand years. ''Mary,'' it is written in the Gospel according to Luke, ''kept all these things and pondered them in her heart.'' As late as 1596, Shakespeare was asking, ''Tell me where is fancie bred, / Or in the heart or in the head.''

Descartes placed the mind a couple of inches above the

head and believed that it interacted with the brain through the pineal body, a small, reddish, cone-shaped structure found in the back of the brain of vertebrates. This structure impressed Descartes because, unlike most brain structures, it was unpaired. Through the pineal gland, Descartes suggested, the mind impels spirits toward the material pores of the brain; the brain then discharges these spirits through the nerves and to the various muscles. Dualism, the idea that the mind and body are separate, was not born with Descartes, but he fashioned it into a ruling idea that continues to permeate much thinking about the brain. In Descartes's time it was also a very useful doctrine: it allowed physicians to explore the workings of the brain without fear of intruding into the realm of the soul and, therefore, of the church. It made possible the coexistence of a sincere belief in a soul and a materialistic attitude toward the mundane, housekeeping aspects of the mind, the brain.

Dualism is no longer necessary as a protective blanket for studies of the brain. Most neuroscientists today are monists: they believe that there is but one ultimate substance—matter— and that the workings of the mind can be explained by, and ultimately reduced to, physiochemical processes. At least that is their modus operandi, the assumption with which they approach their explorations of the brain. While they are still unearthing (at the rate at which they are still unearthing) the basic mechanisms the brain uses to generate and modulate activity, there seem to be no very compelling reasons to suggest that matter cannot account for mind.

This is not to say that all brain scientists feel this way. Some very prominent ones, including several Nobel Prize winners, have been or still are dualists. At the end of his life, Sir Charles Sherrington, whose work on spinal motor reflexes at the beginning of this century won him a Nobel Prize, could say only, "We have to regard the relation of mind to brain as not merely unsolved, but still devoid of a basis for its beginning." On another occasion, he remarked, "That our being should consist of two fundamental elements offers, I suppose, no greater inherent probability than that it should rest on one only."

Sir John Eccles, a protégé of Sherrington's, who in the 1950s pioneered the approach to understanding the brain based on single nerve cells and who won a Nobel Prize in 1963 for his work on the basis of synaptic transmission, has written several books in which he argues for the existence of both a spiritual and a material world. Most scientists, though, view religion as a shortcut to understanding, and they have called Eccles's God the God of the gaps—gaps that are in our present knowledge.

At a conference of Nobel laureates held in 1975 at Gustavus Adolphus College, in St. Peter, Minnesota, at which Eccles outlined his ideas, some participants questioned why we must be so committed to immediate explanation that we will seek an explanation by invoking the supernatural. Why not, they asked, withhold that kind of conclusion and keep looking for a natural explanation? "Eccles has given a philosophical analysis of a problem, not a scientific one," remarked the Belgian cell biologist Christian de Duve.

The physicist Leon Cooper objected to Eccles's belief that if one accepts that mental events are entirely the result of physical events in the body, then man is only a biochemical machine, only an assemblage of chemicals. "I reject the use of the word 'only',"he said. "It reminds me of the people who used to say with a sneer that you are only made of 92 elements, which cost about $1.02. That to me is equivalent to saying that a Shakespeare play is only words, or a Mozart symphony is only notes, or the cathedral at Notre Dame is only stone. . . . If, in fact, it turns out that we can understand even ourselves by ordinary scientific means, and if we are only made of ordinary materials, remember that these ordinary materials are organized in a manner that has to be regarded as extraordinary.''

Indeed, most of those looking at the way in which ordinary materials are organized in the brain have been reaching a conclusion very different from the one Eccles and other dualists reached. Their view, which has been slowly emerging from the research of the last century, is that the brain may just be complicated enough in its interconnectivity, its chemistry, and its physiology to account for mind.

That conclusion doesn't stem from what can be seen of the brain with a naked eye. Nothing about the actual appearance of a brain would cause anyone to reject the belief of medieval philosophers that the brain is far too homogeneous an organ to be able to generate anything like the incredible faculties of the mind and soul. No, the beginning of a higher appreciation of the brain's complexity had to await the development first of the compound microscope and then of a staining technique that allowed scientists selectively to stain a few nerve cells at a time so that they could see an isolated neuron, the basic unit of the brain.

To this day, nobody knows how the Golgi stain, discovered in 1875 by the anatomist Camillo Golgi, works. But by a process that involves treating a very thin slice of brain tissue with a variety of silver-based compounds under very precise conditions, it stains a small, seemingly random proportion of the nerve cells in any slice. Those nerve cells, though, it stains in their entirety. By means of the Golgi stain, scientists saw under their microscopes for the first time nerve cells in all their fantastic shapes, delicate processes, and myriad branchings. Ramón y Cajal, whose youthful ambition to become a painter was thwarted by his father, whereupon he became the finest neuroanatomist of all time, was one of the first to grasp the importance of the Golgi stain. He described his first glimpse of a Golgi-stained preparation in a passage later translated by Sherrington: ''Against a clear background stood black thread-lets, some slender and smooth, some thick and thorny, in a pattern punctuated by small dense spots, stellate or fusiform. All was sharp as a sketch with Chinese ink on transparent Japan-paper. And to think that that was the same tissue which when stained with carmine or logwood left the eye in a tangled thicket where sight may stare and grope for ever fruitlessly, baffled in its effort to unravel confusion and lost for ever in twilit doubt. Here, on the contrary, all was clear and plain as a diagram. A look was enough. Dumbfounded, I could not take my eye from the microscope.''

The sight of the first Golgi-stained preparation, Steven Rose, an English neuroscientist, has written, must have been as great a revelation as when Galileo first turned his telescope on the stars. It was certainly the beginning of a big bang in a still-expanding view that scientists have of the complexity of the brain. For the first time, it seemed that the structure of the brain itself might have something to do with its function.

The intricacy of the cells that Golgi saw with his stain (some looked like tiny uprooted trees with their branches and roots intact; others, like miniature pieces of coral) led him to believe that all the nerve cells in a brain were interconnected to form a nerve net, a single complete tissue. Cajal, though, had the great insight that the varied forms he saw under his microscope represented single cells and the long-sought-after proof that each nerve cell is a distinct entity. He also deduced that the electrical signals sent by nerve cells travel in one direction. They enter a cell through the dendrites and leave the cell at the branched terminals of its axon. Transmission between neu-rons, Cajal theorized, takes place at the specialized points where the axon terminals of one cell come into close proximity with the dendrites of another cell, at the narrow gaps that Charles Sherrington came to call synapses.

Cajal spent a lifetime applying the Golgi stain to virtually every part of the vertebrate nervous system (his elegant drawings are still used today to illustrate many anatomy texts). By looking at many slices of Golgi-stained material from each part of the brain, he built up an inventory of the different cell types in different areas and was struck by the fact that the enormous number of cells in the brain—now estimated at 10^{10} to 10^{11}, or ten to one hundred billion, that is, as many stars as there are in our galaxy—were connected with a high degree of order and specificity, and not randomly arranged, as one would have predicted on the basis of the then-dominant view of the brain. That view, which owed much to Descartes and resembled the view that Lashley later espoused, held that the cerebral cortex, the thin layer of wrinkled gray matter that wraps around the entire surface of the cerebral hemispheres and is most developed in man, acts as a whole for each of the brain's functions—that all parts of the cortex are the same in their capabilities and purposes and are equally able to perform any of the cortex's functions. It could not explain, however, Cajal's findings that different areas of the cortex differ in the kinds of cells they contain and in the ways those cells are interconnected, nor could it explain recent German, British, and French physiological studies that also supported localization of brain function.

Cajal realized that a new theory of brain function was badly needed, and he developed such a theory by combining the new physiological evidence with his own anatomical results. It was called the cellular connectivist view, and it held that different areas of the brain did serve different functions, their nature being determined by the types of cells present and their connectivity. Meanwhile, the dispute about "nerve nets" versus "neurons" continued. For most scientists, the question was settled in favor of neurons by about 1910, but nerve net adherents went on arguing their case until, in many instances, their death. And like many earlier and later scientists whose scientific differences took on a personal element, Golgi and Cajal didn't speak to one another until they met to share the Nobel Prize in 1906.

After Cajal's, the next big leap forward in the understanding of how complex the brain really is came in the twenties when neurophysiologists, those scientists concerned with the function of neurons, began to "talk" to nerve cells. One of the first such conversers was Edgar Adrian, a professor of physiology at Cambridge University, who in about 1925 developed surgical techniques for isolating the axon of a single neuron from those of the cells surrounding it. Adrian's goal was to understand better the electrical signals that nerve cells send. By isolating individual axons, he was able for the first time to stimulate and record from—to talk to—a single cell at a time.

Adrian's conversations with cells took place via electrodes: a stimulating electrode, a long, thin wire that was connected to a power source and that Adrian used to deliver an electrical shock to a single nerve axon, and a recording electrode, with which he detected the axon's response. The recording setup actually involved two electrodes: a "ground," or "reference," electrode, which was positioned in the solution bathing the axon, and the recording electrode itself, positioned at the surface of the axon. The ground and the recording electrode were connected by way of a voltmeter, an instrument for measuring voltage, or the difference in electrical potential between two points (such as the positive and negative terminals of a battery); the signal from the voltmeter was then fed into an oscilloscope, where changes in electrical potential were displayed on a fluorescent screen.

At the beginning of an experiment, before Adrian shocked an axon, thereby stimulating it to fire signals, the potential difference between the ground electrode and the recording electrode was zero. Both electrodes were sitting in the same solution, and both were subject to the same electrical charges in that solution, to the same concentrations of positive sodium and potassium ions and negative chlorine ions that exist in seawater or any bodily fluids. On the oscilloscope, this lack of potential difference was seen as a uniform trace: the line that runs across the oscilloscope's screen and represents the potential difference between the two electrodes over time was straight and flat.

As soon, though, as Adrian used his stimulating electrode to deliver a shock to an axon—a shock strong enough to cause the axon to start firing signals—the potential difference between the ground and the recording electrodes changed dramatically. The recording electrode was now picking up the currents of positively charged atoms that flow around active nerve cells. On the oscilloscope, these currents appeared as the small, rapid changes in electrical potential that neurophysiologists now call spikes.

These spikes, Adrian found as he recorded from the axons of many different types of nerve cells, were always the same size, but their frequency differed greatly. Adrian had discovered what would prove to be a universal law of nervous systems: nerve cells communicate with each other by sending brief electrical signals down their axons; these signals, or action potentials, vary not in size but only in frequency. It was like a Morse code with dots only. The intensity of a stimulus (a noise, a light, or, in Adrian's case, an electrical shock to an axon) is communicated not by the size of the action potentials but by their frequency, as many as one thousand per second; the meaning of a stimulus is determined by the particular nerve cells that respond and by the pathways through which the signals sent by those nerve cells travel into the brain. Action potentials in visual neurons, in other words, look just like action potentials in the nerve cells connecting to the ear or the hand. A sunset, a thunderclap, and a handshake are interpreted differently by the brain because they elicit responses in different nerve cells and because those nerve cells then send signals to different parts of the brain.

At times, in order to learn what nerve cells did when the brain was not receiving any stimuli, Adrian put his recording electrode on axons and just listened to cells. Was every action the result of a preceding stimulus, as was claimed by the advocates of behaviorism, a school of psychology that had its origins in Pavlovian conditioning and maintained that all behavior can be explained on the basis of simple reflexes and the principles of associative condition? Or were there inborn patterns of activity in the nervous system that proceeded even in the absence of any input, as was argued by the ethologists, members of a European school of biology that had arisen in the 1930s largely in reaction to the growth of behaviorism in Russia and the United States and that emphasized the great diversity of animal behavior and the importance of studying animals in natural, rather than in laboratory, environments? What Adrian found when he cut all the incoming sensory lines to the brains of insects was that nerve cells are not waiting patiently for stimuli. Some fire even in the absence of any sensory input. The nervous system, it seemed, was not the tabula rasa that behaviorists had claimed; rather, it did things all on its own.

Since Adrian's work, many such spontaneously active cells have been found in both vertebrates and invertebrates. Neurophysiologists give them such different names as bursters and oscillators; they dubbed one newly discovered cell the Ping-Pong ball because, when the oscilloscope was hooked up to an audio output, a device that transforms changes in electrical potential to sound, the cell sounded just like a Ping-Pong ball that has been dropped on the floor. As Graham Hoyle, a neurobiologist at the University of Oregon, told me, "What you have to realize is that every cell in the nervous system is not just sitting there waiting to be told what to do. It's doing it the whole darn time. If there's input to the nervous system, fine. It will react to it. But the nervous system is primarily a device for generating action spontaneously. It's an ongoing affair. The biggest mistake that people make is in thinking of it as an input / output device."

Adrian's discovery of spontaneously active cells rocked people's notions of themselves; his discovery of the universal action potential set scientists wondering what the mechanism could be that allowed nerve cells to send such rapid uniform bursts of electrical information. Some, including the physiologist J. Z. Young of Oxford University, realized that if you wanted to understand the mechanism that produced action potentials, you would have to put an electrode into a neuron to see what electrical changes were occurring across the nerve cell membrane. The search was on for an axon large enough to accommodate an electrode, and for an electrode fine enough to be inserted into an axon without damaging the cell membrane. Young found the axon, one so large that he thought at first that it was a blood vessel, in one of the ganglia—or collection of interconnected nerve cells—of the common Atlantic squid, *Loligo pealei*.

In 1936, Young brought a squid he had caught off of Long Island in a pail full of inky seawater to the Marine Biological Laboratory in Woods Hole, Massachussets. The squid was more dead than alive, but somehow he managed to convince his at first dubious colleagues that, "if you want to find out about nerve, you've got to work on this axon." He turned out to be right. In 1939, Alan Hodgkin and Andrew Huxley, two English neurophysiologists who later won a Nobel Prize for their work, developed a wire electrode fine enough to be threaded into the squid's fat axon, and the squid became so crucial to the studies on how nerve cells generate action potentials that at least one neurobiologist has suggested that it should have received a Nobel Prize. It was so popular a preparation in the forties that there was a saying that if you were a neurophysiologist and weren't working on the squid, you weren't in business.

The giant axon was able to tell neurophysiologists a great deal about how cells generate action potentials and how the rapid reversal of the electrical potential of a nerve cell during an action potential is caused by a lightning-quick exchange of sodium and potassium ions through special pores in the axon's membrane. This discovery, and the techniques of Hodgkin and Huxley, led the way to a still-expanding view of the diversity and specificity of the ionic channels, those special pores in the membranes of nerve cells, and of the great diversity of nerve cells that these channels produce through their differing distribution in the membranes of different cells.

In order to find out how nervous systems process information, though, researchers needed to move to a very different preparation. A quiet revolution in neurobiology began in the late 1950s when two Harvard neurophysiologists, Torsten Wiesel and David Hubel, used microelectrodes to record the activity of single nerve cells in the visual cortex of anesthetized cats as they projected simple patterns on a screen in front of the cat's eyes. What they found and what gave dramatic evidence that important things were to be learned from looking at one nerve cell at a time was that different patterns made different cells spike or fire action potentials. Some cells were sensitive only to the edges of objects, for example, to edges moving with a particular orientation across a certain part of the cat's visual field; others fired only when cubes, wedges, or doughnuts of light were projected upon the screen. One cell responded with a burst of action potentials when a diagonal black line was moved to the right over a certain part of the screen. If the angle of the line was changed by more than a few degrees, the same cell produced many fewer impulses, and if the same line was moved from right to left, the cell fired only once. Every cell in the visual cortex, it seemed, was looking for just the right combination of features to set it off. Some cells responded to only very simple stimuli, such as lines; others required much more complex patterns.

Hubel and Wiesel ruled out visual experience as the source of this stimuli specificity when they found the same kinds of responses in newborn kittens with no prior visual experience. They also provided profound evidence of how the environment can act on and modify this hard-wired aspect of the brain. Cats raised in a room with horizontal, but no vertical, lines were later found to have few "vertical" neurons; not surprisingly, they responded much better to horizontal images. Furthermore, as neurophysiologists learned to insert their microelectrodes into the areas of animal brains associated with hearing and touch, they found the same sort of phenomenon: cells specialized to respond to certain frequencies, to pressures of specific strengths and duration. Scientists began to speculate that every cell in a nervous system might have its own unique function and that there might even be cells that encoded such complex attributes as the memory of a certain face.

Here, too, was also proof that different animals are endowed with different sensory equipment. Those with little or no ability to discriminate colors have, not surprisingly, few or no cells capable of detecting color. Other animals, we know, have sensory systems capable of detecting events totally invisible to us. A rabbit, for instance, can perceive movement as slow as that of the sun moving across the sky; dogs, as we all know, can hear sound frequencies completely inaudible to humans; bats have sophisticated sonar equipment that enables them to locate moths by bouncing sound waves off of them; some moths, it has recently been found, are able to detect the signals sent by bats and have even developed a defensive move, a sudden tailspin or free-fall, that protects them from attack; snakes are sensitive to the infrared radiation, or heat waves, given off by living organisms. What is incredible to contemplate is that the rabbit, dog, bat, moth, and snake are able to perform these extraordinary feats of perception not just because of the struc-ture—the size and shape—of their eyes, ears, and so on but also because they have nerve cells capable of detecting such events and brains capable of interpreting them. Dogs don't just hear better than we do; they hear different things.

For brain scientists, the experience of talking to cells—showing them a picture, making a noise, giving them a squeeze, and asking them, via an array of electrodes, amplifiers, and oscilloscopes, what they thought of it—was as thrilling as it would be for archaeologists if the dry bits of clay, metal, and bones that they use to piece together a civilization could sud-denly speak and say how they had been used and by whom. It firmly guided the study of the brain toward localization and the properties of individual nerve cells, but it also contained a lesson in humility every bit as great as that taught by Darwin's theory of evolution: our perceptual world, these experiments said, is by no means complete. It is, in fact, only what our neurons are able to tell us, and what our neurons are able to tell us is genetically determined—wired in from birth—and for any animal that is far less than the total reality of what is out there. Our sensory receptors are narrow gateways through which the outside world enters our brains.

For some, this is a bit of a comedown. "We think we have an infinite ability to imagine or create, but we are really very finite," Daniel Alkon told me in one of our many conversations in his office in the library of the Marine Biological Laboratory. "Finiteness begins with how much we can perceive or sense—and our senses are very limited. There are certainly many more dimensions, wavelengths, et cetera that we could perceive but don't. We could be built in such a way that we could take in much more information simultaneously, that we could do the kind of image processing that computers can do. This perspective on the brain is a bit of a depersonalizing one. It's not one you can think of too long and think of yourself at the same time."

Some scientists, of course, were not at all surprised by Hubel and Wiesel's findings. The European ethologists had been arguing for decades that animals are constrained or limited in their ability to respond to stimuli, that they respond only to those stimuli that it makes good biological sense for them to respond to. In fact, many neurobiologists seem to revel in the awareness that our conception of the world is a mere facsimile of what's really out there, an abstracted and greatly reduced reality that has somehow been transformed into the language of the brain, the action potential.

"So what is out there?" I once asked Rodolpho Llinás, a short, wide-eyed neurophysiologist who was born in Colombia and whose questions about the nature of the brain and shock of white hair both date back to when he was thirteen or fourteen.

"I don't know," he said. "I know there is no light out

there. I know there's no color out there. I know there is no sound or taste. But there is something out there, something which I translate and make into a model of something I like.''

It was a beautiful, blue-skied day, and Llinás and I were sitting on a patch of grass overlooking Eel Pond, the small tidal pond around which the village of Woods Hole is built. The boats in the pond were all pointing, as they do in the predominant northeast wind, in the direction of Woods Hole's Great Harbor and, beyond that, to the Atlantic Ocean, and I found it particularly hard to believe that what I was seeing, the balmy August breeze I was feeling, were translations of something else.

"Do you ever forget that it's so?" I asked Llinás, who once told me that he left his very comfortable and affluent life in Colombia when it became obvious that the cook could not tell him what he wanted to know about synaptic transmission.

"No," he answered quickly. "It's part of me. It's so beautiful. It makes life so unbelievable. Not because it's the study of oneself—because it's clear that we didn't make it all, that the world is not just a product of our imaginations. There really is something else out there. But because what is really amazing is that one is: that the brain can do this and do it so well that we are convinced that what we perceive and what is out there are one and the same thing. And the question is how. Other questions are interesting, but they're rather trivial.''

Another time, Llinás, a cultured and admittedly fastidious individual who came to this country to become a neurosurgeon but soon found neurosurgery much too crude for his liking, was discussing with an MBL researcher the propriety of showing certain kinds of preparations during a scientific presentation. They were talking specifically of whether an audience would be repulsed by the sight of a living animal brain in a dish, and Llinás told his colleague of a time when he had produced just that, an isolated, living guinea pig brain, during one of his talks. Someone in the audience had asked, "How do you know the animal is not in pain?"

"I didn't," Rodolpho told the other researcher. "But I was delighted by the question. People were finally understanding that pain—like everything else—is a brain state." In other words, the brain, unconnected to a body, might well perceive its body to be in pain.

It was months before what Llinás was saying began to sink in, and even now concentrating on the meaning of his words is like looking at an optical illusion and trying to keep the patterns from flip-flopping. It's a difficult idea to hold on to. What we think *is* the world is only one version of the world, a version good enough to enable us to get around without bumping into unseen objects or being eaten alive by insects that we do not feel. Pain, that seemingly most authentic of sensations, is just a fiction invented by the brain to help us avoid dangerous situations. Nothing is intrinsically painful (or pleasurable, for that matter). Pain is just the interpretation that brains put on certain events in order to help us survive.

I was beginning to understand, though, I realized one day when I watched John Disterhoft, one of Dan Alkon's colleagues, guillotine a large, white rabbit in order to study the changes that occurred in the rabbit's brain as a result of its having learned a very simple association. The guillotining itself was over in seconds, and Disterhoft (who says that he has adjusted to the sight of electrodes implanted in the brains of rabbits and to the not pleasant task of killing experimental animals because of his conviction that the more we know about brains the better off we will be) assured me that the twitchings of the body of the rabbit in the sink were just reflex actions and would soon stop. I found myself less concerned, though, with what was being felt by the body of the rabbit than with what was being perceived by its brain, a small lump of tissue the size and shape of a walnut meat that Disterhoft was carrying away in a dish.

According to Francis Bacon, the seventeenth-century philosopher, man is the interpreter of nature. Bacon's theory of how scientific knowledge is accumulated is based on this view. For him, science consisted of first observing nature and collecting as many facts as possible and of then running those facts through the mill of logic to come up with hypotheses that could account for them. Finally, by testing those hypotheses through experimentation, one could arrive at the truth.

Even though he was something of a scientist himself, Bacon failed to perceive how deeply the act of judgment was involved in the observation and collection of facts. In another three centuries, he would have known how much our ability to collect facts about the world is restricted not only by our judgment but also by our wired-in sensory capabilities. Man is not the interpreter of nature, as Bacon believed, but a part of nature, as constrained in his abilities to observe natural phenomena as are all organisms.

Bacon's concept of how scientific knowledge accrues and of how hypotheses are developed and rendered precise has been challenged again and again by subsequent generations of scientists and philosophers of science. Some have criticized it because it failed to take into account the importance and necessity of deduction, as well as such nonrational processes as hunches, luck, and insight; others, because Bacon didn't recognize that facts by themselves have very little significance— that they become meaningful only when you have some idea of what you're looking for. The eighteenth-century philosopher David Hume pointed out that it was impossible to arrive at absolute truth through induction: whereas in deduction a conclusion follows logically from its premise and must be true if the premises are true (all insects have three pairs of legs; therefore, if cockroaches are insects, they have three pairs of legs), in induction you cannot justify the movement to the conclusion (cockroaches, moths, bees, and crickets are observed to have three pairs of legs, but the possibility always exists that the next insect observed will not). Rather than absolute truths, there are only relative truths, which depend upon the state of knowledge at a given time.

For all of the redressing of Bacon's scientific method, though, conventional wisdom still has it that science is the search for a pure and objective truth and that scientists are the objective collectors and distillers of facts. Science is also portrayed as proceeding in a straight line pointing forever forward, when it is actually a much more erratic thing that often meanders, runs in place, walks slowly backward, or stops altogether. A good example of this is scientists' investigations into the structure and function of the brain. Over the past 170 years, neuroscientists have zigzagged between a concept of the brain that sees specific brain functions—the response to a specific sensory stimulus, the ability to learn a new task—as localized in specific areas of the brain and one that sees the brain acting in any of its functions as a whole. Cajal's cellular connectivist theory, the dominant view at the beginning of the twentieth century, was, with some differences, a rephrasing of the localizationist view first put forward in the early 1800s by Franz Joseph Gall, the founder of phrenology, a now-rejected system of character analysis that attempted to link personality traits, things like mirthfulness and benevolence, to bumps on the skull. Lashley's view that all areas of the cortex are equal in their capabilities was in many ways reminiscent of the aggregate view of the brain espoused by Gall's scientific opponent Pierre Flourens.

For Flourens, the issue was whether any brain function—even something as simple as the control of a very discrete set of muscles—could be localized to a specific site of the cerebral cortex. By the time Lashley came on the scene in the 1930s, localization of sensory and motor functions was no longer in question (since the 1880s, physiologists had been drawing sensory and motor maps of the cerebral cortex, maps that detailed those areas of the brain corresponding to specific muscles and sensory systems); the issue then was whether such higher mental functions as learning and memory could also be localized. Karl Lashley set out to find evidence for localization, and when he failed in his search, the tide of brain research reverted toward a holist view that held that the mass of the brain, not its specific architecture, was important.

In the mid-thirties, scientists thought that they might soon close in on the nature of the changes produced in the brain as a result of learning, but by the end of that decade, it seemed a poor risk to invest more time in higher psychological functions. From the experiments of Lashley and others, the brain seemed to possess a baffling and almost mystical capacity to function properly despite radical disruptions of its normal wiring. What was needed in order to understand this, at least some scientists realized, was more and better answers on a basic level.

The forties and fifties saw the search for these answers and the piecing together of the elementary vocabulary of the nervous system. With Hodgkin and Huxley's elucidation of the mechanism underlying the action potential, in 1952, some thought that the quest was largely over, that knowledge of the function of the nervous system would flow from knowledge of how neurons transmit impulses. In fact, the picture of nerve cells and nervous systems was to get much more complicated; but these experiments gave scientists faith that, even though the design and operating principles of the brain might be complicated, they were, at least in principle, subject to experimental analysis and lawful formulation. Cajal's cellular connectivist theory began another upswing, and the idea was there that cells and their connections did matter, that you could learn a lot about nervous systems by studying nerve cells one at a time.

So when stories of Penfield's operations on epileptic patients began to circulate in biological circles, biologists were ready to believe. Lashley's assumptions and techniques were questioned, and it wasn't too long before a few investigators began to venture out again into that experimentally thorny but irresistible territory of the physical basis of the brain's higher faculties. They chose to study learning and memory again, in part because of the fundamental importance of those functions to a person's behavior and individuality but mainly because those were the only higher functions that scientists had any way of studying. "No one in their right mind thought that they could solve the problem of consciousness, the mind / body problem," says the Princeton neurophysiologist Alan Gelperin today, "but learning, though complex, was tractable." Pavlovian, or classical, conditioning had given scientists a way to look at how animals form new associations and provided them, at least, with a good operational definition of learning. While there is still very little agreement as to what constitutes consciousness and reasoning, Pavlovian conditioning defined changes in an animal's behavior that everyone could agree represented particular forms of learning.

Having learned the lesson from Lashley well, this new generation of explorers of the mind was concentrating on extremely simple learning tasks—an eye-blink response or the defensive withdrawal of a limb or a gill—tasks that at least offered the possibility of being localized to a defined area of brain tissue. Some of the researchers, including Chuck Woody, now at UCLA, and Richard Thompson, now at Stanford University, chose the difficult task of working on vertebrates, with the idea that even if it took a very long time to locate a site of learning in a rabbit or a cat, whatever principles emerged would most likely also apply to humans. Eric Kandel, inspired by the recent discovery of the structure of DNA and its conservation throughout evolution (the fact that the DNA of all organisms is made of the same four molecules), as well as by the similarity of the nerve cells of vertebrates and invertebrates, felt confident in turning to the much simpler systems of invertebrates. A snail or cockroach is certainly far removed from man, but when nature finds a good solution to a problem, the argument runs, she uses it again and again. Moreover, the nervous systems of snails were a neuroscientist's delight. They might allow investigators to get at the cells involved in a particular behavior fairly quickly and to proceed from there to the specific cellular, molecular, and genetic changes taking place as that behavior changes.

During every period of human history, the brain has been compared to the then-highest level of existing technology. Descartes likened it to the hydraulic machines that pumped water through the fountains of the lavish gardens of seventeenth-century France, fountains whose ingenious arrangement of pipes, canals, and pistons caused figures to dance and play instruments. Eighteenth-century scientists and philosophers of science preferred a clockwork model of the brain, one full of cogs and pulleys, in which the mind twitched the body's limbs like a puppeteer. In the nineteenth century, descriptions of the brain based on electrical attractions, repulsions, and current flow were much in vogue. The development of the telegraph and the telephone led to analogies between the brain and switchboards and exchanges, and the rise of large corporations in the twentieth century brought descriptions of the brain based on corporate structure. When the hologram, a three-dimensional image produced by laser beams, was developed in the 1960s, residual equipotentialists quickly latched on to it as the best analogy for their view of the brain because, like the brain of the animals operated on by Lashley and Flourens, even a small piece of a hologram's photographic plate can produce the complete holographic image. During the later twentieth century, though, by far the most frequently used analogy for the brain has been the computer.

Brains and computers are alike in some ways: both process information; both work with signals that are, roughly speaking, electrical; and both have many elements. But beyond that the analogy starts to fall apart. A computer has many elements, but not nearly as many as a brain. The IBM Personal Computer, for example, has only three million transistors, or on / off switches; a human brain has some one hundred billion cells, each capable of making from one to ten thousand connections and of receiving input from something like a thousand other neurons. What distinguishes a brain from the tissue of any other organ or from anything else that has ever evolved or been made is this interconnectedness. It is estimated that every neuron in a brain is no more than a step or two removed from direct communication with every other neuron. Others have calculated that the number of *possible* connections between all the neurons in the brain quickly exceeds estimates of the number of atoms—10^{84} baryons—in the universe.

It is also said that brains, like computers, are made up of many identical parts. But today some scientists think it's entirely possible, though almost unfathomable, that every nerve cell in the brain is unique by virtue of the types and distribution of ionic channels embedded in the membrane of its dendrites, axon, and synapses. It is this possibly unique set of channels in each cell that enables one neuron to fire an action potential when it ''sees'' a line moving toward the let while the cell next door responds only to a line moving toward the right. A computer is made up of a single signaling unit, the transistor; the brain may have 10^{11}, or one hundred billion, different parts.

Then there's the question of what brains and computers do. As a calculator, a computer is indeed a very useful instrument, but as a brain it is nothing at all. A brain resembles a computer only in its most logical, computerlike functions. A computer operates very rapidly, but can do only a few jobs at a time; the brain is much slower but performs many functions simultaneously. Whereas the computer gives a predictable, determinate output to a given input, the brain's output—Will the animal eat the food placed before it? Will the boy fall in love with the girl at the bus stop? Will the neuron fire and, if so, will it result in the firing of a neuron it synapses on and ultimately in the contraction of a muscle or secretion of a gland?—depends upon a vast number of variables and probabilistic events. The computer is man-made and thoroughly understood; the brain has been created through evolution and is in many important ways not understood.

If the computer is still used as an analogy for the brain, it is because nothing has come along to replace it, and that says something very significant about what we know about the brain. We may be at the end of our analogies for this organ, because we have finally come to realize that there is nothing on earth like it.

Many people experience a kind of automatic distaste when scientists talk about their belief that it is entirely possible to explain the workings of the mind by, or reduce them to, physiochemical processes. Some think perhaps that this means that a simple equation can explain why you plant tulips and your neighbor doesn't. Others don't like the idea of being nothing more than a biochemical machine; still others object to being simplified, demystified, explained. "We all want to be angels," Rodolpho Llinás has said, "not meat." Neuroscientists, though, don't have any illusions that the physical goings-on in the brain are simple, and their confidence in reductionism is not at all simplistic or arrogant. It is, rather, based on the knowledge that the brain is every bit complex enough in its biochemistry, anatomy, and physiology to account for the richness of mind. "There is a fascination almost akin to terror of such complexity multiplied so many times within every individual human's head," Steven Rose, the English neurobiologist, has written. "If consciousness is possible anywhere as a result of the interactions of cells and biological systems, then surely it is here."

The question has always been raised, of course, whether the brain can, in fact, study the brain. The problem is comparable to Godel's theorem in formal logic: the consistency of a logical-mathematical system can never be proven with the aid of that system's methods unless one accepts its incompleteness. There is also the question—the neurological parallel of Heisenberg's uncertainty principle in physics, which states that one cannot know simultaneously the position and the velocity of an electron, since the act of measuring one changes the other—whether one can ever know one's brain completely or whether the act of knowing might change the thing that is known. Neuroscientists are aware of these questions. But they are, if anything, the distant catch-22's of brain research, and most researchers do not spend much worrying about them. Right now scientists are "working on the hunch that they can understand the brain," David Hubel wrote in a 1979 issue of *Scientific American* devoted to the brain, "and for the moment they are doing well."

THREE

The Squishies and the Crunchies

AFTER LEAVING THE National Institute of Mental Health in 1961 to begin his psychiatric residency at the Massachusetts Mental Health Center in Boston, Eric Kandel got in touch with Ladislav Tauc, a cellular neurophysiologist in France who had been studying the membrane and synaptic properties of *Aplysia* neurons for over a decade. Kandel had in mind a series of experiments that would turn out to be highly successful, experiments that would open a new field of research and resonate in the minds of scientists for the next twenty years.

Tauc had immigrated to France from Czechoslovakia in 1949 and was then working at the Institut Morey in Paris, a research laboratory situated on the grounds of what is now the home of the French international tennis tournaments, the Stade Roland-Garros. Having concentrated for many years on the physiology of plant cells, Tauc had chosen to work on *Aplysia* when he arrived in France, not because he was particularly driven by questions of how the brain works but because he had always been interested in cells—and *Aplysia*'s abdominal ganglion was full of large, beautiful cells that he could easily see.

He had stuck with *Aplysia* throughout the late forties and fifties, when many neurophysiologists, under the influence of the growing field of cybernetics and the binomial theory of neuron function—the idea that neurons were very similar to the transistors of computers—abandoned invertebrates to work on cats and monkeys. At that time, neurons were conceived of as little more than on / off switches. What mattered in the question of how the brain functioned, it was thought, was not what the individual nerve cells did but only how they were connected.

"Wiring was everything then," remembers Tauc, a tall, thin man with East European features and an affable, urbane manner. "Many scientists were optimistic that if they could solve the connectivity of nervous tissue, they would understand the brain. The solution was thought to be just a matter of time." But Tauc did not believe this version of the brain for a minute. He knew that synapses were very complex and extremely labile, capable of both turning up and turning down their output; his intuitive conviction was that this plasticity must also figure somehow in the workings of the brain.

Tauc, who is currently the director of the College of France's Laboratory of Cellular Neurophysiology, turned out to be right. The wiring studies, which had been born of the binomial theory of neuron function, had come to a dead end in the seventies. Some had been successful in generating complete wiring diagrams of certain structures in the brain, and yet scientists were no closer to understanding how those structures actually worked. Tauc now feels that his choosing *Aplysia* and showing, by means of the physiology of its neurons, that there was a way to go deeper into the nervous system was the most important thing he has ever done. At the time, though, he was thought to be something of a maverick and more than just a little crazy for spending so much time on such a lowly and, some thought, irrelevant animal.

When Kandel approached Tauc about his interest in using *Aplysia* to explore the basic mechanisms of learning, Tauc recognized in him the same intuition that the key to the brain lay in the properties of individual cells, as well as in their connections, and he arranged for Kandel to spend the following year in his lab. Together, they came up with a protocol for how they would go about asking whether a nerve cell in *Aplysia*'s abdominal ganglion could change its electrical behavior if two distinct inputs to that cell were paired, or delivered to the cell in a particular, closely coupled sequence, in much the same way that Pavlovian psychologists pair two stimuli—flashing light / food, flashing light / food—to produce in an animal a new, "conditioned" response to the previously neutral stimulus of the flashing light.

Tauc and Kandel traveled some three hundred miles south to the coastal resort town of Arcachon, in the Bordeaux region of France, to do these experiments. There, a species of sea hares—called *Aplysia depilans* because their ink was thought to cause hair to fall out—was available locally and could be studied at Arcachon's Institute of Marine Biology. Tauc had tried to have *Aplysia depilans* shipped from Arcachon to his lab in Paris, but he had never succeeded in finding a reliable collector. In the 1960s, he got his animals by asking local fishermen to save any sea hares they happened to net while collecting sea urchins. Even so, the fishermen had a hard time taking these foot-long, swimming snails seriously as a cash crop.

It's easy to understand why. Mottled purple and brown, *Aplysia* look unattractive, are unpalatable, and exude foul-smelling ink when disturbed. Apart from neurobiologists, they have no known predators. They are not even very interesting animals, and, were it not for their mating behavior, many biologists would describe them as placid, antisocial, and out-and-out dull. They are herbivores and feed on a diet of algae, munching on a string of seaweed much as a child eats a piece of spaghetti. All thirty-five of the known species of *Aplysia* live in the tidal or subtidal zones where their food source is abundant. There they use their muscular foot to crawl around, burrow, or attach themselves on the ocean floor. Some species of *Aplysia*, including the one found at Arcachon, can also use their parapodia—wing-like extensions of their foot and body wall—to swim.

Tauc's work on *Aplysia* had also always been hindered by the fact that *Aplysia depilans* could be collected only during two months of the year. No one knows the reason for this seasonality, but Tauc speculates that the sea hares spend most of their time in the open ocean waters and migrate into the large Bay of Arcachon only to mate, the behavior for which the hermaphroditic *Aplysia* are most famous. Any *Aplysia* can serve as either the male or the female for any other. Any *Aplysia* can also act as both a male and a female at the same time; the result is long copulatory chains that are made up of perhaps hundreds of *Aplysia* cupped one inside another and that last for hours and even days. Sometimes, the last member of the chain also moves in position to mate with the first, and the chain thus closes to become a enormous ring of tightly strung snails. Fortunately for the people of Arcachon, who make their living off of its famous beaches and oysters and not the large swimming snails that frequent their waters and couple in wild abandon, *Aplysia* come into season just as the tourists are leaving, in September and October.

Kandel and Tauc's main interest in *Aplysia* was its abdominal ganglion, a tiny, pillow-shaped collection of about one thousand cells located near the animal's gizzard and crop and acting as a miniature brain in controlling the animal's visceral functions—its circulation, respiration, excretion, and reproduction. It is one of eight ganglia or pairs of ganglia in *Aplysia's* nervous systems: all of them have brightly pigmented cells, but the abdominal ganglion's cells are the largest and, therefore, the most accessible to the electrodes of neurophysiologists. This ganglion lays claim, in fact, to the largest nerve cell in all of the animal kingdom, the imaginatively named R-2 cell on the ganglion's right side.

The plan of the two scientists for studying learning in this ganglion was boldly reductionist. They intended to apply learning concepts and paradigms developed around whole, behaving animals to a preparation in which 99.9 percent of the animal was missing and only a tiny ganglion in a dish of seawater remained. Nobody, as yet, had even determined whether a living *Aplysia* was capable of undergoing classical conditioning, and yet Kandel and Tauc intended to open the animal up, take out the abdominal ganglion, then test individual neurons to see if those neurons could modify their behavior on the basis of a previous, associative experience. In short, could the cells, as some might dare to say, learn? Kandel and Tauc wanted to find out if they could change the signaling properties of a single nerve cell by pairing two distinct stimuli, or inputs, to that cell. First they needed to find cells that received input from two unconnected sources. To do this, they attached small stimulating, "cuff" electrodes around the nerves and connectives (bundles of axons) that come into the abdominal ganglion from areas of the animal's body and the other ganglia: the siphon, genital, and branchial nerves and the left and right connectives. Then they poked a recording microelectrode into one abdominal ganglion cell after another. The microelectrode was connected via a wire to a ground electrode in the bath, and both the ground and the intracellular electrode fed into a voltmeter, which read the electrical difference between the inside of the cell and the outside and which was connected to an oscilloscope. Voltage difference as a function of time was displayed on the screen of the oscilloscope. As Kandel and Tauc shocked the various nerves, they watched for the effect on the oscilloscope. If the oscilloscope registered that a cell fired action potentials after they shocked first one and then another nerve, they were in luck.

Once they were in a cell that received input from two unconnected pathways, Kandel and Tauc had to work carefully but quickly. A cell cannot stay alive indefinitely if it has a microelectrode stuck in it; its membrane begins to leak ions, and the cell gradually loses the ability to receive or send signals. Kandel and Tauc could usually count on an experiment duration of only about two hours. During that time, they first adjusted the strength of the shocks they delivered to the two incoming pathways in such a manner that the first one produced in the cell only a small excitatory synaptic potential, a small push toward the threshold at which the cell would fire an action potential. This they called the test stimulus. It would not by itself cause the cell to fire action potentials and was analogous to the conditioned stimulus in classical, Pavlovian conditioning, to the light, tone, bell, or other neutral stimulus that comes to acquire meaning for an animal only after it is paired with a strong shock or food. The shock to the second pathway was adjusted so that it produced a large synaptic potential in the cell and a burst of action potentials. This second shock was analogous to the unconditioned stimulus of Pavlovian conditioning, the stimulus—food, shock—that already means something to the animal when it first comes into the world.

With the microelectrode still in the cell, Kandel and Tauc then paired the two shocks. The first shock that the cell received was the less effective, or test, stimulus—the little buzz. Three hundred milliseconds later (not quite one-third of a second) came the more effective stimulus, the zap that actually produced action potentials. Buzz / zap. Buzz / zap. Buzz / zap. They repeated the sequence for two to five minutes in some ninety cells that they found in the ganglion. In most of the cells, the pairing had no effect upon the cell's subsequent response when the test procedure—the buzz—was presented by itself. In fifteen of these cells, though, the pairing had a remarkable effect. For about twenty minutes thereafter, the cell's response to the test stimulus was greatly enhanced. Previously, the test stimulus had generated only a small synaptic potential; now that potential was much larger and the cell was actually firing action potentials. These fifteen cells, it seemed, had some way of remembering that the weak stimulus had been associated with a much stronger one. And perhaps this had something to do with how animals in Pavlovian conditioning experiments remembered that such initially weak or neutral stimuli as tones, bells, or the sight of a laboratory assistant could be associated with food or shock.

Unfortunately for Kandel, the neurons in which this signal enhancement occurred were unidentified cells, that is, neurophysiologists had not yet described them in terms of a distinctive location, size, or firing pattern. Therefore, Kandel could not count on being able to get back into the same cell in a second animal, and he and Tauc couldn't say much about the mechanism behind the signal enhancement other than to note that it had to involve a facilitation or enhancement of the synaptic potential produced by one pathway as the result of the activity of another pathway. Because it involved two distinct pathways, they called it heterosynaptic facilitation; it was a form of synaptic plasticity, a way in which cells modified their synaptic output, that had not previously been described.

But in their investigations around the abdominal ganglion, Kandel and Tauc had found in an unidentified cell a phenomenon similar to the one that occurred in those other unidentified cells. This was therefore a phenomenon they could begin to analyze. In the giant cell in the right half of the ganglion, the largest of *Aplysia*'s neurons, they could also produce an enhanced response to a weak test stimulus (the buzz), but this response, they found, was not pairing specific. That is, it occurred after the strong zap was delivered ten times by itself or ten times in conjunction with the less effective buzz. This phenomenon immediately struck Kandel as being analogous to what psychologists call quasiconditioning, or sensitization.

Sensitization, a kind of behavioral modification that some like to consider a form of learning, is an increase in a response to a weak stimulus that follows a strong one. It is, as some might explain it, the reason you might jump out of your chair during a showing of Alfred Hitchcock's movie *Psycho* when the man behind you sneezes. Sensitization puts an animal in an aroused state. It has received one noxious stimulus and is preparing itself for another. Like the pairing-specific signal enhancement in unidentified cells, the phenomenon in the giant cell also entailed some sort of heterosynaptic facilitation, an enhancement of one pathway as a result of activity in another. Because Kandel and Tauc could get back into this cell, though, they could begin to ask where this facilitation occurred and what it involved. Did it occur in a cell upstream—or presynaptic—to the giant cell? Or was it the result of a change in the giant cell itself? For example, were its membrane properties altered in such a way that the cell now reacted more strongly to the same amount of synaptic input?

These were some of the questions that Kandel and Tauc began to address. They soon ruled out a change in the membrane properties of the giant cell. They also ruled out the possibility that facilitation was due to a decrease in inhibitory input to the giant cell. They were left with the idea that this form of heterosynaptic facilitation occurred in a cell upstream to the giant cell and involved an increase in the excitatory output of the less effective pathway. At this point, Kandel and Tauc could only suggest what caused this increase, but they felt that the most likely explanation was an increase in the release of excitatory neurotransmitter from the axon terminals of the test pathway.

Kandel and Tauc also suggested two ways in which this type of enhancement might occur only when the two stimuli were delivered in a specific and closely linked sequence. "The nonspecific process of heterosynaptic facilitation could become specific," they wrote in 1965, "if there were axon terminals which could undergo presynaptic facilitation only when they themselves had been invaded by an action potential some hundreds of milliseconds before the impingement of the priming stimulus. Specificity could also be achieved by means of appropriate convergence and divergence in a complex neural circuitry."

In other words, the kind of non-pairing-specific facilitation (or signal enhancement) that they had found in the giant cell could provide the basis for pairing-specific facilitation in either of two ways. Perhaps the axon terminals of some unidentified cells had in them a sort of "internal gating mechanism" such that those terminals could undergo facilitation in response to input from the strong pathway only if they had received input from the weak pathway fractions of a second earlier. Alternatively, specificity could be brought about not by an internal gating mechanism but rather by the way that inputs to different pathways travel through a ganglion and converge on particular neurons. It was possible, for instance, that the cell in the abdominal ganglion that was responsible for producing facilitation of certain unidentified neurons received input from both the weak and the strong pathway, but that it would fire (thereby producing facilitation of those unidentified cells) only when those two pathways were stimulated at the same time. Stimulation of either pathway by itself would not suffice to fire this hypothetical neuron and bring about facilitation; only when signals from both pathways converged or summated on the neuron would facilitation occur.

Four scientific papers came out of the four short months that Kandel and Tauc worked on *Aplysia* together. Kandel was elated about the work and viewed the experiments as obvious and powerful analogues for associative conditioning and sensitization. Tauc, on the other hand, wanted to interpret the results much more cautiously. "My idea was very simple," he says. "I wanted to find something in the cell that lasted a long time—memory—then find out if it could tell us something about learning. I looked at the findings from a cellular neurophysiological point of view and didn't want to insist too much on correlations between what was going on at the cell membrane and an animal's behavior. Kandel was different, though. Coming from a background of psychiatry, he was at ease in the jargon of learning." Kandel wanted to go too far, in Tauc's view, in saying what these experiments meant and in applying the results to the very complex issues of animal behavior. They disagreed sharply about how the papers should be written, and their disagreements can to a large extent be explained by differences in their training: while medical training stresses the global, biology always deals with the particular.

When Kandel returned to the United States in 1963, he set up shop in the basement of the Massachusetts Mental Health Center (the Boston Psycho, as it was known to its staff) and was appointed director of the laboratory of neurophysiology, as well as a staff psychiatrist. By then, he was not the only investigator in this country who was interested in exploring questions of learning and behavior in *Aplysia*. Once the snail had been introduced in the United States by Angelique Arvanitaki and taken up by Felix Strumwasser, numerous researchers were quick to see the advantages of its nervous system. By the late sixties, the animal's popularity among neuroscientists was so great that it spawned a brisk cottage industry of *Aplysia* collection on the West Coast; only edibility could have made *Aplysia* a hotter item. The other scientists who were taking up *Aplysia,* however; came from a tradition different from Kandel's, and they approached *Aplysia* with a different philosophy and a different set of questions.

Most of these other scientists had been trained in biology rather than in medicine and were heavily influenced by ethology. While Pavlov and the behaviorists believed that associative-conditioning paradigms represented universal forms of learning whose rules applied to all animals, the early ethologists suspected and went on to prove that animals don't all learn the same things, or the same things equally well. Their background in biology made them very conscious of the great diversity of behavior among species, and they reasoned that animals learn best what it makes good biological sense for them to learn. While behaviorists thus persisted in their attempt to discover universal principles of learning—the interstimulus interval that gave the best learning, the rate at which learning was acquired or forgotten, and so on—using one or two species of animals (usually pigeons and rats) in highly artificial learning situations, ethologists were busy finding numerous examples of how different animals learn differently. Honeybees, for example, were found to associate an odor with a food after just one pairing, whereas it took them three trials to associate an odor with a color and more than twenty to associate it with an object of a certain shape. A herring gull quickly learns to distinguish its young from all the others (though all young gulls look identical to a human observer), but it has no aptitude for recognizing its own eggs and readily accepts substitute eggs of different color, shape, pattern, or size.

In the heyday of behaviorism, when its advocates were arguing that all behavior is learned and the result of reinforced stimulus / response associations, the ethologists challenged these conclusions with convincing examples of innate (*instinct* and *instinctive* had been cloudy, if not dirty, words since their overuse by Freud) behavior—behavior that couldn't be explained as the result of an external, triggering stimulus but that seemed, rather, to be generated by something within the organism itself. Neurophysiologists like Edgar Adrian got into the fray when their recordings from single cells in invertebrate nervous systems showed that nervous systems were not quiet places waiting for incoming stimuli. Instead, many cells were spontaneously active.

By vigorously shaking the foundations and assumptions of behaviorism and by then reinforcing the remaining structure with lessons from biology, ethology would over the next twenty years make learning theory more profound and powerful than even Pavlov had imagined it to be. In the sixties, though, the two disciplines were still battling it out. And their differences were readily apparent in their approaches to the nervous system. Both disciplines were interested in the neural basis of behavior, but whereas neuroethologists tended to study innate, wired-in behaviors (which undoubtedly represent the greater part of an invertebrate's total behavioral repertoire), researchers trained in psychology or physiology gravitated toward learned behaviors. While neuroethologists began by looking for nerve cells that were spontaneously active, Kandel was interested in finding normally quiet cells whose activity he could modulate. Schooled in medicine, with its emphasis on one species—man— Kandel was initially biased toward a universal form of learning generated by some universal neural mechanism; neuroethologists, by contrast, started with the diversity of animal behavior, a diversity they knew would be reflected in the underlying neural architecture and physiology. Finally, whereas neuroethologists were interested in animals in their own right and in the behavior of unrestrained animals, physiologists and psychologists tended to be interested in animals only insofar as they could provide insights into how humans work. "I think it's important to understand the adaptive significance of a behavior and how an animal behaves in a natural environment," a neuroethologist might say.

"I don't give a damn about *Aplysia*," Tom Carew, formerly a learning psychologist in Kandel's lab, told me. "I want to understand how my daughter works, but there are problems working on my daughter."

Because he studied learning in what was traditionally a biological stronghold—invertebrates—Kandel was, in the sixties, in a very strange position. Neuroethologists were out of sympathy with his learning paradigms; learning psychologists were only just beginning to see the benefits of working with invertebrates. Kandel was to transform this neither-fish-nor-fowl position into an accepted approach to learning and to gain for it a level of support that would leave many neuroethologists in his scientific dust.

Flush with his recent discovery of the phenomenon of heterosynaptic facilitation and a three-year, $66,164 grant from NIH's Institute of Neurological Diseases and Blindness, Kandel found that one of his first tasks upon his return from France—to find a reliable source of *Aplysia*—was easy but, in the end, somewhat disappointing. Felix Strumwasser had already located a good and reliable collector in Rimon Faye, a graduate student in biochemistry at UCLA who paid for his diving hobby by collecting marine specimens for research labs, but when

Kandel began experimenting on this new species of sea hares, *Aplysia californica,* he found that he couldn't replicate the results he had gotten in France. Kandel didn't understand then what he was to find out later, namely, that the species *Aplysia californica* and *Aplysia depilans* differ in many respects. But his intuition told him to lay those analog experiments aside and look instead for a behavior that was controlled by the abdominal ganglion and that might be capable of undergoing a modification as a result of experience—Kandel's definition of learning. If he could find such a behavior, he could begin to study memory—the process by which that learned information was stored in the nervous system and made use of at a later time.

Since Kandel's familiarity with associative-conditioning paradigms was only a passing one, it was essential for him to recruit a postdoctoral student for his lab who was well grounded in the subjects of learning and behavior. Ten years earlier, this would have been a difficult task since most psychologists would have balked at the idea of working in invertebrates (there isn't a biologist whose tongue doesn't trip over that prepositional phrase, especially when trying to make the distinction between it and its sister phrase *in vertebrates*) or in cellular neurophysiology. But Kandel's timing was just right. By the mid-1960s, psychologists were beginning to recognize that a great deal could be learned from talking to nerve cells one at a time, and the advantages of using invertebrate nervous systems were becoming known. It helped that Kandel himself was a physician yet felt that snails were sufficiently important to devote his time to them. So even though Irving Kupfermann, a graduate student in psychology at the University of Chicago, hadn't heard of Eric Kandel when he got a phone call from Wess Frazier, a student in Kandel's lab in Boston and an old friend of Kupfermann's from Stanford University, he almost immediately said yes when asked if he would be interested in studying learning in *Aplysia*. He had, in fact, been looking for a lab in which an animal with a simple nervous system was being used to study learning, but he hadn't been able to find one in this country. He had been all set to go to Chile to study leg-lifting paradigms in cockroaches when his phone rang.

While Kandel and two of his other postdoctoral students worked on mapping the cells in the abdominal ganglion and studying their connections, synaptic properties, and inhibitory and excitatory pathways, Kupfermann, who was also gradually being broken into neurophysiology, set out to study the behavior of *Aplysia* and to look specifically for behaviors controlled by the abdominal ganglion. He knew the organs whose movements were controlled by nerve cells in the abdominal ganglion, among them the heart, the gill, and the siphon. Since, ideally, the behavior the investigators chose to study was one that they could easily observe and repeat, he first turned his attention to the gill and the siphon, organs located in *Aplysia*'s mantle cavity.

Turned on its side, *Aplysia* resembles a purple egg omelet with a head. The flaps of the omelet are its parapodia, the fleshy wing-like extensions of the foot that project up laterally and meet but are not joined on the animal's backside; inside the omelet is everything else: the enclosed visceral cavity that houses the animal's internal organs and the mantle cavity. All mollusks have a mantle cavity. In *Aplysia*, it contains the gill, as well as the openings of the excretory and reproductive tracts, and is covered by a fold of skin, the mantle shelf that holds the snail's residual shell. At the rear of the animal, the mantle shelf extends to form a cylindrical siphon, which normally protrudes out of the mantle cavity between the two parapodia and which serves both as an exhalant funnel for seawater circulating through the animal's mantle cavity and as a receptor for tactile input.

Kupfermann really began to focus on the siphon when he found that if he touched either the siphon or the mantle shelf, the siphon, mantle shelf, and gill all quickly withdrew into the mantle cavity. This behavior, a simple defensive reflex that allows *Aplysia* to bring these organs under the protection of its mantle shelf and parapodia, looked perfect for their purposes. Not only could it be easily observed, but its underlying neural circuitry should be fairly simple, because it was a reflex, and reflexes, in order to be fast, must involve short chains of cells (some reflexes entail just two cells, a sensory and a motor neuron; the reflex that controls the constriction of the pupil in response to a bright light involves four or five). "It wasn't that we were interested in gills and siphons," says a member of Kandel's lab, "but the gill and the siphon looked like a place where we could study learning."

Kupfermann had no success in his first attempts to get the siphon withdrawal reflex to undergo classical conditioning by, for example, pairing a touch to the siphon with some neutral stimulus—a tone, light, odor, or the like—but in very early, informal experiments he did find that the behavior of the siphon could be, if not conditioned, at least modified. If Kupfermann poked the siphon once, it underwent a brisk withdrawal. If he poked it ten times in a row, it withdrew much less. This was an example of the ubiquitous phenomenon of habituation, a phenomenon first described by Charles Sherrington in his studies of spinal-cord reflexes. Now it was being studied with renewed interest by Alden Spencer, Kandel's good friend and colleague from NIMH days, who was then writing a review on habituation that would greatly influence Kandel's thinking.

Defined as "a decrease in a behavioral reflex response as

a result of repeated stimulation,'' habituation is an extremely useful phenomenon. It allows us to ignore stimuli that have lost novelty or meaning—the clothes on our backs, traffic noise, the sensation of grass between our toes—and get on with the business of living and survival. Though some psychologists and biologists don't consider habituation learning, because it involves a decrease in an existing response rather than the formation of a new one, most consider it a very simple but important form of learning. Habituation is thought to be the first learning exhibited by infants; a Columbia University psychologist has found that the ability of one-year-olds to habituate to the repeated presentation of a visual stimulus correlates well with various measures of intelligence obtained later, when those same children are four. Kandel and his group might have preferred to be studying classical conditioning, but habituation was what they had, and it looked both real and tractable.

After only two years at the Massachusetts Mental Health Center, a period during which Kandel had been promoted from research associate to instructor in the Harvard Medical School's Department of Psychiatry, he was offered a position as an associate professor in the Departments of Physiology and Psychiatry at the NYU School of Medicine. He leapt at the opportunity both because it would allow him to return to his hometown and because it meant that he would be able to join forces once again with Alden Spencer, who had also just taken a position on the NYU staff. He must have expected that the move would be a long-term one, for before leaving Boston he signed a $40,000 mortgage on a three-story stucco and wood trim house in the Riverdale section of the Bronx. The house, which dates back to 1910 and has a view of the Hudson, is where Kandel and his family have lived ever since.

At NYU, Kupfermann, Spencer, and Kandel formed a small research nucleus that was soon expanded by the arrival of Vincent Castellucci, a dapper neurophysiologist born and raised in the Canadian woods, and Harold Pinsker, a physiological psychologist from Berkeley who had recently abandoned the Lashley-type ablation studies of monkey brains that he had done for his Ph.D. thesis. He made his switch from monkeys to sea snails very quickly one day, after a new professor at Berkeley took him aside to say, "You know, Harry, this thing you're doing is just a piece of shit. You're never going to learn a thing about the nervous system this way. You're throwing away the wrong part of the animal. If you're interested in what that piece of the brain that you're taking out does, you've got to study it directly."

"It took me about thirty milliseconds to realize that he was right," says Pinsker, a small man with fine features, a strong, square jaw, and eyes the color of turquoise. The same professor went on to tell Pinsker about Kandel, and before the year was out, Pinsker was in New York.

There the NYU group had begun seriously to examine the behavioral features of habituation of the siphon withdrawal reflex. If they were to understand the neural basis of this simple form of learning, they had to know as much as possible about its observable characteristics—the kinds and number of stimuli that produce habituation, the length of its duration, the kinds of stimuli that can produce a quick disruption or "dishabituation" of the habituated reflex, and so on. When the time came for them to define the neural basis of habituation, their explanation would have to be able to account for all of these characteristics. Otherwise, they might not be looking at the right answer.

One of their first tasks was to design an apparatus to hold the *Aplysia* in place with its parapodia pulled back so that they could observe the behavior they were interested in. They came up with a seawater aquarium the length of an *Aplysia* with a head clamp at one end and clamps at either side for each parapodium. They also needed a way to quantify the behavior—how far the siphon withdrew—so that the reliance solely on an observer (and his bias) could be eliminated from the experiment. They couldn't devise a good way to quantify siphon withdrawal, but they found that the amount that the gill contracted during this reflex could be simply measured by placing the gill on top of a photoelectric cell whose output (as recorded on a polygraph) was directly related to the area of the photocell that was uncovered as the gill contracted in size. The photocell's signal, then, was directly proportional to the amount the gill contracted. The delivery of the stimulus that causes the defensive reflex—Kupfermann's initial poke to the siphon—was also taken out of the experimenter's hands and quantified. The tactile stimulus to the siphon now took the form of a brief jet of seawater squirted out of a device usually reserved for the cleaning of teeth—a Water-Pic.

At the same time that they worked on the behavior, finding out, for instance, that habituation in *Aplysia* resembled that in vertebrates in six out of the nine features Spencer had outlined in his review of this simple form of learning, Kandel's group were also beginning to puzzle out the neural circuitry—the motor, sensory, and possible interneurons—that mediated the reflex. The setup they used closely resembled the one for the behavioral studies, but now they wanted to be able to get inside the nervous system and relate specific neurons to specific movements. It was Kupfermann who figured out that if he made a slit in the back of an *Aplysia* restrained by the head clamp, he could go in and lift out the still-attached and still-functional abdominal ganglion, pin it to a small Lucite stage that sat just above the animal, and then poke it with microelectrodes.

The first cells they looked for were the motor neurons, those nerve cells that are able to transform the electrical signals of the nervous system into a muscle contraction, in this case into the withdrawal of the gill and the siphon. They started with them for the simple reason that motor neurons are fairly easy to identify: if you've managed to insert a microelectrode in one and if you drive or fire it by injecting a bit of electrical current, you'll see a movement.

The Kandel group was lucky to have found very early one motor cell that controlled movement in the siphon (this serendipitous finding also strongly influenced their decision to focus on this reflex), but a more systematic approach demanded that, starting at the gill and siphon, they inject dye into the nerve that projects from the abdominal ganglion to those organs. Those cells in the abdominal ganglion that first fill with dye, then, are closest to the output end of the nervous system and most likely to be motor neurons. Inserting a microelectrode into one dye-filled nerve cell after another, they stimulated the cell, then watched for a movement of the siphon and the gill. If there was no movement, they knew they were not in a motor cell. If there was movement, they then had to check that the cell they were in was itself a motor cell and not just connected to one. By this method, they found four motor neurons involved in contracting the gill and siphon. From the size and shape of the synaptic potentials in those motor neurons (the signals those neurons received when the siphon was touched), they realized that the motor neurons received both direct and indirect connections from sensory neurons. In other words, the sensory neurons, those cells able to take an environmental stimulus— a squirt of water from a Water-Pic—and turn it into the language of the nervous system, synapsed directly onto the motor neurons, but they also synapsed onto interneurons that in turn fed into the motor cells. Whether these interneurons, nerve cells that are neither sensory or motor, were excitatory or inhibitory (that is, whether they promoted or inhibited action potentials in the neurons they connect to), they did not know. They also knew very little about the sensory or input side of the reflex circuit. However, they had enough information to begin to ask the question that interested them: Where do the changes occur that account for habituation?

For four years and at all hours of the day and night, the Kandel group worked on the behavioral and neural analysis of habituation in *Aplysia*. It was, as one postdoctoral student described it, "a labor of love." Pinsker, Kupfermann, and others all remember clearly the enthusiasm, dedication, and exitement that was present, the sense that they were working on something very important. There was much talk of "going for it" or "going after this thing," and the morale of the group was extraordinarily high. The lab definitely had the trappings of what some like to call "an invisible college," a group of scientists working in a single research tradition usually led by a charismatic leader who formulates the group's basic assumptions and sets the research priorities. For the Kandel group, the basic assumptions were that animals with simple nervous systems could be used to discover general mechanisms of learning and memory and that learned information was stored in specific circuits and cells. And like other examples of invisible colleges—the most famous being the phage group at Caltech in the 1940s, which used bacterial viruses, or phages, as they are usually called, to study the physical basis of genetic transmission—the Kandel laboratory began to develop its own research style and atmosphere and even to adopt a group sport, baseball. They called themselves aplysiologists, and they strove to be at the same time both as rigorous and as relaxed as possible. Many of Kandel's postdocs and colleagues came to dress in a similar, neat but casual fashion, favoring corduroy and tailored shirts, and to emulate Kandel's energetic but very polished way of presenting data, as well as his intense manner of questioning speakers at symposia and conferences.

Kandel, who still spent much of his time at the laboratory bench, kept the morale of the group high by heading frequent staff meetings, by exhibiting an unfailing interest in the daily progress of the work, and by the excitement he conveyed about the significance of what they were doing. Jimmy Schwartz, Kandel's friend from medical school, joined the staff of NYU as an assistant professor of microbiology in 1964 and remembers meeting Kandel again in their new guises of university professors. "Why don't you work on something really important?" Kandel asked him. He was referring to the molecular biology and genetics of learning and memory, the study of the actual molecules that a neuron uses to change its behavior. The problem quickly sparked Schwartz's imagination, and within a few years he had phased out his work in bacterial genetics and was totally immersed in *Aplysia*. Kandel's enthusiasm was so great that it even rubbed off on the electrical-engineering student who had the part-time job of building and fixing the electronic equipment used in the lab. As Jack Byrne applied his engineering skills to problems of constructing better recording setups and more-automatic training devices, he sensed that something very significant was going on in Kandel's lab and wanted to be a part of it. He became involved less and less in electrical engineering and more and more in neurophysiology.

When Kandel, Kupfermann, Pinsker, and Castellucci were ready to ask where in their system changes might occur that would account for habituation, they generated a "laundry list" of all the possible explanations for habituation. The first item on the list was sensory adaptation, the possibility that habituation was due to a change in the part of the sensory cell located in the skin of the siphon, with the result that the sensory cell came to respond less to the same squirt of water from the Water-Pic. Another possibility was muscle fatigue: after repeated stimulation, the muscles might run out of the chemical substances they need to contract. Both of these possibilities could result from changes outside of the abdominal ganglion, changes in the animal's periphery. It could also be that the change occurred in the ganglion—inside the animal's central nervous system. One possibility was that habituation was due to an increase in the output of any inhibitory interneurons in the circuit such that the motor neurons would receive less of a push toward the threshold at which they would fire. A second possibility was that a change had occurred at the synapse between the sensory and the motor neurons. After repeated stimulation, either the sensory neurons were able to release less and less excitatory neurotransmitter or the motor neurons' receptors for that neurotransmitter became less and less sensitive.

Once they had drawn up this list, the NYU researchers began going through it, crossing off the possibilities one by one. They were able to rule out sensory adaptation by showing that habituation still occurred when they bypassed the siphon (and therefore the sensory receptors in the siphon skin) and stimulated the siphon nerve directly. Muscle fatigue was eliminated when they found that the size of the withdrawal response was the same before and after habituation training by putting an electrode into the motor neuron and stimulating contraction directly by injecting current. This left the possibility that habituation was associated with some change within the ganglion. They began examining the nature of this change by inserting a microelectrode into one of the motor neurons that control the withdrawal reflex and recording the synaptic potentials in that cell during habituation training. The squirting of water on the siphon produced, at first, large synaptic potentials in the motor neuron, a burst of action potentials, and a large contraction.

When the squirts were repeated, though, the size of the synaptic potentials decreased, as did the number of action potentials. If they restored the full reflex response by letting the animal rest, they found that the synaptic potential also returned to normal.

What could cause the decreased synaptic potentials? Kandel and his colleagues were able to rule out an increase in the inhibitory input to the motor neurons. They could eliminate a change in the membrane properties of the motor neurons that would cause those cells to respond less to the same amount of excitatory, depolarizing neurotransmitter. They were left with only two possible explanations: either the sensory cells released less neurotransmitter after habituation training or the transmitter receptors in the membrane of the motor neurons were now less sensitive. In 1969, Kandel didn't yet have the data to choose between these, but he favored the first one. As it turned out, he was correct.

Because these habituation studies marked the first time that a specific instance of learning had been correlated to changes at particular cells and synapses, they were the first test of the hundreds of theories that had been posited since philosophers and investigators had begun thinking about the nature of learning. "The question," says Pinsker, "was no longer what was logical, but what was biological." In this simple form, learning didn't involve any of the electrical or chemical fields proposed by Lashley and the Gestalt psychologists; nor did it seem to involve the formation of any new connections between cells. It happened too fast for that. Rather, habituation in *Aplysia* was due to a change in the functional effectiveness of previously existing excitatory connections, meaning that the capacity for behavioral modification was actually built into the snail's neural architecture. This evidence that learning did not involve the formation of new connections between neurons had the ring of truth. "The nervous system does not have the advantage of muscle of being able to get bigger," says Rodolpho Llinás. "Whatever it's doing during learning, it cannot be making *more* proteins; otherwise you'd see great differences in the sizes of brains—and you don't."

After four years of experimentation, Kandel's group was ready to publish the work on habituation and dishabituation. They were able to present their results as a trio of back-to-back papers in a March 1970 issue of the prestigious journal *Science* because, as they argued, this was the first time that scientists had been able to go completely from input to output—from behavior to the underlying neural circuitry—without any missing links. Reaction to the papers was generally enthusiastic. Many biologists and psychologists thought the work immensely important and looked forward to watching as the rest of the story unfolded, as Kandel and his group probed the mechanism of decreased neurotransmitter release in habituation and studied different kinds of learning. They knew that Kandel would want to know whether short-term and long-term learning took place at the same synapses and involved the same kinds of changes. Did sensitization and other forms of learning also entail preexisting connections? Did different types of learning—habituation, sensitization, and associative conditioning—share similar mechanisms? Some other scientists, though, played down the importance of Kandel's work. A number of vertebrate physiologists and psychologists believed that the physiology of the invertebrate *Aplysia* might have little bearing on what happens in animals further up the evolutionary ladder. Other researchers were less than enthusiastic because the findings dealt with habituation, which—involving, as it does, a change in an existing response rather than the formation of a new one—they didn't define as real learning.

Kandel and his group were happy to think of habituation

as a simple form of learning; but at the same time they were worried that *Aplysia,* the animal in which they had invested considerable time, might not be capable of undergoing classical conditioning, a modification of behavior that almost everyone agreed was learning. They had reason to worry. Their own efforts had failed to produce classical conditioning in the sea hare (Kupfermann had been unable to get *Aplysia* to learn to withdraw its gill and siphon in response to a neutral stimulus like a light, even after presenting the snails with light and a strong poke many times). And *Aplysia,* which labs around the country had taken up enthusiastically in the sixties, was now being abandoned as investigators became disillusioned with its extremely limited behavior and discouraged with the poor results from their own efforts to produce learning. Graham Hoyle, who has described *Aplysia* as ''an unbelievably boring, stupid animal, really just a feeding, copulatory machine,'' became so disgusted with *Aplysia* that, only half in jest, he gave demonstrations of how the animal's behavior hardly changed once its entire nervous system was removed. More recently, he has said that *Aplysia* neurons are so easy to work with that even his janitor could stick one. Neuroethologists decided that behavior and not the ease of experimentation should be their guide and moved toward other invertebrate preparations, which though they might lack the big cells of *Aplysia* and other mollusks—or the squishies, as they became known—had at least behavior in their favor. Many chose to work on insects—or crunchies—animals that already had been shown to undergo rapid and vigorous conditioning but which caused great frustration because they had small, unpigmented neurons and ganglia encased in tough, hard-to-penetrate sheaths. Others began looking into carnivorous mollusks like the *Pleurobranchaea,* with the idea that more aggressive eating habits would endow these snails with a more interesting—and possibly conditionable—feeding behavior. The trade-off was that feeding would certainly entail a far more complicated underlying neural circuitry, which it might take years and even decades to unravel.

As one after another neurobiologist switched from *Aplysia,* Kandel and his group were heavily criticized for letting their choice of preparation dictate the direction of their research when they should instead be choosing an animal to suit the questions they wanted to ask. Kupfermann got his own laboratory at NYU and spent several years trying to see whether some behavior other than the siphon and gill withdrawal reflex could be made to undergo classical conditioning. He tried to get *Aplysia* to run mazes and to learn to associate particular foods and odors with a subsequent bad gastrointestinal reaction—all without success. Sometimes the results looked promising at first, but always they turned out to be either sensitization or artifact. Any sign of a real associative change disappeared as Kupfermann ran the numerous groups of controls necessary to prove that a change in an animal's behavior is the result of its having learned a relationship between two closely paired events and not, for instance, of its state of arousal, hunger, or fatigue.

So, in spite of Kandel's success with habituation, there was a time, a long time, when it seemed that his hunch that the sea hare was just the right animal in which to explore a whole series of questions about the basic mechanisms of learning and memory was in fact wrong. It might just be that *Aplysia* hadn't evolved the necessary machinery for conditioning, that it was capable of only such lower forms of learning as habiituation and sensitization. In this case, Kandel and his colleagues had spent a lot of time puzzling out a neural circuit that wasn't capable of entertaining the questions they were really interested in. Their carefully analyzed circuit for gill withdrawal was, in the words of one researcher, "all dressed up with no place to go."

FOUR

The Mind of the Snail

WHAT MOST OF US KNOW about the origins of associative conditioning is that sometime around the turn of the century, a Russian scientist rang a bell and noticed that a dog had begun to salivate. The real story has just as much to do with serendipity, though it reveals that Pavlov, who had already won a Nobel Prize for his studies of digestion when he discovered the paradigm to which he would devote the rest of his life, was somewhat less observant than he first appears.

During his studies of the chemical composition of salivary fluid, Pavlov had devised a way of collecting saliva for analysis that involved placing a tiny tube into the salivary ducts of dogs, then inducing salivation by squirting a meat powder into their mouths. Pavlov, who was said to be totally incompetent at the practical aspects of life—he never bought a pair of shoes for himself, for instance—but perfectly capable of attending to even the smallest details in the lab, happened to notice that after this procedure had been repeated several times, the dogs began to salivate even before they received the meat powder, at the moment when the assistant who had given them the powder in the past walked into the room. This unplanned response interfered with the course of the Russian physiologist's experiments, yet he immediately recognized its importance. Salivation at the sight or taste of meat was built into the animal, Pavlov reasoned. It was, as he would call it after Sherrington's spinal-cord reflexes, an unconditioned reflex; it differed from those reflexes that were controlled by the spinal cord in that the cerebral cortex was involved. Salivation at the sight of the assistant, on the other hand, was a reflex that the dog had acquired through experience. Pavlov called it a conditioned reflex or, because it dealt with the previously unapproachable question of how animals learn, a psychic reflex. His great insight was to see that the formations of these conditioned reflexes could be studied as objective occurrences in the cerebral hemispheres, that they opened up windows on the mind.

Pavlov didn't publish his work on psychic reflexes for twenty-five years, a practice he defended by asking, "How can I write papers when the field is developing so quickly?" But it is clear that he appreciated two somewhat different uses of the paradigm that came to be known as classical conditioning. One, which isn't well known outside of scientific circles, is that classical conditioning can be used as a means of approaching the objective study of the brain. If you can train animals to make different responses to different stimuli, you have a means of communicating with those animals and of determining quite precisely their perceptual capabilities. One way, for example, of asking whether a dog can see colors is to determine if lights of different colors can produce different responses.

The second use of classical conditioning is the one familiar to us. Pavlov realized that inborn reflexes—salivation at the taste of meat—must form a significant part of the behavior of all organisms but that an even more significant portion of behavior cannot be inborn. That we respond if our hand touches a flame is almost surely inborn. But that we respond to a shout of "Fire!" is not. Somehow, we have come to associate the word *fire* with the flame itself, so either the word or the flame produces in us the appropriate response. For Pavlov, then, the study of conditioning was the study of laws governing the formation of associations in the mind—the study of learning.

From his extensive studies of the conditions under which his psychic reflexes were formed, Pavlov postulated some basic governing laws about conditioning, laws that survived intact for many years but began to fall apart, one by one, during the late 1960s and 1970s when some psychologists—under pressure from ethologists—began experiments that would fundamentally alter the understanding of the nature of Pavlov's paradigm. One of these laws was that conditioning involved the simple, mechanical association of two events—any two events to which the animal is sensitive—that occurred closely together in time. A rat hears a bell and is given food a half a second later. After twelve such experiences or pairings, the rat begins to produce a new, "conditioned" response to the bell and now jumps about excitedly at the sound of the bell alone. For Pavlov, the formation of this new response depended only on the length of time between the sound of the bell and the arrival of the food. Half a second was deemed by Pavlov the interval that produced the best learning, and that time frame remained engraved in stone for learning theorists for more than forty years.

Then, in 1970, contiguity, or the idea that conditioning could occur only if two events were closely paired in time, was dealt a blow when John Garcia, a psychologist at UCLA who was influenced by some of the ethological arguments against behavior theory, decided to test rats in a situation they might encounter in real life. Rats aren't made to hear bells or get shocked on the foot, Garcia argued. Rats are made to get around in the world. How would they learn, he wondered, outside of the very artificial setups of the laboratory? To begin to find out, Garcia fed rats a distinctive-tasting food—vanilla, for instance—then poisoned them sublethally with a compound that took several hours to take effect. What he found, and what flew in the face of behavior theory, is that when the rats were tested the next day, they remembered the vanilla perfectly. They wouldn't go near it even though the length of time between their taste of the vanilla and their subsequent sickness was up to twelve hours—a very far cry from half a second. Farmers had known about this phenomenon, which they called bait shyness, for a long time (if they were going to poison a rat with a particular bait, they knew, they had better be successful the first time around because they wouldn't have a second chance), and patients undergoing radiation or chemotherapy were all too aware of it as they found themselves unable to eat foods they associated with the nausea induced by their treatments. It was only in the 1970s, though, that Garcia forced psychologists to look at this phenomenon and its implications for the theory of learning.

By the time Garcia performed his now-famous experiments with the rats, another psychologist, Robert Rescorla, then at Yale University, had recently injected into behaviorism the idea that events came to be associated in an animal's mind not just because they were closely paired in time or contiguous, as Pavlov believed, but also because one event came to predict another. Rescorla demonstrated this by giving two groups of animals the same number of paired presentations of, for instance, light and shock. One group, though, also received interspersed presentations of light alone. That group didn't learn to form an association between light and shock nearly as well as the other. For these animals, Rescorla reasoned, light was not nearly as good a predictor of shock. Indeed, if he gave that group enough presentations of light alone (more than the number of paired light and shock presentations), light would come to predict not shock but the absence of shock; the animals would take it as a cue to relax.

The idea that animals used classical conditioning to make predictions about the occurrences of external events got its greatest momentum from the experiments of the psychologist Leon Kamin at Princeton University. His experiments had the psychological community buzzing for many years and led to a fundamental rethinking of how conditioning works. Kamin took rats and exposed them to sixteen trials in which a noise was followed by an electric shock. The rats then got eight trials in which they were exposed to simultaneous noise and light, then to shock. Since rats learn beautifully to associate either noise and shock or light and shock, Kamin expected that the results of this experiment would produce a very robust conditioning to both the light and the noise. What he found instead was that the rats produced barely any response to the light. His explanation, borne out by much additional experimentation, is that since the rats already had a very good predictor of shock in the noise, the light was redundant, and the rats could somehow block its association with shock. Rather than associating any two events closely linked in time, as Pavlov believed, animals could, it seemed, block the formation of new associations if they were redundant and added no new information. Rather than operating mechanically, they were somehow evaluating each new stimulus as it came along and comparing it with what they already knew.

The experiments of Garcia, Rescorla, and Kamin supported what ethologists had been telling behaviorists all along. Animals learn that which evolution has prepared them to learn; they learn best the things that are of adaptive significance. More important than the absolute amount of time between two events is the biological sense of what is being learned and the predictive value of the conditioned stimulus. It is so important, for example, for a forager like a rat to be able to sample a lot of foods, measure their effects, and then either return to them or avoid them in the future that it has evolved a mechanism for storing and associating tastes and ill effects for up to twelve hours and after only one pairing. Yet it might not associate the sound of a bell with nausea, no matter how many times they were paired. But what also emerged from this work was the realization that rather than being just the highly artificial learning paradigm that some ethologists had claimed it was, associative conditioning might represent a powerful and, perhaps, universal form of learning for the very reason that it gave animals a way of learning causal relations and of making predictions about the world.

"It made one think," Eric Kandel once told an audience at Princeton University, "that perhaps the reason animals learn classical conditioning so readily and the reason it has been such an attractive laboratory model is because it represents a way of learning causal relationships, relationships which the brain has evolved to handle. Animals evolve in a context of environmental pressures, and those animals that know how to relate cause to effect will have a better chance of survival. So perhaps classical conditioning represents an actual thing that is loaded in the brain."

At the same time that ethologists were adding biological relevance to Pavlov's learning theory (and pointing out instances of learning that could not be explained in terms of conditioning—the rapidity with which newly hatched chicks come to recognize their mothers, for example, or a bee's ability to locate its hive), behaviorism was being attacked on another front by psychologists with a more cognitive approach. The issue here was the mind.

Disgusted by the highly subjective, introspective psychology of the nineteenth century and by the Freudian use of such ambiguous, undefinable terms as *the subconscious, instinct,* and *motivation* to define behavior, some of Pavlov's followers had come to assert that the only aspects of behavior that can be studied are the observable ones, not the inner forces. B. F. Skinner and John Broadus Watson rejected concepts of mind and consciousness and went so far as to say that a person's observable behavior was synonymous with his mental life. For them, the mind might as well be an empty black box. They could find out everything they needed to know about it by analyzing stimuli and responses, inputs and outputs. The brain could be full of cotton wool for all that it mattered, Skinner once said.

Cognitive psychologists, on the other hand, emphasized the richness of the mental representations that must intervene between stimuli and their responses (the "shadow," perhaps, that T. S. Eliot was referring to when he wrote, "Between the idea / And the reality / Between the motion / And the act / Falls the Shadow"), and they were fond of pointing out instances in which behaviorists were unable to explain even their own results in terms of reflexes. One of these results was something that Pavlov himself had first described and had called second-order conditioning.

If a dog is exposed to a procedure in which a tone is paired with an electric shock, after a number of trials the tone reliably elicits the conditioned response of crouching and shaking. That's first-order conditioning, and the first phase of higher- or second-order conditioning. Now, suppose the dog is subjected to two types of procedures on alternate days. On some days, tone / shock pairings occur as usual; on others, a light is paired with the tone, and no shock is presented at all. After a while, the animal starts showing the conditioned fear response to the light even though it has never seen the light and the shock together.

The phenomenon of second-order conditioning pleased

behaviorists by increasing ways in which conditioned reflexes could form and by thus lending indirect support to their contention that these reflexes were at the root of all learned behavior. It showed how a person's associations with the relatively rare unconditioned stimuli of the world could grow: someone's unconditioned fear of thunder, for example, could be associated by first-order conditioning with lightning, then by second-order conditioning with an increase in wind, a drop in the temperature, a darkened sky, or the like, until just a sudden breeze was able to start his heart racing. However, second-order conditioning was extremely problematical in that it could not be accounted for in terms of an immediate, stimulus/response reflex. The dog's response to the light is elicited not by the tone but by some internal or mental representation of the aversiveness of shock that it retains and uses to pair with light. Similarly, the person who is terrified of thunder holds in his mind an internal representation of thunder that can then come to be associated with an initially innocuous stimulus such as a darkened sky or an increase in wind. Behaviorists also had problems with Kamin's experiments in which an animal blocks the formation of an association. There, as in second-order conditioning, the animal had to be keeping in its brain some sort of mental representation against which it could measure the new stimulus. That mental representation, cognitive psychologists said, was mind.

Mind was not, therefore, as these experiments showed, the empty black box that behaviorists had claimed, but rather something with content and something very clever—clever enough to keep track of conditioned and unconditioned stimuli and somehow estimate the probabilities that if a bell rings, a shock will follow; clever enough, too, to decide which is the best response to make. And, most amazing, all this cleverness had to have as its basis physiological mechanisms built into cells and circuits of cells: compounds that might have a life of only half a second, an ion channel that might stay open for up to twelve hours, a reset mechanism in a circuit that might ensure that every time a stimulus is presented by itself, the association between two events is weakened. The possibilities are endless; it only remains for cellular neurophysiologists to find out which of these many theoretically possible mechanisms cells actually use.

Chris Sahley, a young Yale University psychologist who is the undisputed master at teaching snails the tricks of associative conditioning, gets fidgety when people start talking about minds, especially the minds of snails. It must be because of her training in behavioral psychology. At the same time, her sympathies with the concerns and methods of ethologists have taken her further than anyone else in finding out just how smart snails are. She expected big differences in the way in which snails and humans learn; instead, she has found remarkable similarities. It is in fact her work that gives Kandel and other researchers the confidence that what goes on in a snail's ganglion is going on in the cerebral cortex of humans as well.

After Pavlov discovered associative conditioning, numerous scientists, interested in whether this form of learning was universal, tried to find associative changes in a variety of animals, ranging from chimpanzees to flatworms. The vertebrates were quick learners, but most of the experiments with invertebrates failed, it is now known, because investigators used stimuli—lights and bells—that were tantalizing to humans but totally irrelevant to a snail or a worm. Later, using the ethological theories of the sixties and the seventies and the idea that experimenters should concentrate on behavior and stimuli that have adaptive significance for the animal, researchers suddenly began to succeed with invertebrates. In 1962, insects were found to be capable of conditioning, and since then the list of invertebrate learners has grown to include starfish, hermit crabs, leeches, bees, fruit flies, octopuses, crayfish, and numerous species of snails. No one is saying that these animals are as smart or as capable of learning as mammals. It is clear that innate, wired-in behaviors form a much greater proportion of invertebrates' repertoires than they do of vertebrates', but it is also clear that the ability to learn from experience was not tacked on late in evolution: it exists in some of the simplest and most primitive animals on earth.

Chris Sahley was still an undergraduate in the late 1960s when much of the work on invertebrate learning was being done. She was not even the first to find associative learning in a snail; Jack Davis and George Mpitsos, at the University of California at Santa Cruz, would do that in 1973. While working in the laboratory of Alan Gelperin at Princeton University, she was, though, the investigator who would go further than anyone else in analyzing associative learning in snails.

Like the rest of the psychologists who spend their time teaching snails tricks, Chris Sahley, now in her mid-thirties and with a manner so relaxed and open that you suspect when you are talking with her that she has just finished a daily workout of some sort, is only mildly interested in the snail's ability to learn, per se. But, she believes, if snails are going to be used as the main preparations in which to study the cellular and molecular basis of mental functions like learning and memory, it will be nice to know, at least, that the behavioral (observable) features of learning in snails resemble those of learning in humans, for that will give us some indication that the underlying mechanisms might also be the same.

Along the way, Sahley's studies have given her a higher opinion of snails. ''I tend to think about animals differently than other people,'' she says. ''When I hear people being chauvinistic about humans, I have to say, 'Come on. Give me a break. We definitely have language and fantastic capabilities, but you also have to appreciate that there are some very fundamental similarities between us and invertebrates.' When I teach learning theory to undergraduates, I show them the similarities between how invertebrates and vertebrates learn, and they love it. You have to talk about commonalities, not differences.''

''Did you ever doubt that snails could learn?'' I asked Sahley one day as we sat in the small, windowless room off her lab at Yale that was serving as her temporary office.

''No, but I guess I did start out thinking that learning in invertebrates would be very simple, that it would operate on simple concepts like stimuli pairing, but perhaps not on predictability or contingency,'' she replied. ''Then, as I got further into my work and tested for predictability, I found that slugs seemed to be using the same principles that operate in humans. And I thought, Why not? We all have to live in the world. We all have to extract causal relationships from it. The sun comes up; it's daytime; it's warm. The snail must learn to move away from the light and into the dark. Dark, for it, predicts a moist, cool environment, and that environment is essential for the snail since it cannot regulate its internal temperature.''

When Sahley first started working with slugs (technically, a land mollusk with only a rudimentary shell) as a postdoctoral student in Alan Gelperin's lab, there was good evidence, she says, that certain marine snails and the slug could undergo a pairing-specific or associative change in behavior. Those experiments had been done by neurophysiologists unfamiliar with learning theory, though, and pairing was about as far as they went. With her background in psychology, Chris was also interested in whether her slugs could learn predictability, blocking, second-order conditioning, and so on.

Sahley had had much exposure to biology students and ethologists as a graduate student at the University of Kentucky in the mid-seventies, and when it came time to put her training to work on *Limax Maximus* (the common garden slugs that Alan Gelperin had chosen to work with, in part because he was able to get them from neighborhood children for ten cents apiece instead of the ten dollars it cost for a marine snail like *Aplysia*), she was all ready to turn to a natural situation. She knew that her slug was a generalized herbivore—that it foraged for a wide variety of foods—and that it was attracted to odors. Thinking that it would be in the slug's best interest that, if it tasted something it didn't like or that made it sick, it wouldn't be attracted to the odor of that thing again, she decided to try getting the slugs to learn to associate certain odors with certain tastes. It was, as she says, a "natural CS / US [conditioned stimulus / unconditioned stimulus] pairing."

Garden slugs don't eat very often (contrary to the experience of most gardeners), and they must be starving in order to do so. Sahley therefore decided not to use feeding itself as a test of the slug's ability to learn, but rather food preference. "You have to be kind to your animals or you'll never see learning," she explains. "You can't ask a starving animal not to eat. Learning is such a small part of an animal's total behavior that you can't have it working against everything else, its sexual drives, state of satiation, circadian rhythms, et cetera."

In rats, a shifting of food preferences had been found to produce very strong learning, and Sahley opted for a similar setup for her slugs. She would pair an odor that the slugs liked to home in on with a disagreeable taste and see if she could shift their food preference. All slugs, she found, prefer potatoes to their normal laboratory diet of rat chow, but if she paired the odor of potatoes with the bitter taste of quinine ninety seconds later, she could shift their preference to rat chow.

Everyone had thought that slugs would be slow learners, but this happened after just one trial, 90 percent of the time. It was learning that was, in the jargon of psychologists, very robust.

It was also the most dramatic learning ever demonstrated in invertebrates, but Sahley was not satisfied to stop there. She also wanted to know if the odor of potatoes came to predict to the slug the taste of quinine. The experimental protocol she used was basically the same, but now in addition to the same number of potato / quinine pairings, one group of slugs also received some presentations of potato odor alone. Not surprisingly, these slugs didn't learn to avoid potatoes nearly as well; for them, it didn't always predict quinine.

Next Sahley tried blocking the formation of the slug's association of potatoes and quinine. First, she had slugs learn to pair carrots—another preferred odor—with quinine. Then she alternated presentations of carrots and quinine with presentations of carrots, potatoes, and quinine. The outcome was the same as that for Kamin's rats: because the slugs had a perfectly good predictor of quinine in the odor of carrots, they failed to make an association between potatoes and quinine. These results flew in the face of traditional behaviorist theory, as well as our historical stinginess in acknowledging the presence of properties like mind and reason in the rest of the animal kingdom. Not even the ganglia of these slugs were empty black boxes; rather, they had stored within them a "mental" representation of carrots and quinine against which potatoes measured up as redundant.

Sahley also succeeded in getting the slugs to show second-order conditioning. In the first phase, she produced strong first-order conditioning by pairing the odor of potatoes with the bitter taste of quinine. In the second phase, she got those animals to make the additional association between potatoes and carrots. Though they had never experienced carrots with quinine, they now avoided the previously tempting carrots as much as they did potatoes.

The next question, said Sahley (who notes that in just ten years psychologists have gone from asking *if* invertebrates can learn to *what* they learn), was what was actually going on in the slugs' heads—ganglia—during this process. Do the slugs form an association between the smell of carrots and the smell of potatoes (which because it is associated with quinine brings about an avoidance reaction), or do they make a direct association in their "minds" between carrots and the avoidance reaction? Amazingly, psychologists have a way of distinguishing between the two possibilities. They take an animal that has undergone second-order conditioning; then by repeated presentations of potatoes alone, they extinguish—or make the animal forget—his first-order association of potatoes and quinine. Under these circumstances, if the first interpretation is correct, the animal won't remember that potatoes are associated with anything it would like to avoid and will continue to be attracted to carrots. If the second alternative applies, it will avoid carrots as before.

"When I tried these experiments, it was a riot," Sahley says. "I couldn't figure out what was going on. In some experiments, it seemed that the first thing was happening and in others the second." She was at this time interviewing for her current position as an assistant professor of psychology at Yale, and while in New Haven talking to various department members, she happened to mention her mixed-up findings to Bob Rescorla. Rescorla laughed; he had recently found the exact same thing in rats and thought he had the explanation for it. In phase two of second-order conditioning, if the two stimuli—potatoes and carrots—are presented simultaneously, the animal forms an association between carrots, potatoes, and the aversive qualities of quinine. If carrots are presented before potatoes, however, the slug associates the smell of carrots with its conditioned response to potatoes—avoidance.

Incredibly esoteric? Yes and no. What it means for Sahley is that the nervous system operates differently if two stimuli are presented simultaneously from the way it works if they are presented sequentially. "There's something different going on," she says, "because the internal representations that the animal is forming are different." And when Sahley finally maps the neural circuit in the garden slug that controls these feeding preferences and begins to use electrophysiological and biochemical techniques to study the cellular and molecular basis underlying the shift in food preference, this kind of information is going to give her a very precise criterion for how things can happen. With these detailed behavioral studies, she is erecting a kind of scaffolding that will guide her in her investigations of the mechanisms underlying learning. Her scaffolding is far more detailed than that of the others in the field, most of whom started and finished their behavioral studies with simple pairing. Sahley will know now to look for a mechanistic difference between simultaneous and sequential presentations of two stimuli. "It's these kinds of things that are the most fascinating to me," she admits. "Like other psychologists, I tend to jump in at the complex end. Biologists start figuring out the simple things first."

"What does your mother think about what you're doing?" I had the nerve to ask Sahley at this point in our conversation.

"Oh, my mother. I have lots of good stories about my mother," she replied with a grin. "Let's see. 'Have you finished your experiment yet?' she's always asking me. Or, 'If you do good work with slugs, will they let you work on real animals?' " Sahley laughed. To her, slugs are real enough.

And what does it mean that the garden slug, the bane of a cabbage grower's existence, is capable of internal representations? Sahley, who tends to interpret the results of her experiments cautiously, says that it means only that slugs can do things on the basis of a knowledge that they have rather than needing a tone or some other stimulus to which they then react. Its greatest meaning, perhaps, is only in relation to the long-standing behaviorist position that most behavior can be accounted for by stimulus / response reflexes. But did it also mean that snails or slugs are conscious—or able to perceive their own perceptions?

Naively, I expected neurobiologists to have the answers. But when I asked Alan Gelperin, Chris Sahley's postdoctoratal adviser, about consciousness and the slug, he set me straight. "Neurobiologists have no special insights into consciousness," he told me. "They have no way of approaching consciousness. How do you even go about asking if an animal is conscious? That's the problem. For a nonverbal animal, what are the essential defining features that will allow you to attribute to it consciousness? Nobody has any answers to these questions for chimpanzees, much less snails."

He added, though, that many forms of learning neither require nor imply consciousness. You can learn all kinds of things without being aware that you have learned them—think of all the fine motor adjustments required to learn to ride a bicycle or throw a ball a certain distance. Also, humans, rats, and other animals can learn some kinds of simple associations very well while they're anesthetized and unconscious. So can animals that have intact spinal cords but whose brains have been removed—animals that nobody would argue are in possession of consciousness. Such a spinalized animal, as it is called, is capable of associating a shock to one of its limbs with a mild tactile stimulus, with the result that after a few such pairings it comes to withdraw its limb when presented with the tactile stimulus alone.

Consciousness, then, is not essential for learning, and the fact that snails and slugs learn says much more about how the capacity for changing behavior based on previous experience came very early in evolution; it was not, as human chauvinists from Descartes on have thought, a recent development, added on once humans—or even vertebrates—came into existence.

The slug's ability to block associations and to form second-order associations means it can hold in its ganglia internal representations of the world around it. This holds out hope for the study of the mind. The mind of a human is certainly many orders of magnitude more complex than anything that goes on in a slug, but what is going on in slugs satisfies, at least, the definition of mind of many psychologists and philosophers. Therefore, because snails and slugs have relatively simple nervous systems, scientists have been able to use them to begin to explore "the cellular basis of mentation," as Kandel puts it—the content of the mind.

FIVE

The Rest of the Field

WHAT SNAILS OFFERED TO scientists, then, was the possibility that, in the same cell and with the same microelectrode, they could fix their attention on the psychological and the physiological at the same time. And scientists were justifiably excited. Here was a chance, yes, to study the cellular basis of learning, but also to approach the cellular basis of dualism, to begin asking the question of how it is possible that a mind emerges from a collection of single cells. Kandel was the first to appreciate this, but by the 1970s his work had inspired several other investigators to try their luck with these "simple systems" as well. Like Kandel, they would study learning because learning was at least operationally defined through Pavlovian and instrumental conditioning paradigms. But while Kandel was studying habituation and, later, sensitization, they would put all their emphasis on associative conditioning.

Chris Sahley's postdoctoral adviser, Alan Gelperin, was one of these investigators. In the late 1960s, Gelperin, a young biology professor at Princeton University, was at a crossroads in his career. He had been trying to study learning in a crunchy—the praying mantis—but was frustrated because raising these insects in the lab was extremely difficult and because "their neurophysiology just wasn't any good," meaning their neurons were too small to record from. At the time, Gelperin had read Tauc and Kandel's papers and was eager to pursue his own questions about associative conditioning, but he didn't have a suitable animal with which to work. *Aplysia* was expensive and, besides, Kandel seemed to have had that animal covered early on. It was then that Gelperin happened to pay a visit to a friend of his who ran a small natural-history museum. There, in one of the aquariums, he saw a brown, two-inch-long female garden slug with its eggs; its scientific name was *Limax maximus*. Curious about *Limax*'s potential experimental usefulness, Gelperin brought the land slug and its eggs back to his lab and began examining its nervous system as well as its possibilities for associative learning. Now, some fifteen years later, the efforts of Gelperin and his postdoctoral student Chris Sahley have given *Limax* the title (among those who study snails) "queen of the learners."

Limax's educability, some say, is the result of Gelperin's and Sahley's sympathy with ethology and concern with using natural stimuli; others give more credit to the snail's own intelligence, to the fact that its nervous system is highly centralized or concentrated and, therefore, more like the nervous system of a lower vertebrate than, for instance, is *Aplysia*'s. Centralization and cephalization (the tendency for nervous systems to become concentrated in the head or cephalic region) are the major directions in the evolution of brains. Whereas *Aplysia*'s ganglia are small and distributed over the snail's length, *Limax*'s are mostly clustered in a large mass at its head. But the same characteristics that may make *Limax* a smarter snail than *Aplysia,* its greater number of interneurons and therefore its capability, perhaps, of forming more associations, also makes those associations much more difficult to analyze. Any advantages that *Limax* offers because of its abilities to learn turn into disadvantages when it comes to studying the cellular basis of that learning. *Limax*'s small, clustered cells are hard to get at with a microelectrode, and this makes the determination of which cells are involved in a given behavior extremely difficult and time-consuming. Sahley estimates that it will take her ten to twenty years just to figure out the circuit of neurons that are involved in her learning paradigm—the shifting of the snail's preference from potatoes to rat chow. Finding the changes that take place in those cells during learning will take even longer. She is in this for the long haul, though, and seems to accept that time frame. When her mother asks, "Have you finished your experiment yet?" she has to laugh, for it may well be that the work with *Limax* will not be completed in her lifetime. Gelperin, who now has a joint appointment at Princeton and at Bell Laboratories in New Jersey, also continues to study *Limax*.

Another early entrant in the field opened up by Kandel was William Jackson ("Jack") Davis, a Californian biologist with blond hair and classic good looks that make him look more like many people's idea of a ski instructor than a neurobiologist. Davis was interested in learning not for its own sake but because learning was the only one of the higher mental processes that had been at all defined and that therefore was approachable or "tractable" at a cellular level.

"Really, if I had my druthers," says Davis, who divides his time between his large family (he has six children) and his interests in ecology and neurobiology, "I would like to know whether we can understand the most complicated things that people do and are in terms of individual nerve cells, but that's unrealistic. You have to move down from the most complicated things like personality to problems that are at least partly defined—like learning. And you have to move down from people. At this point, it's learning in a snail that's tractable, but its really the more complicated questions that give me my philosophical push.''

In 1969, when Davis began experimenting on the large and carnivorous marine slug *Pleurobranchaea,* there were some tantalizing hints that invertebrates, including snails, could learn, but no hard scientific evidence. Davis, though, had no doubts about their abilities. He had always been impressed by the abilities of the fleas in European flea circuses and knew that sometimes ''scientists were the last to figure things out.'' He did have his doubts about whether he as a human being would be able to come up with the right stimuli for these highly aggressive snails to learn to associate. Humans are very visual, but most snails see poorly if at all. They also don't hear well, so it was unlikely that they would use either their undeveloped visual or auditory senses to learn with.

Davis solved the problem by trying mentally to put himself in the body of a snail and ask himself how he would learn. ''What a snail does do well is feel and smell,'' he says. ''So I began by playing around with a probe, touching the snail here and there. An innocuous touch to the head, I found, elicits a 'bite-strike'—or feeding—response. Then I tried changing the seeming, built-in inevitability of this response by shocking the snail every time it responded to the probe in that way.''

Soon, the California neurophysiologist found that he was able to condition his snails not to feed—to bite-strike—when touched by the probe. His next task was to show that this change in behavior is pairing specific, that is, that it is not just the result of sensitization or some other nonassociative phenomenon. To do this, Davis had to run control groups in which the probe and shock were delivered at different times and to show that the animals in these groups failed to learn. ''This was the trickiest party,'' he remembers, ''because these snails have a very different sense of time than we do. It's as if everything is in slow motion for them. The only way we could get the experiment to work was to abandon all the usual dogma about 'optimal intervals between the conditioned and the unconditioned stimulus.' In order to get our control animals not to show a change, we had to poke the snail with the probe, then wait for thirty minutes or so before we delivered the shock. We started off in high speed—pairing the unconditioned and conditioned stimulus over milliseconds—then went to middle speed, but it wasn't until we moved to low speed that we could show pairing-specific changes.''

Davis's perseverance paid off, and in 1973 he and a graduate student, George Mpitsos, were the first to report that snails were capable of reliable associative learning. Since then, Davis has switched from tactile to chemosensory stimuli (instead of the probe, he now pairs the odor of ground-up squid with electric shock), and he has begun to look for the cells responsible for feeding. That experience has been a deeply humbling one. *Pleurobranchaea* was chosen as Davis's experimental animal because it was supposed to have a ''simple'' nervous system. True, its nervous system is far less complicated than that of a vertebrate, but, says Davis, it is still enormously complicated. When Davis and his colleagues began taking it apart, they found that hundreds and hundreds of cells were involved in feeding. '' 'Simple systems', I soon realized, was an indication of our level of thought rather than the actual level of the system,'' Davis says now. He and his colleagues have been working on this simple system for fifteen years, and only in the last three has Davis expressed confidence that he can bring the project to completion in the next fifteen years.

Daniel Alkon, a staff investigator with the National Institutes of Health's in-house research program, was a third scientist to enter the field and the most similar to Kandel in training and background. Like Kandel, Alkon graduated from medical school, and after completing his internship in medicine, he trained in neurophysiology under Mike Fuortes at NIH's Laboratory of Neurophysiology. Alkon didn't have any formal psychiatric training, but he was deeply impressed by psychoanalytic theory and had read Freud in medical school. Both Alkon and Kandel were physicians, interested in human problems, who had questions about the nature of learning that could be answered only in snails. Neither started with an interest in the behavior or biology of snails; at least in the beginning, their interest in these animals was largely confined to their usefulness in the study of learning. Nor was either of them overly concerned with performing Chris Sahley's type of detailed behavioral analysis. The goal of both was to find an example of learning, then get as quickly as possible to the cellular mechanisms that explained that learning.

This is very apparent in the way that Alkon approached the question of learning. Instead of starting out—as Gelperin and Davis did—with a behavior, then looking for the neural circuitry behind that behavior, Alkon began with an understanding of neural circuitry, then looked for a behavior that he could map onto it. It was an unorthodox strategy, but one that was to put him far ahead of Gelperin and Davis and, for several years, Kandel, in what many observers were beginning to see as a race to understand the cellular and molecular basis of learning and memory, a race that insiders and outsiders alike felt would culminate in a Nobel Prize.

Thirteen years Kandel's junior, Alkon first became aware of the older man's early work on habituation in 1970 during his internship at Mount Sinai Hospital in New York. Alkon had been interested in the basic mechanisms of learning for several years, but since he believed that real learning was associative in nature, he tended to dismiss Kandel's experiments with habituation. "If there had been anything to that work," he once told me, "I'd be working on *Aplysia* now."

Alkon, a short, slightly heavy man with strongly sculpted features, long, brown eyebrows that curl upward, and an intense, humorless expression, is known for slighting remarks like that, and his talk is liberally salted with such statements as "I knew at a very early age that I was exceptionally bright"; "I was very much in demand then"; "_____ is the antithesis of my idea of a scientist"; and "This field is mostly bullshit"—statements that soon irritate even an initially sympathetic listener. They seem to be part of an almost automatic behavior on his part to put down others and promote himself, a trait that has not made him a favorite among his colleagues. At the NIH laboratories in Bethesda, Maryland, where Alkon spent the years 1970–74, he is said to have been so unpopular as to be the target of practical and even cruel jokes by some of his colleagues. One thought of putting random-noise generators in Alkon's equipment to slowly drive him mad; another fulfilled Alkon's request for a recently systhesized chemical but sent it to him in a vial on which the lid had been epoxied shut.

Over the years, Alkon has succeeded at NIH because he is ambitious, bright, and persistent and publishes frequently. But his deeply ingrained habit of disparaging almost anyone and everyone has made for strained relations with many of his co-workers. Among the seventy or eighty scientists who have worked with Alkon over the past sixteen years, there are those who see eye to eye with him, but others have found him difficult, if not impossible, to work with. Not surprisingly, the morale in Alkon's lab is sometimes low; a number of his colleagues have left because of irresolvable differences. Alkon, meanwhile, dismisses those he does not get along with as either less intelligent or less committed to "finding the truth" than he is.

Alkon, who was raised in a middle-class suburb of Philadelphia, always knew that he would be involved in some sort of scholarly pursuit, but he didn't realize that he wanted to become a scientist until late in his college career. Coming out of a childhood he describes as having been "full of turmoil" on account of an extremely tyrannical father, Alkon first flirted with literature and dropped out of school altogether before completing the honors thesis in biochemistry that convinced him that research was the thing he loved to do. He received a degree in chemistry from the University of Pennsylvania, then decided to go on to medical school because, he says, of "an urge to help people," an impulse that came from the problems in his own family. "I'm a physician for a reason," he told me. "I've seen enough mental suffering in people that I know to make me want to help." While at the Cornell University Medical School, Alkon became familiar with psychoanalytic theory and interested in how individuals reinforce and reenact their past conditioning throughout their lives. He spent a great deal of his time working with mentally ill patients, and one of his first scientific publications was on the effect that the early loss of a parent had on the probability of someone's becoming a psychiatric patient.

Alkon's readings in psychiatry and his attempts to resolve the events of his own childhood led him to wonder, as he puts it, about "the degree to which an individual can expand his freedom of choice." How can we learn to break old, destructive patterns? How could he change his own fearful expectations stemming from the events of his past in the new relationships in which he became involved? Alkon read up on learning and relearning and found that, on a very basic level, nothing was known about the mechanisms they entailed. A critical determinant of people's behavior was what they had learned; yet scientists knew very little about how we learn or how we can change what we have learned. It was obvious to Alkon that if psychiatrists knew more about the basic physiology of learning, they could help their patients more effectively.

At this time, Alkon stopped reading and began to develop his own theories about the brain and learning. He started with a purely armchair approach. How would he design a brain that could learn? What were the essential elements of learning? He came up with some ideas. One was that learning was associative: it involved the association of different kinds of stimuli (visual, tactile, auditory, and so on) because those stimuli had occurred together in time. But how were these stimuli associated in the brain? Alkon learned a lot about this, he says, without doing a single experiment or opening a single book.

"I made, for instance, the observation that I could associate something within a fraction of a second," he told me, "and this gave me the insight that an explanation of learning based on the growth of new connections between cells—new synapses—would be ridiculous. I was forced to realize that for some associations the pathways already exist in the brain."

And this brought him to a second conclusion: "That with whatever ability I have to perceive something, I could at will associate it with anything else just because I decided to. The wiring had to be already there. What does that mean? That a lot of the function of the billions upon billions of synapses in the brain is to provide the possibility of any stimulus converging with any other, to provide the framework for learning. We are, after all," Alkon notes, "above all else machines that learn."

Alkon pursued this line of reasoning, and once he had finished with his internship at Mount Sinai Hospital, he went to NIH's Laboratory of Neurophysiology as a research associate in the Public Health Service. There he began looking for an animal with which he might be able to test his ideas. Rimon Faye, the California collector who was supplying most of the *Aplysia* to Kandel's lab, sent Alkon many different animals to look over. From among them, Alkon chose *Hermissenda,* an inch-and-a-half-long, brightly colored, shell-less marine snail with yellow and blue racing stripes. Because of its covering of fleshy, plumelike spikes—external extensions of its respiratory system—*Hermissenda* looks like the snail's colorful answer to the porcupine. Unlike porcupines, though, these small snails are extremely aggressive and eat everything, including each other.

Alkon's choice of *Hermissenda* was based in part on the dissimilarities between its nervous system and that of *Aplysia.* Like *Limax, Hermissenda* has a nervous system that is highly centralized in a ring of ganglia around the animal's esophagus. But to Alkon this represented an advantage. If he wanted to associate two different kinds of sensory input, he didn't want the ganglia that processed those inputs to be strung out over the animal's body. Far better that they were in the same location (where he could poke them at the same time) and connected by short, easily analyzable connectives. *Hermissenda* also had a big advantage over *Limax* in that its ganglia were covered by almost no connective tissue, for this made the nerve cells very easy to penetrate. But there was another major reason behind the choice of this particular snail, namely, that Alkon already knew from the work of a Stanford graduate student that at least one of *Hermissenda*'s sensory systems—the eye— was fairly simple. Whereas the human eye has some one hundred million photoreceptors (nerve cells specialized to receive light), each of *Hermissenda*'s two eyes, tiny black dots at the base of the snail's tentacles, has only five.

In his NIH laboratory, Alkon put microelectrodes into these five photoreceptors and recorded from them for a full year. He determined, for instance, that there were two different kinds of photoreceptors in the eyes of *Hermissenda* (he called them Type A and Type B), which were characterized by their behavior in darkness, their action potentials, and their connections with each other. Both types of cells fire action potentials in response to flashes of light, but while the Type A cells are quiescent in darkness, Type B's fire bursts of action potentials, or spikes. Type B photoreceptors are also mutually inhibitory (when a Type B cell fires, it sends inhibitory signals to other Type B cells), and they inhibit Type A photoreceptors; Type A receptors, by contrast, have few if any interactions with each other. Using microelectrode recordings and dye injection techniques with which he could trace the actual course of the cells and their axons, Alkon also began to examine how the photoreceptors interact with the fourteen cells of the snail's nearby optic ganglion (a small mass that, like the eye, is located just outside the much larger cerebropleural ganglion) and where these cells actually end up. Axons from both the photoreceptors and the optic ganglion cells travel in a common tract into the cerebropleural ganglion, where they terminate in a spray of fine endings.

While studying these structures, Alkon couldn't help noticing the snail's primitive vestibular, or balance, organs—its statocysts—located, as they are, right next to the eyes and optic ganglia. The statocysts, tiny spheres lined with disk-shaped nerve cells and filled with a clear fluid and a cluster of tiny crystalline particles called statoconia, tell the animal which way is up. They are analogous to the inner ear in humans. The disk-shaped cells have long hairs that project into the center of the sphere. When the statocyst is tilted, the crystalline particles fall to the lowest point, bending the hairs of particular hair cells. Those cells are excited and send signals down their axons and into the cerebropleural ganglion. Because the statocysts are so close to the eyes, Alkon thought that the vestibular pathway would be a great second pathway for the associative-type experiments he had in mind.

But no one had ever recorded from a cell as small as a hair cell. One cell was only a five-hundredth of an inch in diameter (some two hundred times smaller than the giant cell in *Aplysia*'s abdominal ganglion), small enough to put any scientist off. It was several years, therefore, before Alkon finally decided to give these cells a try. When he did, he found that putting a finely drawn microelectrode into a hair cell was entirely possible and, most important, that he could obtain excellent recordings from them. The very first time he stuck a microelectrode into a hair cell, Alkon also flashed a light on his preparation and watched the screen of the oscilloscope closely. The hair cell had been firing bursts of action potentials, but it changed the frequency of those potentials in response to the light. Alkon had in effect just asked the hair cell if it received input from the visual system, and the cell had answered yes. Alkon promised himself that he was "going to have a try at this." He was going to try to get these snails to associate a visual and a vestibular stimulus, then study how that association took place.

First, though, Alkon wanted to know more about the wiring of the statocysts and about the interactions of the two systems. The electrophysiology of the statocyst, he found, was a simple but elegant parallel to the organ's function. When the animal is tilted and the statoconia fall to the lowest point, they compress the hairs of those hair cells located on the side that the statocyst is tilting toward. By putting microelectrodes into two hair cells simultaneously, Alkon discovered that an excited hair cell inhibits the hair cell on the opposite side of the statocyst. It sends signals, in other words, that prevent that cell from firing. Only the hair cells at the lowest point of the statocysts are active at any time, therefore, and this gives the animal an accurate reading of which way is up. Alkon also found more evidence that the hair cells receive input from the visual system and new evidence that photoreceptors receive input from hair cells as well. If he stimulated the hair cells of one statocyst to fire, Alkon found that he interrupted the normal response to light of the photoreceptors in the eye on the animal's other side.

In all, Alkon, who believes that one of the features of a good scientist is persistence, spent three to four years at this painstaking kind of analysis, stimulating and recording from pairs of cells in hundreds of animals, learning when and how specific receptor cells respond to a particular stimulus and how they interact with other cells. By 1973, he had a very good idea of how the visual and vestibular systems were wired and was ready to try out associative conditioning. The question he faced now was what stimuli he should attempt to pair. He thought of changing an animal's orientation, then flashing a light, as well as of several variations on this idea, when a colleague at NIH suggested that he "just shake the thing up."

"I thought about it," says Alkon, "and it made a lot of sense. In the wild, *Hermissenda* exhibit positive phototactic behavior. That is, they crawl towards the light because they find their food in the brightly lit, shallow water. When they're in turbulent water, they respond by clinging to the bottom, by decreasing their movement and the size of their foot. Maybe, by giving a snail repeated paired presentations of turbulence and light, by 'shaking an animal up' while flashing a light, it would be possible to change the snail's natural response to light.''

Alkon attempted to do just that. He placed containers of snails on rotating platforms and turned on a diffuse light for 45 seconds before and then during a 25-second rotation cycle. Rotation was followed by 105 seconds of rest, then another round of light paired with rotation. After training periods of three hours, Alkon tested his snails by seeing how long it took them to crawl into a spot of light and by comparing that with their average time before training. He first reported learning-associated changes in phototactic behavior in a 1974 paper entitled ''Associative Training of *Hermissenda.''* Most of the other investigators in this growing field, however, were quick to point out that the changes Alkon had found could very well be due to the nonspecific phenomenon of sensitization rather than to true associative learning. Shaking the snails up must sensitize them and change many of their normal responses; Alkon had not shown that it was those animals which received rotation in conjunction with light that showed the greatest change in phototactic behavior.

Alkon's next steps were to recruit a learning psychologist, someone who could help in sorting out sensitization from associative learning, to the work on *Hermissenda* and to move his laboratory up to the Marine Biological Laboratory in Woods Hole. Since its foundation in 1888 by a group of fifteen biologists who had raised $11,000 for the purpose of establishing a seaside laboratory, MBL had been a predominantly summer research facility; in the late 1960s, though, it had begun to encourage year-round investigations and programs in the hopes that the full-time usage of the laboratory might ease some of its budgetary strains. NIH was among the first to respond to MBL's overtures, by moving its Laboratory of Biophysics up to Woods Hole; Alkon was appointed assistant chief of the new "extramural intramural" lab. Not all of his colleagues were pleased by his promotion, but Alkon was chosen at a time when some of the higher-ups at NIH were wondering whether the scientists in the Laboratory of Biophysics were studying anything at all that was relevant to human problems and human diseases. They felt that Alkon's tremendous persistence, energy, and interest in learning would infuse new spirit and energy into NIH's in-house research program.

In 1978, after Alkon had settled in to his new and somewhat cramped quarters in MBL's Lillie Building, he and Terry Crow, a psychologist from California who had abandoned classical conditioning in cats to work on snails, were able to publish the results of experiments that showed clearly that *Hermissenda* was capable of an associative change in its response to light. Crow had used the basic skeleton of Alkon's original conditioning paradigm but had filled it out with additional, exhaustive controls and had made several important changes. He fully automated the training procedure so as to remove any investigator bias, and he also changed how rotation was delivered to the animals so that the effects of rotation could be better defined. Instead of shaking the snails up on rotating tables, Crow started spinning them around in individual glass tubes on the turntable of a record player. Most important, he changed the timing of light and rotation to one that was more likely to favor an associative change.

Alkon was not the first to find associative conditioning in snails, but now that he had it, he was all ready to jump into the study of the cellular correlates of his associative change. Alkon already understood the circuitry of the cells that must be involved in *Hermissenda*'s learning; in the race to understand the basis of learning and memory, he was well out in front.

While Alkon was beginning his rise through the ranks of NIH and paving his way for an analysis of the basic mechanisms of learning in *Hermissenda,* Eric Kandel's group at New York University was continuing to make remarkable headway in understanding the basis of habituation and then sensitization, habituation's functional opposite. They had also started to address a question that had long fascinated psychologists: What is the relation between short-term and long-term memory?

One of the oldest observations in regard to memory is that recent memories are more easily disrupted than old ones. A woman who becomes unconscious after being hit on the head is more likely to remember—when she wakes up—the name of her fifth-grade teacher than that of the new neighbor she met the day before. This instability of recently acquired memories has led to the idea that short-term and long-term memory are different phenomena, brought about by different mechanisms. They undoubtedly occur in parallel, but short-term memory, it has been widely believed, is just a short-lived phenomenon, a temporary record an animal can use, while the long-term memory of a telephone number, face, technique, and so on is in the process of being fixed in the brain. Because short-term memories are extremely labile, it was thought that they might involve the continuous activity of loops or circuits of neurons, activity that could easily be disrupted. Long-term memory, on the other hand, was believed to be inscribed in the brain in less erasable ink, perhaps through changes in the effectiveness of existing synapses or (less likely) the formation of new ones.

Until the early 1970s, though, theories on the relation between short-term and long-term memory were purely speculative. There was no evidence on which to base them, since no one had been able to localize within the brain any site of memory, much less compare it in the long- and short-term forms. In 1972, Kandel was the first to accomplish a study of this kind after finding that the gill withdrawal reflex, the reflex already shown to be capable of undergoing habituation for short periods of time, could also habituate for days and weeks. True, some scientists don't regard habituation as learning, and this was only habituation in a snail, but their findings indicated that long-term habituation was not a completely different process from the short-term phenomenon but, rather, a continuation and extension of the changes that occurred early on.

When Kandel and his colleagues looked at an animal whose gill withdrawal reflex was profoundly depressed (habituated) and would remain so for weeks, they found that the motor neurons controlling gill contraction showed a decreased post-synaptic potential in response to a stimulus to the siphon, just as they had in short-term habituation. The decrease was even greater, though, so great that in some cases when Kandel put a microelectrode into a sensory cell and a microelectrode into a motor cell, then fired the sensory cell, he found that he couldn't pick up any response in the motor neuron at all. Whereas short-term habituation involved a transient decrease in synaptic effectiveness, long-term habituation led to a prolonged decrease in synaptic effectiveness and a profound functional inactivation of previously existing synaptic connections. This extension might have been brought about, Kandel speculated, though changes involving the cell's DNA or through structural rearrangements in the cell.

For short-term habituation, at least, Kandel and his group were soon able to determine the cause of the decrease in the postsynaptic potential in the motor neurons. In 1970, they had been left with the two possibilities: a decrease in the sensitivity of the neurotransmitter receptor molecules in the dendritic membrane of the motor neurons or—the possibility favored by Kandel—a decrease in the amount of neurotransmitter released by the sensory neurons every time an action potential swept into their terminals. Now, in 1974, they were able to distinguish between these.

Neurotransmitter, as Bernard Katz of University College London had shown in the fifties, is not released from the synaptic terminals of nerve cells as single molecules, but rather in "quanta," or packets of many molecules. Each packet contains roughly the same amount of transmitter (several thousand molecules), which is thought to be stored in small membrane-bound vesicles. When the vesicles fuse with the synaptic membrane, it is believed, they release their contents to diffuse the millionth of an inch across the synaptic gap and interact with the receptors in the membrane of the postsynaptic cells.

Since the number of transmitter molecules in each quantum, or packet, does not usually change, the number of quanta released by each action potential is a fairly reliable index of the total amount of transmitter released. By analyzing the number of quanta released, one can tell whether the total amount of neurotransmitter has changed. Using a sophisticated method of analysis, Vincent Castellucci and Kandel looked at quanta release during habituation training and found that the number of transmitter quanta released per impulse in the sensory neuron did decrease. The sensitivity of the receptor in the membrane of the motor neuron remained the same.

Short-term habituation of the gill withdrawal reflex in *Aplysia* was brought about, then, by a change in the amount of neurotransmitter released from the sensory cell, the cell that took input from the environment (a squirt of water from a Water-Pic) and converted it into electrical signals. But what could cause this decrease? Since the concentration of calcium in the synaptic terminal was known to control quanta release, a change in it was the most obvious thing to look at.

Just as countries regulate the traffic across their borders, cells of every type regulate the substances that cross their membranes. They spend a great deal of energy making sure that they have just the right internal environment of sugars, proteins, and ions (electrically charged atoms) in order to go about the business of being a muscle, liver, blood, or nerve cell, and they use pumps, carriers, and custom-designed channels or pores in the membranes to bring in desirable elements and keep out undesirable ones.

Calcium, which exists in solution as a small, positively charged atom, is under heavy prohibition. Most cells have evolved elaborate means of keeping calcium out, with the result that the concentration of calcium is much higher in the fluids surrounding cells than on the inside of the cells. This difference in concentration—or concentration gradient—means that, given an opportunity (an opening into a cell), calcium ions will rush inside a cell, flooding it with calcium until the internal and external concentrations of calcium are about equal and the gradient is eliminated.

Neurons—cells that specialize in sending rapid signals over relatively long distances—take advantage of this calcium gradient in performing their jobs. They use a quick influx of the normally restricted calcium ions to trigger the release of neurotransmitter, and they employ for this purpose special pores or channels. These channels, made of proteins embedded in and spanning the nerve cell's membrane, are usually closed to the passage of calcium; they open only briefly (by changing their shape) in response to the electrical changes that take place as a nerve cell fires an action potential. When they open, many calcium ions flow quickly into the synaptic terminals of a nerve cell and bring about the release of neurotransmitter.

As they were studying habituation, it occurred to Kandel and one of his graduate students, Marc Klein, that the amount of calcium that entered a nerve cell during an action potential might be variable rather than fixed and that this variability could be responsible for the decrease in neurotransmitter release that they had found during habituation. Perhaps, they thought, habituation training somehow reduced the number of calcium channels that could open during an action potential. Fewer open channels would mean that less calcium entered and less neurotransmitter was released. Alternatively, perhaps the same number of calcium channels opened but for a shorter time. The effect would be the same: less calcium is allowed to enter, less neurotransmitter is released, the sensory neurons send a weaker signal to the motor neurons, and the contraction of the gill and the siphon is reduced.

Kandel and Klein would have liked to directly study the flow of calcium into the synaptic terminals of the sensory neurons, but they faced an insurmountable problem. The synaptic terminals in these cells, like those of most neurons, are far too small to accommodate a microelectrode. They are, in fact, only about five times the diameter of a typical microelectrode, and the two neurophysiologists had to settle for looking at the calcium currents in the sensory neuron's cell body, then inferring from those currents what might be happening at the synapses, about one millimeter away. They began studying the calcium currents of sensory neurons during habituation and did find a progressive decrease in the duration of the part of the action potential that was due to calcium, a decrease that paralleled the decrease in the release of neurotransmitter. Since the 1940s, ionic channels in the nerve cell membrane had been known to be at the basis of the action potential; now it seemed that channels might be at the basis of learning and memory as well.

Meanwhile, the New York University team of investigators had also acquired a much better knowledge of the cells that control gill and siphon withdrawal (they had found a cluster of twenty-four sensory neurons that responded to tactile input to the siphon, six motor neurons that produced movement of the gill, and three identified interneurons) and had begun to study sensitization. Sensitization, as we have seen, is another elementary form of learning, but one in which a strong or noxious stimulus enhances an animal's reflex response. Depending on the pattern and duration of training, sensitization can also last for short or long periods of time. It is the opposite of habituation and can restore even completely inactivated synaptic connections produced by long-term habituation. Sensitization resembles classical conditioning in that activity in one pathway facilitates reflex activity in another, but it differs from classical conditioning in that it does not require the specific temporal association of the two stimuli. The similarities between the two learning phenomena, though, have led some to speculate that sensitization is somehow related to associative conditioning, that conditioning may in fact build upon sensitization.

Gill and siphon withdrawal in *Aplysia* was shown to undergo sensitization when Kandel and colleagues gave the snail a strong shock to either its head or its mantle region, then observed that the length of time for which the siphon withdraws when it receives a harmless touch is greatly increased. When four brief shocks are given to the snail on four consecutive days, this enhanced response persists for at least one whole week and is not fully abolished after three.

Then Kandel and his colleagues began looking at how this behavior translated into changes in neural activity. They were somewhat surprised to find that the changes occurred at the same location as those governing habituation—the synapses between the sensory and motor neurons. In sensitization, however, the changes were opposite in direction, the output being turned up. In snails in which Kandel and his colleagues simulated sensitization by opening the animal up, then delivering a shock to the neural connective that runs from its head to its abdominal ganglion, they found that enhanced gill withdrawal is correlated with an enhanced postsynaptic potential in the motor neuron. Now, when a sensory neuron fired, the motor neuron was *more* likely to fire and the gill to contract. Just one zap to the head connective was enough to produce this enhancement for almost fifty minutes.

The next question was the same as it had been for habituation. Was the change in postsynaptic potential due to a change in the sensory (presynaptic) cell or in the motor (postsynaptic) cell? Was the sensory cell releasing more neurotransmitter, or were the receptors in the membrane of the motor neurons now more sensitive to the same quantity of transmitter? In their search for answers, Castellucci and Kandel did the same kind of quantal analysis they had done for habituation. Sensitization, like habituation, they found, involved a presynaptic mechanism, a change in the number of transmitter quanta the sensory neurons released. This time, though, the number of quanta was *increased* while the sensitivity of the receptors remained the same.

Kandel and his group already had evidence that the short- and long-term forms of at least one kind of learning—habituation—entailed similar mechanisms and the same locus; now they were finding that different kinds of learning could also act at the same locus in the same cell by turning neurotransmitter release either up or down. This was certainly not the on / off switch that brain scientists of the fifties had imagined neurons to be; it was, rather, much more like a rheostat, the device that controls a light dimmer. These results on sensitization also caused Kandel to dust off the mechanism that he and Tauc had proposed years before for the phenomenon resembling sensitization that they had found in the giant cell in *Aplysia*'s abdominal ganglion. In Arcachon, Tauc and Kandel had discovered that they could enhance postsynaptic potentials in the giant cell by giving one pathway to that cell a large zap, then looking at the cell's response to a small shock to another, unconnected pathway. At the time, they had called this phenomenon "heterosynaptic facilitation" and suggested that it had, most likely, a presynaptic mechanism. For sensitization of the gill withdrawal reflex, quantal analysis now allowed Kandel to state that the facilitation was indeed in the sensory (presynaptic) cell.

Kandel was also ready to suggest a physical basis for this new phenomenon. The pathway of the sensitizing stimulus (the zap to the head connective), couldn't contact the sensory neurons at their dendrites or cell body, those places where nerve cells receive most of their incoming signals; otherwise it would itself trigger action potentials. But perhaps it did contact the sensory neurons at their synaptic terminals. There, Castellucci and Kandel suggested in 1976, a signal from the sensitizing pathway would act not to generate an action potential but to increase the number of transmitter quanta that would be released if the sensory cell fired an action potential. In Kandel's experiments, this happened when *Aplysia*'s siphon was squirted with water. In the early 1980s, Kandel and his colleagues would find support for this theory when they traced the course of the axons of the interneurons known to carry the sensitizing stimulus. By examining stained, thin serial sections of the abdominal ganglion under an electron microscope, they discovered that the synaptic terminals of these interneurons did indeed contact the sensory neurons near the sites where they released neurotransmitter.

But what could the transmitter from the sensitizing pathway do to the terminals of the sensory neurons in order to increase the transmitter release? Calcium currents were involved, Kandel and his colleagues soon discovered, but in sensitization, not surprisingly, the calcium influx was increased. More calcium came into the sensory neuron terminals of a sensitized animal, and therefore more transmitter quanta were released. But this was the last step, the end result of sensitization. Kandel had no idea how many other steps there were between the binding of neurotransmitter from the sensitizing pathway to the receptors in the synaptic terminals of the sensory neurons and the increased calcium influx resulting from an action potential in those neurons. Through a series of good hunches, he and his colleagues began to find out.

The first hunch was that the small, intracellular molecule cyclic AMP (cyclic adenosine monophosphate) might somehow be involved. Cyclic AMP is one of several intracellular messengers known to mediate the actions produced by hormones on muscle and other target cells in the body. Most hormones do not enter the cells whose function they regulate; they only knock on the door, so to speak, by binding to receptors in the cell membrane. The binding triggers the manufacturing inside the cell of many molecules of cyclic AMP. Cyclic AMP, then, acts as a so-called second messenger in carrying out the hormone's—the first messenger's—effect. Since the late 1950s, when Earl Sutherland at Case Western Reserve University discovered the cyclic-AMP second-messenger system through his study of how the hormone epinephrine (which stimulates the heart and increases muscular strength) acts on its target cells, it has been found that cyclic AMP is extremely important in regulating the functions of many cells and that some neurotransmitters—like hormones—exert their effects through the cyclic AMP second-messenger system. Moreover, it had been known since 1962 that brain tissue contains one of the highest concentrations of cyclic AMP of any body tissue. It is not so surprising, then, that Kandel was curious whether cyclic AMP played a role in the activity of nerve cells in *Aplysia*'s abdominal ganglion.

The first indication that cyclic AMP had any role at all came in 1972, when Kandel and his colleagues electrically stimulated the connectives to the abdominal ganglion for fifteen minutes, then assayed the entire ganglion to see if cyclic AMP levels had changed. The long-lasting stimulation, they found, produced a twofold increase in the level of cyclic AMP that lasted for forty-five minutes. In order to determine which transmitter substance was responsible for this effect, they briefly bathed whole abdominal ganglia with eight different neurotransmitter substances that had recently been found to act by stimulating cyclic AMP. Only three—serotonin, which in mammals is thought to be involved in temperature regulation, sensory perception, and sleep; dopamine, thought to be involved in the regulation of emotional responses and the control of complex movements; and octopamine, a neurotransmitter known to be active in some invertebrate nervous systems—were able to cause the increase in cyclic AMP synthesis. Further experimentation showed that, of those three, only serotonin was effective in actually mimicking presynaptic facilitation of the gill withdrawal reflex, in increasing the amplitude of the excitatory postsynaptic potentials in the gill motor neurons. An additional indication that serotonin might be doing this through cyclic AMP came when they showed that the injection of cyclic AMP into sensory neurons also produced this facilitation and enhancement. This was just the beginning of the Kandel group's foray into the biochemistry of learning, but it was enough for them to generate a tentative model in which cyclic AMP some-how regulates the levels of intracellular calcium in the cell. However, it was also the origin of an assumption later to be called into question—namely, that the neurons that mediated sensitization in *Aplysia* used serotonin as their neurotrans-mitter.

From the early to middle seventies, then, Kandel's inves-tigation into the mechanisms of learning progressed from cel-lular neurophysiology to biochemistry. For Kandel himself, whom colleagues describe as having an extraordinary combi-nation of scientific assets—an excellent memory ("He can remember details from an experiment published a year ago," says Kupfermann, "and the exact page they appeared upon"), great intelligence and imagination, a knowledge of many dif-ferent areas of science and an ability to pull these areas together, and very good organizational and political skills—it was a time marked by tremendous personal advancement and recognition. In 1974, at the age of forty-five, he was elected to the National Academy of Sciences, an elite organization whose members compose just over a half of one percent of all the scientists living in the United States but include a very high percentage of Nobel laureates. The election carried with it enormous pres-tige and put Kandel in great demand to serve in various sci-entific "gate-keeping" functions (on NIH research panels that review the grant proposals of other scientists, for example, or as the editor of one or another scientific journal). It also meant that he could publish his findings very quickly in the *Proceed-ings of the National Academy of Sciences,* a publication founded so that the academy members could communicate rapidly with each other, avoiding the long, prepublication delays of the other, "refereed" journals, which require that every paper is first approved by one or two reviewers.

In the same year, Kandel and his colleagues were also invited to move to the College of Physicians and Surgeons of Columbia University, in New York, and form there the nucleus of the new, multidisciplinary Division of Neurobiology and Behavior. With the move to one of the nation's six most prestigious academic institutions and the election to the National Academy, the amount of money available for Kandel's research increased dramatically. In his last year at New York University, his research efforts received about $83,000 of NIH money. In 1976, just two years after his coming to Columbia, the level of government support for his work was up to $625,000 a year, a sum that included funds from one large project grant, two individual research grants, and a career development award.

Despite his success at getting grants, Kandel, like many other research scientists at the time, was extremely worried by the fact that the growth of NIH's funding had slowed down markedly since the late sixties (and President Johnson's famous call to the research establishment to produce fewer heads-in-the-clouds studies and more concrete results) and was by the early 1970s barely able to keep pace with inflation. Kandel coped with what might be a threat to the future of his research by tapping outside sources—private foundations—for money, something the charismatic psychiatrist would prove particularly good at. In 1975, the Klingenstein Foundation, which funds primarily research on epilepsy, awarded Kandel the first of the grants that would add up to $750,000 over the next eight years. Several years later, he would also attract the interest of the McKnight Foundation (for a sum of $450,000 over a period of five years) and the Office of Naval Research (for $750,000 over a three-year period). At the same time, his NIH funding was continued at slightly increasing levels.

Kandel was adept at soliciting support for his work, but the effort and the time involved forced him, in about 1974, to stop working at the laboratory bench and to devote himself full-time to raising money, to directing the activities of his lab, and to performing his numerous gate-keeping activities. He sometimes misses "getting wet" (poking and dissecting) but realizes that it just wouldn't be an efficient use of his time.

"Eric provides the umbrella (the money and space) under which this work can go on," says his colleague of many years, and weekend tennis partner, Vincent Castellucci. "But he also stays very much in touch with the work. When he's in town, he makes the rounds every day and sits in on an experiment for an hour or so. He also is up on all the latest techniques and on what's happening in different fields. I consider myself an avid reader, but I'm always one step behind Eric."

Although the 1970s brought tremendous recognition to Kandel, they were also marked by several scientific disputes that seemed to cast the significance of Kandel's work with *Aplysia* in a somewhat different light. These controversies came to influence greatly how Kandel was perceived by other neuroscientists.

One of these disputes was with Harold Pinsker, an early postdoctoral student of Kandel's who left Kandel's lab in 1972 to form his own lab at the Marine Biomedical Institute in Galveston, Texas. There he began to study the neurophysiology of intact, behaving snails.

Pinsker explains this choice of research problems as follows: "At NYU, we were supposed to be the big-deal people who had tied together behavior and neurophysiology. But I began to think more critically about this once I was out of Kandel's lab—out of the magic circle—and writing my own grant proposals. Then I realized that, in all of the time at NYU, we had never conducted an experiment where we did behavioral and neurophysiological experiments on the same animal, on the same intact animal. It was outrageous because even when you're dealing with a simple reflex, the things that go on in an opened-up and restrained animal are not necessarily the same things that are going on in an intact animal.''

Pinsker thought it was important to do these experiments and designed a protocol in which he opened an *Aplysia* up, surgically implanted ''cuff'' electrodes around the siphon nerve, and sewed the snail back up. He was then able to record from the siphon nerve as the animal withdrew its gill and siphon under these somewhat more natural conditions. He found that there was a whole component to the siphon withdrawal reflex that disappeared when that reflex was examined in an animal locked into a restraining apparatus and slit open (a position, notes Pinsker, that none of us would care to be in). That component (called the Interneuron II network), and not Kandel's simple reflex, Pinsker and his colleagues then went on to determine, was what was largely responsible for habituation in intact animals.

''You can imagine that this discovery disturbed certain proprietary interests with regard to what was going on in this reflex,'' says Pinsker cautiously. When he tried to publish a paper on these results in the *Journal of Neurophysiology,* where Kandel was an associate editor, the paper, which was sent to one of Kandel's colleagues for review, encountered long delays. Only after it was returned to the journal and then given to a second reviewer was it finally accepted and published, some one and a half years after its original submission, a rather long time even by the standards of scientific publishing. To Pinsker, who says he is reluctant to rehash scientific issues that have ''kind of resolved themselves in a reasonable fashion,'' the important thing is that the paper was eventually published and that ''people can take our results into consideration when evaluating Kandel's work in a reduced preparation.''

Ken Lukowiak, a scruffy, long-haired neurophysiologist

who climbs mountains and builds health care facilities in Nepal when he is not sticking electrodes into cells, was another scientist whose work was at odds with that of Kandel and his colleagues. He says now that he had no idea of the controversy he was walking into when, in the early 1970s, he began to study learning in *Aplysia.* At the time, Lukowiak was a graduate student in the laboratory of Jon Jacklet at the State University of New York at Albany. Since the laboratory was not well funded, Ken and another graduate student had agreed that they would share each *Aplysia:* the other student would get the abdominal ganglia, and Ken would get everything else. That was how Lukowiak happened to find that you didn't need the abdominal ganglion to get habituation of the gill withdrawal reflex. Lukowiak's ganglionless snails habituated just fine using only the cells of their peripheral nervous system, small groups of isolated neurons that course under the skin of mollusks and innervate the internal organs, as well as the foot and appendages. Vertebrates also have peripheral nervous systems, but they are usually limited to the internal organs.

Lukowiak's finding that gill withdrawal could habituate in *Aplysia* that lacked abdominal ganglia threatened to upset Kandel's applecart. Here, on the one hand, was Kandel saying that he had localized the cells and identified the changes responsible for habituation and, on the other, was Lukowiak contending that learning can take place without those changes, without even the ganglion in which Kandel said those changes occurred. Here was a prominent scientist claiming that he had a very analyzable system in which to study learning, while a mere graduate student countered that, no, the system seemed to have many variables.

The clash between Lukowiak and Kandel over peripheral versus central control of learning took the form of several stormy encounters at scientific meetings. Because of the disparity in size and resources of the laboratories involved, there were those who saw the graduate student and the Columbia professor as David and Goliath figures. In 1974, Lukowiak and Kandel argued at a small conference held at Newport Beach, California, and Kandel told Lukowiak that his results were all wrong. Later, Lukowiak gave a talk, then found himself being grilled about his findings by about twenty of Kandel's co-workers. He is said to have handled it well, including the suggestion of one of Kandel's colleagues that he would be better off working on a different problem because he was just delaying the Columbia team's research by making it repeat experiments. To this Lukowiak simply replied, "F___ you."

Then, in 1975, at a Society for Neuroscience meeting in New York City, Kandel and Lukowiak got into a shouting match. The chairman of the session at which they were airing their differences suggested that they start behaving like adults and recommended that the best way to resolve the dispute was in the lab. Some six months later, Lukowiak and two of his colleagues went to Kandel's Columbia lab to collaborate on experiments that essentially proved Lukowiak right: like the abdominal ganglion, the peripheral nerve net can mediate habituation. After Lukowiak left, Kandel and his colleagues went on to publish reports acknowledging this, and adding evidence that suggested that you could basically choose which system—central or peripheral—you brought into play by adjusting the strength of the stimuli delivered to the siphon (a strong stimulus to the siphon would excite peripheral components of the nervous system; weak to moderate stimuli were mediated by the cells in the abdominal ganglion). On the basis of his continued research, Lukowiak disagrees. "It's not that neat," he says. "No matter what stimulus is used, the peripheral system always plays some part in habituation."

Despite their unresolved scientific differences, Lukowiak,

who is now a professor at the University of Calgary, in Canada, and Kandel are on much better terms these days, and Lukowiak says that the shouting match at the New York meeting was a kind of catharsis for their relationship. Their clash, though, left much of the neurobiological community with the lasting impression that, rather than seeing Lukowiak's work as a new piece in a very large and incomplete puzzle, Kandel had chosen to respond to it as if it were a threat to the model of learning he and his colleagues were building in New York. Kandel came to be seen by a number of scientists as someone who didn't want the complexity of real life to get in the way of his ''simple system.''

SIX

The Manifold Neuron

INSERTING A MICROELECTRODE into a nerve cell, according to Juan Acosta-Urquidi, a postdoctoral student in Alkon's lab in the early eighties, is like sticking a broomstick into a balloon.

Or shimmying into a tight pair of pants, says Greg Clark, a young neurophysiologist working with Kandel.

It is how neurophysiologists spend much of their time, an everyday procedure, but one still far too difficult for scientists to take wholly for granted.

To neurophysiologists of the 1940s, sticking a finely drawn glass tube through the membrane of a nerve cell in order to record the electrical activity of the inside of a cell was a radical act. No one knew if the cell could survive such treatment, if it might not, instead, deflate, burst like a balloon, or somehow lose its ability to transmit electrical signals. It was a big surprise to everybody when the cells into which the first microelectrodes were stuck didn't fall apart. On the contrary, their membranes seemed to form a kind of seal around the glass intruder, then go about their business. After a period of hours, the membrane tended to become increasingly leaky to ions, but until then the cells transmitted action potential after action potential as though no one were watching.

At first, neurophysiologists thought that only the largest nerve cells would be able to tolerate a microelectrode inside of them. But in the years since the first landmark experiments with microelectrodes, in 1946, scientists have succeeded in inserting into increasingly tiny cells microelectrodes that are not that much finer than the ones used originally. It is now fairly commonplace to record from inside one of the tiny neurons in a mammalian brain, a feat unthinkable forty years ago.

Intracellular recording has always been technically difficult. In some ways, it is even more difficult today than when it was first tried since most of the easy experiments on the big cells have already been done, and scientists are now attempting ever more arduous maneuvers. Sticking one cell with a microelectrode is difficult; sticking four different cells in the same ganglion with four different electrodes, then maintaining those cells and those electrodes over the course of a long experiment, is almost impossible. Neurophysiologists do it, but at the rate of only about one successful experiment for every week of trying.

"Nine-tenths of what we do is a dismal failure," Bob Hawkins, an investigator in Kandel's lab has told me.

"Every step of an experiment adds to the probability of failure," says Jack Byrne, the electrical engineer who converted to neurophysiology after observing the goings-on in Kandel's lab. "There are so many variables. First, you have to have a healthy animal, then a good dissection and good electrodes. Then you have to find the cells you want and impale them without damaging either the cells or the electrodes. Finally, you have to be able to hold that cell, record from it, and do whatever else the experiment requires—changing solutions, squirting in neurotransmitters, dyes, and inhibitors, voltage clamping, et cetera. I'd say we probably average about one successful experiment a week. The thrill is when you do have one of those. It makes your day; it makes your week. You can live on it for a while.''

"What keeps me going?'' Hawking laughed. "Stupidity . . . and optimism. I'm an incurable optimist. I always think the next experiment will work. Plus, the physical activity— the dissecting and desheathing—is not unpleasant. It's like basket weaving, mildly therapeutic. People think that science is all cerebral, but there's a lot of manual labor.''

"These experiments demand an impossible measure of patience,'' said a researcher at MBL who had just completed his first successful experiment of the summer, an experiment that followed the dissection and unsuccessful analysis of 324 synapses in 324 squid giant axons. "Most people would not be able to endure it.''

Despite such complaints, its doubtful that these scientists would rather be doing anything else. All of us may have a need to know, but scientists, it is said, have a need to know that what they know is really so. Research allows them to pose questions about an infinite number of things and then attempt to answer them. Also, it's one of those rare human endeavors that, for many of its practitioners, make time fly. On the other hand, it can and does consume as much time as a scientist is willing to put into it, and it happens that many seem to come to a point in their careers when they have to make a very conscious effort to sustain a life outside the lab.

Alkon used to put in what he has called a twenty-five-hour day, but in the ten years since his first child was born, he has made a point of coming in at nine and leaving around five, an extremely unusual schedule for a scientist. "It's difficult to

juggle work and family,'' he admits, "but I do it because my
children come first. They are my greatest source of pleasure.''

For Jack Davis, achieving a balance between research and
other aspects of life is also difficult, but worth working at. ''A
lot of people are 101 percent scientists,'' says Davis. ''That's
all they do with their time, and it's difficult to compete with
people like that. To me, though, you've only got one shot at
life and you've got to enjoy it. You can't enjoy it by becoming
so specialized that you can't think about anything else. Science is a system that selects for highly competitive, full-time
people. But if the system won't let me into heaven, I don't
think I want to go.''

Some freely acknowledge that science is something of an
addiction for which they quite willingly give up the trappings
of a normal family life. Rodolpho Llinás, who regularly puts
in a thirteen-hour day at the lab (he goes home for dinner, then
works late into the night), says, ''Science is somewhere between
an addiction and an avocation. I don't think that you can become
addicted unless you have an avocation.''

''It's an addiction for me,'' Jim Bower, one of Llinás's
postdoctoral students (and perhaps the only researcher who takes
his squid home to fry and eat after he's through experimenting
with them), told me once. ''I can't imagine putting in a nine-
to-five day. I love my family, but I can't see taking a two-
week vacation with them. Being the kind of family you always
see walking down the streets of Woods Hole in the summer.
You know, the father in front, the children in the middle, and
the wife four steps behind.''

In neurophysiology, a field where most of an investigator's
time is spent dealing with technical difficulties, superstitions
about what will work and what won't become surprisingly

important, almost as important as experience. If a technique—
a new type of electrode, a different enzyme, a change in the
angle at which the electrode is inserted—works one day, scientists will go on using it long after they're knee-deep in
technical difficulties again. For one of Alkon's postdocs,
preparation—the actual dissecting and desheathing of the ganglion—is 99 percent of the experiment. "If I can see a cell, I
can stick it," he says. Every time he starts an important experiment, he prepares a fresh batch of enzyme solution that he
uses to remove the ganglion's outer connective tissue.

For others, the microelectrode is key. Electrodes must be
wide enough to pass current but fine enough to get into a cell
without damaging it. Their tips must be stiff enough that they
can get through things, but flexible enough that they will not
break easily. To the naked eye, the tips of these electrodes, a
mere ten-thousandth of a millimeter wide, are invisible, and
one of the first lessons a neurophysiologist-to-be learns is to
give these delicate instruments a wide berth so as to avoid
accidentally destroying them. Using one of those notoriously
temperamental machines—micropipette pullers—most scientists pull their electrodes out of round glass tubes; others swear
by triangular tubes because of their increased capillary action.

Then there is the question of how to get the microelectrode
into a cell. The electrode, which is filled with a concentrated
solution of potassium chloride, is inserted into the clamp of a
micromanipulator and connected via a lead in the potassium
chloride solution to an electronic amplifier. A second electrode—the ground, or reference, electrode—is placed in the
solution bathing the axon or ganglion and then also connected
to the amplifier. The amplifier boosts the small signal that it
receives and feeds it into an oscilloscope, which displays the
potential difference between the two electrodes as a function
of time. The ganglion (or axon) to be impaled is, at this point,

sitting under the microscope in a small dish. It is held in place by pins (or sometimes cactus spines, because they are finer than any pins) and is immersed in the bathing solution, usually running seawater. Using the microscope and the gross controls on the micromanipulator, the experimenter guides the electrode until its tip just touches the outside of the cell to be poked. It's there, the experimenter knows, when the reading on the oscilloscope screen begins to jump around, a signal that means the electrode is picking up the positive charges of the molecules that tend to cluster on the outside of a membrane. Some investigators use an audio hookup to turn these small changes in voltage into sound, hair-raising shrieks that are reminiscent of Jimmy Hendrix's recording of "The Star Spangled Banner" and that tell the investigator what he cannot see. Others work in silence.

Once the electrode is in position, there are a variety of methods of getting it through the millionth of a millimeter thick membrane and into the cell. Some investigators like to dial in, using the fine adjustment knob on the micromanipulator. Others buzz in, by sending current through the electrode and causing its tip to vibrate. A few tap in, by gently hitting the micromanipulator, and occasionally an investigator will just sit and wait, apparently hoping that the electrode will enter of its own accord.

Watching an electrophysiological experiment is not most people's idea of fun. The odds are that it won't succeed. Most of the time is passed in silence; many experiments take place in the late hours of the night, when interruptions are rare. Once the investigator has brought the electrode to within stabbing distance of the cell, he usually swivels his chair away from the operating table (where four or five micromanipulators may be poised above a ganglion the size of a speck of dust) and toward the box containing his electronic equipment, a tall rectangle holding a bewildering array of amplifiers, stimulators, audio monitors, and oscilloscope, as well as an oscillograph for recording what crosses the screen of the oscilloscope. He begins adjusting dials and pushing buttons. The silence continues, broken only now and then by "We're in. We're in the cell. Nope, we're out again."

Like the investigator, an onlooker watches the electrical correlates of these words on the face of the oscilloscope. "We're in," and the horizontal line that runs across the screen of the oscilloscope and corresponds to the difference in electrical potential between the bath electrode and the intracellular electrode suddenly drops down the screen to minus seventy millivolts, the cell's resting potential. "We're out again," and the line jumps back up to its previous position. "We're in. It's holding steady," and a continuous and relatively "blipless" line runs across the oscilloscope's screen again at about minus seventy millivolts. That's good. It means that the cells' resting potential is not fluctuating. The cell is healthy; the electrode hasn't damaged the membrane. It isn't leaking ions.

The investigator now has to check to make sure he's in the cell that he wants to be in. Very few cells are absolutely identifiable from their size and position alone; most are distinguished mainly by their signaling properties and / or the cells they connect to. The methods of checking differ for different animals and cells, but when Alkon wants to check that he's in one of *Hermissenda's* Type A photoreceptors, he turns off the lights in the lab to adapt the cell to darkness, then flashes a light and watches the oscilloscope to make sure that the cell shows a characteristic response. When one of Kandel's postdocs wants to verify he's in one of the siphon's sensory neurons, he shocks the nerve that runs from the siphon to the abdominal ganglion and waits several milliseconds for the sensory neuron to fire an action potential.

If the electrode is in the right cell, well and good. It's time to put the second electrode in. Most electrophysiological experiments require two electrodes in the same cell: one to record the voltage (the electrical difference between the inside of the cell and the bath); the other to inject current into the cell. Using these two electrodes, the investigator can set or "clamp" the membrane of the cell at whatever voltage he wants, then study the comings and goings of different kinds of positive and negative ions across the cell's membrane at that voltage. He sets the desired voltage, then flicks a switch that turns on the circuit for "voltage clamp." The current electrode will now automatically inject just the right amount of current to maintain the cell (that is, to offset the naturally flowing ironic currents) at the voltage the investigator has chosen. The trick, of course, is to get the current electrode into the same cell without knocking the voltage electrode out.

Two electrodes in a single cell may be all that an experiment requires, but an investigator might well want an electrode or two in a postsynaptic, or follower, cell and perhaps intracellular electrodes with which to inject dyes, chemical inhibitors, neurotransmitters, or a variety of other special solutions into the desired cells. All of this he must accomplish in a set amount of time (to guarantee the healthiness of the cells and, therefore, the validity of the results); if he doesn't, the preparation is thrown out and he begins again. If luck is running with the investigator, at the end of a day or the end of the week, he may have a piece of data—the effect, for instance, of calcium on the opening and closing of a particular ionic channel in the membrane—that he can fit into his much larger puzzle.

If this sounds difficult, it is. It grows more so every year as researchers come to use methods like the "patch clamp," a technique in which a tiny section of a cell's membrane is sucked up into a microelectrode in order that the opening and closing of just one or two ionic channels can be studied in isolation. The technical aspects of their work, many investigators have told me, are totally unpredictable. They can get what you want in minutes, days, or not at all.

"What people don't realize," says Rodolpho Llinás, "is how amazing it is that we know anything about these things at all."

If luck, as Pasteur said, favors the prepared mind, one of the most prepared minds in the history of science must have been that of the eighteenth-century Italian anatomist Luigi Galvani, the man who discovered that nerves transmit electricity. Certainly, the observation on which his discovery is based is one of the luckiest ever. One day, Galvani happened to have some frogs' legs hanging by a copper wire off the iron balustrade of his balcony (whether for culinary or other purposes, history does not record). When the wind blew them such that they touched the iron railing, Galvani noticed that the legs twitched. The only way he could explain this was by postulating that the stuff that runs through nerves and causes muscles to contract is electricity. What was happening, then, when the legs touched the iron was that they were completing the circuit of an incredible makeshift battery.

With its overtones of animal magnetism, Galvini's observation sparked the public's imagination. In terms, though, of how scientists thought nerves and nervous systems work, it did little at first except give new meaning to the ancient doctrine of "vital spirits," those spirits that were long thought to course from the soul to the brain and from the brain to the nerves and muscles. Not until the early twentieth century did researchers actually begin to develop theories that would account for bioelectrical currents.

Cells at this point were known to have what is called a resting potential. That is, the inside of all cells was known to be negative with respect to the outside. In part, this is because within cells there is a much higher concentration of negatively charged proteins than there is outside in the extracellular soup. If you push an electrode through the membrane of any cell, then place another electrode on the outside of the cell and attach the two via a voltmeter (a device that measures the difference in electrical potential between two points and is commonly used to test batteries, look for short circuits, and so on), the voltmeter will record a difference in electrical potential. For most cells, this difference—the cell's resting potential—is on the order of seventy to one hundred millivolts, or about one-tenth of a volt. The inside of cells is about one-tenth of a volt negative with respect to the outside.

All cells have resting potentials; only nerve cells, though, have developed the ability to use this potential to send signals to other cells. One of the first theories on how nerve cells actually do this was posited by Julius Bernstein of the University of Halle, in Germany. In 1902, he proposed that the action potential sent by a nerve cell involved a temporary breakdown of the resting potential, a change in the permeability of the nerve cell's membrane, with the result that a nerve cell suddenly lost negatively charged ions and its inside went from minus seventy millivolts to a point at which there was no difference in electrical potential between the inside and the outside of the cell.

Bernstein's theory remained the dominant one until the 1940s, when the English neurophysiologists Hodgkin and Huxley began putting it to the test by inserting electrodes into the squid's giant axon. With an electrode inside the axon, they found that an action potential was accompanied not just by a breakdown of a nerve cell's normal resting potential but by its reversal. During an action potential, a point inside a nerve cell goes from minus seventy millivolts to *plus* forty millivolts with respect to the outside, then back down to minus seventy millivolts—all in the space of about one-thousandth of a second. To Hodgkin and Huxley, it was apparent that the mechanism responsible for these rapid reversals of electrical potential was going to be a good deal more complicated than the one proposed by Bernstein. It was also apparent that this mechanism resided in the membranes of nerve cells.

Every living cell—from the single-cell amoeba to one of the one hundred billion nerve cells in the human brain—is surrounded by a cell membrane, an outer covering through which the cell's business with the outside world is conducted. Only a millionth of a millimeter thick, the membrane consists of two layers of fatty lipid molecules, which, under the electron microscope, have a characteristic sandwichlike appearance of two parallel dark lines separated by a lighter space. The lipid bilayer is pretty much the same for all cells; what distinguish the membrane of a nerve cell from that of a red blood cell are its proteins, its particular set of membrane-associated enzymes, pumps, channels, receptors, and structural proteins. These molecules, embedded in and sometimes spanning the membrane, endow cells with their special capabilities and characteristics.

As Bernstein hypothesized, the resting potential of cells results from the unequal distribution of electrically charged particles across their membranes. This, in turn, results from the cell's large, intracellular collection of negatively charged proteins and from the membrane's differential permeability to specific ions (or electrically charged atoms). Since charged molecules and ions cannot simply diffuse through the fatty membrane (for the same reason that oil and water don't mix), permeability means that proteins embedded in the membrane must act to carry, pump, or channel the charged particles through the membrane. This is true for all cell membranes. What makes a nerve cell different from the rest of the cells in the body is its capacity to turn the energy inherent in this resting potential into a signal—an action potential. The nerve cell is excitable, and this excitability arises from the ability of its membrane to undergo transient changes in its permeability to specific ions. It is now known—or if not known, at least suspected with a high degree of conviction—that these changes in permeability arise from the presence of channels in the membrane that allow ions to pass in and out of the cell. Somewhat like sluice gates, these channels can be opened and closed.

At rest, the membrane is impermeable to sodium ions, which are among the ions that play a major role in this signaling ability. They, along with negatively charged chloride ions, are major constituents of the extracellular soup in which cells live. They carry a positive charge and are found at a ten times greater concentration outside the cell than inside. Because opposites attract, the positively charged sodium ions tend to cluster about the outside of the membrane, drawn to the negatively charged proteins on the inside. Because all particles tend to flow down-hill—that is, from regions in which they are highly concentrated to regions of lower concentration—sodium ions are also drawn toward the cells for another reason. They are stopped from entering a cell and thereby flowing down both their concentration and electrical gradients by the membrane.

A second principal actor in the action potential is potassium. Because the membranes of all cells are studded with many permanently open channels through which positively charged potassium ions can freely flow, membranes are, at their resting potential, permeable to potassium ions. The concentration of potassium is thirty times higher inside cells than on the outside. Given the downhill flow of ions, this may not seem to make sense, but potassium is torn between a tendency to flow down its concentration gradient and outside the cell and its electrical attraction to the negatively charged protein molecules on the inside. Its concentration in the inactive nerve cell is a delicate balance between the two gradients—electrical and concentration.

The action potential, as Hodgkin and Huxley found, takes full advantage of all of these gradients. It begins when a stimulus (either electrical or mechanical) renders a small segment of an axon permeable to sodium by opening up special sodium channels in the cell membrane. Driven by both their electrical and their concentration gradients, sodium ions rush into the cell, making neighboring regions of the axon less negative and, therefore, triggering the opening of those sodium channels nearby. In this way, the action potential moves down the axon without losing strength. It is propelled by an influx of sodium that will continue until the combined concentration and electrical gradients for sodium are all but eliminated. At any discrete region of the axon, that takes only half a millisecond, at which point the inside of the cell in that region is now forty millivolts positive with respect to the outside. That area of the axon now enters a transition phase during which this new potential difference across the membrane triggers both the closing of the sodium channels and the opening of a new kind of potassium channel. Potassium is expelled from the cell through these channels, driven by its repulsion from the like-charged sodium ions as well as by its own concentration gradient, and the cell is quickly repolarized. In another half a millisecond the inside of the cell in that region has dropped back down to its resting potential of about minus seventy millivolts. Meanwhile, the action potential continues to journey down the axon—triggering the opening of more sodium channels, the influx of sodium, the efflux of potassium—until it sweeps into the synaptic terminals, where it opens calcium channels, causing a short, rapid influx of calcium and the release of neurotransmitter.

That is the end of the action potential, but the cell now has an excess of sodium and calcium ions and a dearth of potassium. Calcium is quickly taken up or bound by a special intracellular protein, calmodulin. But to return the cell to its state before the action potential was fired, sodium must be expelled from the cell and potassium pulled back in. This is the job of some other proteins embedded in the membrane—sodium pumps—and, unlike the downhill mechanisms that drive the action potential, requires a great deal of energy. A full 40 percent of the energy expended by a nerve cell, it is estimated, goes into replacing sodium with potassium. The pumps are working against the concentration gradients of both potassium and sodium, as well as against the electrical gradient of sodium. They are, in effect, winding up high-energy springs that the cell will later let fly.

Nobody has ever seen an ionic channel, those proteins that are the basis of the action potential and, therefore, of all our thoughts, emotions, actions, and ideas, but the proof of their existence is compelling, and in recent years two such channels have actually been manufactured by means of sophisticated recombinant DNA techniques. At first, though these channels were just theoretical constructs that made sense out of what was known about the behavior of nerve cells, their rapid changes in permeability to sodium and potassium. Evidence for their existence was only indirect: charged ions cannot pass through the lipid bilayer no matter what the potential difference across the membrane; the speed at which carrier proteins and membrane pumps can move ions across the membrane—about two hundred ions per second—is not nearly great enough to account for the known effluxes and influxes of ions during an action potential. Therefore, the argument ran, there must be such things as ionic chanels, holes in the membrane that open and close in response to voltage changes and that can allow the passage of twenty thousand sodium ions or an equal number of potassium ions in just one-half of a millisecond. In some cells, these holes or channels exist in unimaginable concentrations—up to ten thousand channels per square millimeter of membrane, an area smaller than the size of one hole in a window screen. They quickly turn an impenetrable barrier into a leaky, one-way sieve.

Not much is known for sure about how these channels open and close, but the best guess is that the channel proteins are charged molecules that align themselves in the electric field of the membrane in much the same way that iron filings align themselves with the lines of magnetic force between two magnets. Just as moving those magnets changes the distribution of the iron filings, changing the voltage across a cell's membrane causes a realignment of the membrane-associated proteins and a change in their three-dimensional shape or conformation. That change can mean that one protein now has a hole through which sodium ions can pass or that another protein is suddenly closed to the flow of potassium.

In their proposed mechanism for the action potential, Hodgkin and Huxley needed to hypothesize the existence of only two types of ionic channels, voltage-sensitive sodium channels (which open when the inside of the cell is made more positive by about fifteen millivolts) and "delayed rectifying" potassium channels (which open when the cell is about forty millivolts positive). Since the publication of the sodium theory, though, scientists have turned up evidence for at least ten additional channel types, and many more, undoubtedly, remain to be identified. These channels differ in the type of ion that they let pass, their distribution in nerve cells, and their sensitivities, that is, what triggers their opening and closing. Not all channels respond to changes in voltage; some are "chemically gated" instead. Much as a lock opens when the right key is inserted and turned, they open when a specific chemical (usually a neurotransmitter) binds to a receptor associated with the channel protein. Binding also causes these chemically gated channels to undergo a change in shape, thereby opening them up to the passage of ions. Other channels are sensitive to chemicals as well as to changes in voltage.

But what is the purpose of all these different channels? Like Hodgkin and Huxley's channels, some of the more recently discovered ones are found in almost all nerve cells. These play key roles as translators: at the dendrites of a nerve cell, they translate the chemical message of a neurotransmitter into electrical currents; at the synapses, the calcium channels already discussed translate the electrical signal of the action potential into the release of neurotransmitter.

Chemical-sensitive sodium and chloride channels carry out the first job. When molecules of neurotransmitter diffuse across a synaptic gap to bind to their custom-made receptor molecules embedded in the membrane of a connecting nerve cell, binding causes a change in the shape of the channels associated with those receptors. This change opens the channels, and ions rush into the cell. If they are sodium channels, positive sodium ions pour inside, creating small, local, positive currents that push the cell toward the point at which it will fire an action potential. The message delived by the neurotransmitter will be excitatory. If the channels are chloride channels, the effect will be just the reverse. Now, binding of the same neurotransmitter produces an influx of negative chloride ions that will make the inside of the cell more negative than before and less likely to fire. Chloride ions, in other words, carry inhibitory messages. Since a neuron may receive information form up to one thousand other neurons, its dendrites might at any moment be receiving many small, local influxes of chlorine ions as well as of sodium ions. Much as streams and tributaries flow into the main branch of a river, these small, "synaptic" currents flow toward the initiation zone of the neuron. There the cell adds up all of the information it is receiving, and if it finds itself depolarized—or more positive—by a threshold amount of about fifteen millivolts, it starts firing action potentials.

Unlike sodium and chloride channels, other ionic channels are far from universal in their distribution. They are found only in certain nerve cells and play extremely subtle roles in the behavior of those cells. As the different holes of a flute or a clarinet allow those instruments to produce their many different sounds, so these different kinds of channels, producing innumerable tiny gusts and spurts—or currents—of positively and negatively charged ions, enable nerve cells to act in many different ways. "These channels allow cells to do many more tricks than just the action potential," Rodolpho Llinás once said. They are indeed responsible for the fact that one neuron is a spontaneously bursting cell that produces rhythmic bursts of action potentials without any synaptic input at all, while another is a silent cell that requires a long, slow stimulus before it will fire. They are also the reason that cells react to an injection of the same amount of positive current in quite different ways: one neuron might respond with a long train of action potentials, while a second shows no response at all; a third cell might bark—or fire—once, then remain silent.

A good example of how ionic channels do all this comes from the first attempt by scientists to link even a simple behavior in an animal to a specific ionic conductance. The study was on the inking reflex in *Aplysia* and was carried out first by

Tom Carew at Columbia and then by Jack Byrne after he left Kandel's lab in 1976 to take a position at the University of Pittsburgh. In it, Carew and Byrne, who is now a professor at the University of Texas Medical School at Houston, were able to pin many of the observable characteristics of that reflex on an unusual potassium conductance.

Like squid, octopuses, and certain other mollusks, *Aplysia* has an ink gland in its mantle cavity, and when the snail is greatly disturbed, it releases a dark purple substance into the water. Like siphon and gill withdrawal, this is a protective mechanism for the snail, but one that can't be used very often, since it takes days for ink reserves to build up again.

Inking in *Aplysia* is controlled by nerve cells in the abdominal ganglion and is reflexive; that is, the nerve cells that mediate it are separated by no more than one or two synapses. It differs dramatically, though, from the well-studied gill withdrawal reflex in its response to stimuli. Whereas gill withdrawal has a low threshold and, like the knee-jerk response in humans, is graded, inking requires a very strong, long-lasting stimulus and, like a sneeze or cough, is an all-or-none response. Both reflexes can be triggered by stimulation of the same sensory neurons; but the three motor neurons that control the release of ink from the snail's ink gland differ from the motor neurons controlling gill withdrawal. It is in these motor neurons that the key to the behavioral differences between the two reflexes lies. Ink motor neurons, Carew found, have a high resting potential (that is, they are more negative on the inside than most neurons). Sometime later, Byrne discovered that they also have an unusual conductance. Whereas an injection of positive current into the gill motor neurons results in their firing an action potential, the same current injection into the ink motor neurons results in the opening of "fast" voltage-dependent potassium channels, through which positive potassium ions are quickly expelled from the cell. This brisk loss of potassium, in effect, shunts the incoming positive current and usually succeeds in returning the ink motor neurons to their resting potential. Only a long-lasting and strong stimulus can overcome the potassium shunt enough to bring the ink motor neurons to fire. By chemically inactivating this unusual potassium channel, Byrne found that he could turn an inking motor neuron into a gill motor neuron; that is, the could make it respond to depolarization in the same way that a gill motor neuron does.

Twenty years ago, scientists tried to understand the output of a particular circuit of neurons by making wiring diagrams of its excitatory and inhibitory connections. That wiring is just one aspect of the brain is clear from a study like Carew and Byrne's. Important are not just the excitatory and inhibitory connections but also the characteristics of the cells themselves. How an individual neuron is able to shunt or magnify a given synaptic input by turning on or off ionic currents through its membrane obviously has as much to do with its subsequent behavior as the fact that it gets any input at all. "With all of these different channels operating in different combinations in different cells," comments Jack Byrne, "the brain seems much more complex, but also much more interesting. You don't need complex circuits to produce neural modification; you can do it all within a single cell and you have billions of cells each with that capability. The real challenge is going to be finding out what it's all there for."

One scientist, at least, thinks he has an idea. Clearly, the great variety of ionic channels allows nervous systems to produce a greater diversity and flexibility of behavior than could be achieved by wiring alone; according to Rodolpho Llinás, though, it may also provide the answer to one of the most fundamental questions regarding nervous systems: "How is it that I am a collection of a hundred billion nerve cells, yet I think and act as one?'' Llinás first began to consider that the answer to this question might lie in cells' blends and symphonies of ionic conductances after he began studying a particular type of nerve cell in the brain of a guinea pig, a cell whose eleven ionic conductances endowed it with some rather unusual properties.

"These cells," Llinás told a symposium at MBL several years ago, "have the usual sodium, delayed-rectifying potassium and calcium conductances, as well as several calcium conductances not previously described and a host of potassium conductances. When all these conductances are put together, you find that they are almost perfectly matched to allow the cells to oscillate at the frequency of eight per second without firing an action potential. These cells don't oscillate because they're told to; they oscillate because it's what they do best."

Later, Llinás and I talked about what this kind of oscillation—the regular fluctuation between two electrical values—might mean. "If nerve cells only have private conversations," he said, "that is, if they only communicate by synaptic transmission, it's hard to put it all together, to understand how I can be one as a thinking process, yet so many different neurons. All kinds of mass properties can happen, though, when cells are intrinsically capable of oscillating at about eight per second. The brain marches. This ability of cells to oscillate must mean that the brain marches. And it must march so that if one cell gets off the beat, the others will know it immediately."

"Just think for a moment of how large our brain is," Llinás continued. "It weighs one and a half kilograms and has billions of neurons; yet when you put electrodes to the surface you get an organized set of electrical events. It's unbelievable. It's so fat, so immense. How dare it oscillate at regular intervals? It's as if the two ends of the galaxy were talking to each other. What it means is that a whole lot of cells must be doing the same thing at the same time.''

This theory will be difficult to prove, Llinás admits, and the finding of so many different conductances in a single cell is both good and bad news. ''We are understanding a lot,'' he says, ''but the system is not getting any easier.'' That is certainly true. Recognition of the still-increasing variety of ionic channels has added another thick layer of complexity to a system already complex by virtue of its numbers and interconnectivity. Indeed, some scientists are beginning to suspect that it might just be possible that every nerve cell in a nervous system is different from all the other cells by means of its distribution and type of ionic channels and its connectivity. As Gerald Fischbach, a recent president of the Society for Neuroscience, has said, ''One of the great embarrassments in neurobiology is that we don't know whether there are thousands, millions, or billions of electrophysiologically distinct neurons.'' Neuroscientists wonder where they are going to find the genes for all these distinct types of neurons and still have any DNA left over to account for all the other proteins necessary to build a complete human body. It's possible, though, that environment and experience play a great role in the differentiation of neurons and that, therefore, very large numbers of actual ''brain genes'' are not required.

Nervous systems generate behavior, and they enable animals to make predictions about the world around them. That seems simple enough. So does the fact that they can accomplish this only by causing a muscle to contract or a gland to secrete (''Secrete or contract,'' some neurobiologists are fond of saying). But that is all that is simple about brains and nervous systems, and scientists are beginning to realize that there may not be a limit to the number of ways in which nerve cells can carry out these ends. Neurophysiologists may never discover all of the conductances and combinations of conductances possible in nerve cells. And that is just one layer of complexity. The variety of substances that nerve cells transmit or secrete is another and one that has also just recently come to be appreciated. Twenty years ago, it was thought that the brains might use only three or four chemical messengers; now, they are suspected of using hundreds. Some of these messengers have effects that last for just ten milliseconds; others seem to linger for minutes, hours, and even days. Some cause or inhibit action potentials; others produce a wide variety of less direct effects that include making a cell or a circuit either more or less excitable by opening or closing ionic channels. Some act only at synaptic junctions; others affect any number of cells that happen to have on them the right receptors. In short, so much for wiring diagrams; now it seems that nerve cells don't even need to synapse with each other in order to have a functional connection.

In the midst of this seemingly endless variability of nervous systems, most investigators are confident that generalities will emerge, that nervous systems do follow rules, and that scientists can discover those rules through the close analysis of circuit after circuit, cell after cell. Yet neuroscience today is in a period of analysis—not synthesis—and just as nerve cells must oscillate, brain scientists must continue to unearth new phenomena, marvel at yet another elegantly orchestrated circuit, and hope that the mechanism they just discovered in a leech or a praying mantis is perhaps also used elsewhere in other species.

Not everyone can stand working in this atmosphere of ever-increasing uncertainty and variability. Once I asked a physiologist at Woods Hole how she was able to go on in the face of the untidiness of her findings, of life itself, and she told me about a friend of hers who is a taxonomist. "He's extremely confident about everything in life," she said. "But physiologists are different; they have to deal with a lot of variables, and they have to like it."

Those I asked do.

"Things are getting very sloppy, and I love it," Juan Acosta-Urquidi told me. "We used to think that the whole brain was like a computer; now, it's more like there's a computer in every cell. I started out believing that biology—life—could be reduced to physics. Now, I'm not so sure."

"You have to understand that there are no final answers in science, that you can only solve partial problems," Ladislav Tauc explained. "Every time you climb a mountain, there are new ranges in front of you. I'm perfectly satisfied to go over as many mountains in my lifetime as I can."

"You'd get dizzy if you thought about the whole brain all the time," said Paul O'Lague, a neurophysiologist at UCLA. "You have to restrict yourself to the simplest system possible."

"Tackle the next solvable problem" was another physiologist's admonition. "You're just happy if your observed results equal your predicted results. It's hard to explain what keeps you going. You've just got that itch."

Perhaps the most farsighted comment came from Rodolpho Llinás, who unabashedly admits that his ultimate goal is to answer the question "What am I that I can think about my existence?"

"One only gets lost," Llinás said, "if one is looking for something in front of one's nose."

SEVEN

In Search of the Engram

LADISLAV TAUC, the Czechoslovakian physiologist who introduced Kandel to the ways of *Aplysia,* believes in science, he tells me, but he wouldn't want scientists running the world. He tells a story that illustrates why. Until just a few years ago, electrophysiologists recorded the electrical phenomena they observed in nerve cells by taking Polaroid snapshots of the screen of their oscilloscopes. All the windows of electrophysiology labs were for this reason blacked out with cardboard and tape, and most of the "setups" or "rigs" were ringed by long, floor-to-ceiling, black curtains. In the sixties, when NIH planners were considering the construction of a new neurophysiology laboratory, an investigator in Mike Fuortes's lab suggested that they could save money and spare neurophysiologists a lot of trouble by erecting a building without windows.

"Like a lot of scientists," says Tauc, whose hunched shoulders are evidence of the many hours he has spent bent over microscopes, "he just couldn't understand the difference between a building with blacked-out windows and one with no windows at all." Nor did the investigator turn out to be very farsighted. Today, most neurophysiologists no longer need to work in the dark, because it's now possible to digitalize the information from an oscilloscope and feed it directly into a computer. Fortunately, NIH decided not to follow the neurophysiologist's suggestion.

Owned and operated by the 730-odd scientists who are the members of its corporation, the Marine Biological Laboratory, or MBL, is a world run by scientists—but it hasn't done so badly. In the almost one hundred years since it was founded, it has been able to avoid the large gaffes deemed inevitable by Tauc. Somehow, it has always managed to make the changes necessary to its survival (to adapt, as biologists would say) and yet to remain true to its original goals of being a diverse, top-notch biological research facility as well as a teaching institution. Today, there might be a tinge of self-satisfaction at MBL ("MBL doesn't build ugly buildings," the current director told a group of townspeople who were concerned about the facility's latest plans for expansion; it has in fact put up several undisputed clunkers), and some scientists worry that the desirability of spending a summer at MBL has made it a dangerously cliquish and inbred place. But on the whole, MBL continues to be an institution remarkable for its lack of pretense, bureaucracy, and fat. It is an institution that operates on a human scale. You can feel it in the library, which is open twenty-four hours a day and run on an honor system, and in the bare-bones economy of many of the laboratories and the limited number of simple cottages that MBL rents to scientists and their families who cannot afford the resort rates of Woods Hole's summer rentals.

A meeting—and mating—ground for fundamental biologists (nobody knows exactly how many scientific marriages have resulted from summer encounters in Woods Hole, but estimates run very high), MBL is a place that students and senior scientists alike get easily hooked on and then work to find ways to come back to year after year. "MBL has become essential to the happiness of me and my family," one postdoc told me. "I like my children playing with children who know what topsoil is."

MBL provides senior investigators, who spend much time at their winter institutions in teaching and administrative duties, with a chance to get their hands dirty, to actually sit at the lab bench and do their own experiments. It is also a place where, as one scientist puts it, "everybody who is anybody has the opportunity to work with everybody else in the same category."

"At the lectures here," another MBL scientist has commented, "you hear the stuff that is going to appear in print over the next two or three years."

For students enrolled in MBL's seven prestigious and highly competitive courses in neurobiology, parasitology, embryology, marine ecology, and physiology, life in one of MBL's dorms offers freedom from the mundane tasks of daily living—dealing with landlords, making beds, preparing meals, and the like—and the chance to become totally immersed in a new field. These students, who include a few highly qualified undergraduates, graduate students, and postdoctoral students, as well as established scientists from other fields (one of the students in a course that I sat in on was a member of the National Academy of Science, a world-renowned biochemist who was using the summer at MBL to test the waters of neurobiology before he decided whether to take the plunge and switch fields), spend mornings in lectures and the afternoons and evenings in the lab. They're there many times until twelve or one, when they will break for a beer at the nearby Captain Kidd. Because the instructors know how easy it is for the students to burn themselves out on such a schedule, during the dinner break they organize class games of volleyball and softball; on Sundays, they lock the students out of the lab all day.

The immersion pays off, though. Graduates of MBL's course in neural systems and behavior (a seven-week class in which twenty students are taught by a constantly changing staff of some twenty faculty members) are able to go home and actually set up a neurobiology lab. They know how to use the latest equipment and techniques; they have met many of the top scientists in their field and heard firsthand about their research. Along the way, they have also gotten glimpses of the mixture of dog work, serendipity, frustrations, and ideology that is the basis of most scientific achievements—and have been instilled with a special MBL ethos. The courses, the tuition for which is $750, are not graded, but students are aware that each of the instructors will take back an assessment of his or her capabilities and motivation; the only diplomas are the highly coveted T-shirts designed by each year's classes and worn like badges by students and teachers alike.

MBL is not the center of neurobiology that it was in the thirties, forties, and fifties, when investigators there developed such techniques as the voltage clamp and began working on the squid's giant axon and when the Monday night neurophysiology lectures got so heated that they became known as the Monday night fights. But it is still a major crossroads in neuroscience, as well as in embryology, ecology, parasitology, and developmental biology. Some one hundred neurobiologists from all over the world come to MBL each summer to experiment on the ten thousand squid that the laboratory's full-time collectors net each year; many others come to work on countless other animals whose nervous systems have proved useful for study. Attracted by the facilities for raising and maintaining marine animals—all the labs have running seawater, for instance—a number of them, including Felix Strumwasser, William Adelman, and Dan Alkon, are staying year-round.

Like most of the labs at Woods Hole, Dan Alkon's, on the third floor of the brick, three-story Lillie Building, is far from being either modern or spacious. The main lab where Alkon's neurophysiological studies are conducted has only about 150 square feet of floor space, which is divided into a dissection area and three electrophysiological setups. Because Alkon is working with light-sensitive cells—photoreceptors—the areas are separated by curtains and the windows are blacked out. The atmosphere is reminiscent of certain Moscow apartments described by Dostoevski, apartments with tiny, interior, windowless rooms that are shared by two or three families and in which one unlucky denizen is always being climbed over by the other ten. If there are more than two or three people in Alkon's lab at the same time—and there are often five or six—they tend to get in each other's way. Elaborate tangos are frequently performed by those occupying one seat or position at the dissecting table and others who need to get by. The summertime, of course, with its surge of summer students and researchers is the worst. Then it gets so bad, Alkon's secretary told me, that "sometimes they line up outside the door." Or work in shifts. Some of Alkon's postdocs come in only at night.

"Is this a formal arrangement?" I asked Robin Forman, a postdoc who was just starting his research day at six o'clock in the evening.

"Sort of."

"How does the crowding affect the work?" I asked Juan Acosta-Urquidi.

"It's awful," he said. "Tensions can't help but build up. With Dan, you don't exactly have an easygoing atmosphere to begin with, but the overcrowding makes things a whole lot worse."

Alkon would like additional space for his neurophysiologists, but he doesn't have it, for two main reasons: lab space at MBL is expensive, and year-round space tends to be restricted because of the tensions between MBL's year-round investigators and its summer researchers. The latter are afraid that year-round research is going to change the character of MBL and diminish the caliber of its research by, among other things, bringing in less than top-knotch scientists or reducing the amount of space available for summer researchers. In spite of this, Alkon has over the years managed to spread out and expand, and he now has a spacious office in the new wing of the library, special animal quarters, and at least three additional, small labs devoted to the biochemical and anatomical study of learning in *Hermissenda* in different parts of the Lillie Building. The neurophysiologists, though, are still confined to quarters so small that there is no room for desks and that they must use tables in the library instead. "It's not ideal," says Alkon, "but I can't complain. I'm one of the best-funded investigators at NIH."

On the second floor of Lillie, and immediately below Alkon's neurophysiology lab, Eric Kandel also has a year-round lab. A poem on the door, entitled "Cloned Poem: Habituation is Royalty and Habituation in *Aplysia*" and written by Michael Newman, an editor of the *Paris Review,* lets you know you're in the right place. Inside is an *Aplysia* factory; refrigerators and aquariums are filled with *Aplysia* at every stage of development: tiny, free-floating larvae, juveniles, and adults that are presided over by Joe Bidwell, a young water chemist who runs the *Aplysia* mariculture lab. Joe hopes to be able so completely to define the conditions under which these snails thrive that he can eventually raise *Aplysia* in artificial seawater. Then researchers in Illinois or Missouri will be able to bred their own stock of *Aplysia*. In the meantime, he raises adult *Aplysia* from juveniles supplied to him from California. His goal for the next few years is to produce eight thousand adult *Aplysia* a year—enough to meet the needs of the Columbia University lab and to supply other labs as well.

Kandel, who has very commodious quarters in New York City, spends very little time at MBL, and is not in fact a member of MBL's corporation. His lab at MBL, though, is a reminder to Alkon of Kandel's position in the field of invertebrate learning (you have to worry when the editor of the *Paris Review* starts writing poems about the competition's research) and of a relationship that Alkon says is the ''most unpleasant experience of his scientific career.'' Though some of Alkon's former colleagues would vouch for the fact that Alkon's relationship with Kandel is certainly not the only unpleasant experience of his career, the animosity between these two researchers is well known in scientific circles. Over the years, the syntax of their relationship has been punctuated by blowups at scientific meetings, by failures of the two scientists to cite each other's work, and by Alkon's outspoken attacks on the assumptions and methodology of the Columbia lab's research and on Kandel for what Alkon perceives to be his attempt to play down the importance of the *Hermissenda* work. To Kandel and his colleagues, Alkon's nose is out of joint because he would like more recognition than he is getting.

That Alkon and Kandel have an antagonism that goes beyond the usual grating of scientific egos seems obvious. Less clear are its roots. How much can be attributed to Alkon's difficult personality, his arrogance, and his outspokenness and how much to the fact that, in this growing field of research, Alkon was Kandel's greatest scientific competitor, the man who from the early 1970s on looked as if he might be able to get at the cellular mechanisms of associative learning the fastest? A third factor in the relationship between the two scientists, one that might have made Kandel particularly sensitive to Alkon's irritating qualities is that with their short statures, prominent noses, brown eyes, curly hair, and staccato, clipped manners of speech, the two men look and—on the surface—act so much alike that they could be mistaken for brothers. Their academic backgrounds are also similar, and their colleagues tend to use many of the same adjectives—*ambitious, arrogant, manipulative*— in describing the two men. Alkon, though, lacks Kandel's wit, humor, and immense congeniality—not to mention his knack for creating an enthusiastic research atmosphere.

"They hate each other's guts, but they're very much alike," says a scientist who knows both Kandel and Alkon well. If it's true that we're hardest on the people who most resemble us, Kandel might well have had it in for Alkon because Alkon is someone in whom he can see much of himself.

Alkon, characteristically, does not see that his personality might have played any part in the developing hostilities with Kandel. When he and Kandel first met, at a talk that Alkon gave at the NIH in 1973, Alkon had for years been openly disparaging of Kandel's work with habituation (it wasn't real learning, he said), yet he prefers to remember himself at that meeting as the young scientist eagerly seeking the approval of an established investigator. After Alkon's talk, Kandel came up and introduced himself, and they discussed the work on *Hermissenda* and one of Kandel's grants. According to Alkon, who happened to be sitting on the panel that was reviewing this grant, Kandel wanted to be sure of his support. Alkon says that he voted in favor of the grant but that ultimately it was not funded, leaving Kandel furious. He believes that Kandel saw him as the culprit and that it was this that got their relationship off on the wrong foot. Possibly. But it's equally possible that Kandel had heard about Alkon's criticism of his work on habituation and already had a somewhat negative opinion of him. Or perhaps their difficulties arose sometime later—when it became clear that Alkon could zero in on the cellular basis of learning in *Hermissenda* or when Alkon was pressing to be recognized for having found associative conditioning in *Hermissenda* though he had not yet run the control groups that Kandel and his colleagues, as well as other investigators in the field, felt were necessary to sustain such a claim.

Whatever the genesis of their hostilities, one of its public manifestations has been in the scientific literature of the field, in the way that Kandel and Alkon have recognized—or failed to recognize—each other's work in their own publications. The failure of scientists to cite others for ideas and experiments that have influenced their work—citation amnesia, as it is sometimes called—goes far beyond a lack of scientific courtesy. In a world in which the state of knowledge is constantly changing, all a scientist really has to his credit is priority, the fact that he found a certain phenomenon first; when that priority is not recognized, his lifeblood is taken away. Also, since the history of science and the advancement of knowledge depend not only on the actual performance of experiments but also on whether the experiments are remembered, a conscious failure by one investigator to cite another's work may be seen as an attempt to write history in such a way that the contributions and influence of the other scientist are excluded. This, at least, is the effect a well-established investigator can have on someone who is just starting out and has, as yet, few collaborators and a small reputation.

By the time Alkon came on the scene of invertebrate learning, Kandel was already getting some one hundred citations a year, a number that greatly underrepresents his actual influence, since citations are indexed to only the first author of a paper and since Kandel, from the early seventies on, when he stopped working at the laboratory bench, usually appeared as the last author on his jointly authored papers. This reflects a tradition observed in many laboratories: the scientist who puts in the most time at the bench gets the position of first author. In the mid-seventies, Alkon, on the other hand, was getting only about twenty-five citations a year, and most of these appeared in his papers. If there were to be a game of citation amnesia, it is clear, Alkon would have more to lose.

Alkon started out citing Kandel (his 1974 paper on the associative training of *Hermissenda* contains two, rather slighting references to Kandel's work on habituation and sensitization), but he soon stopped, he says, when he realized that Kandel and his colleagues weren't reciprocating. There is no mention of Kandel's research on learning in any of Alkon's papers from 1975 to 1978; the citations begin again in 1978, once Terry Crow and Alkon began publishing papers together. During the time that Crow, a personal friend of one of Kandel's close colleagues, was with Alkon, the citations to Kandel's work were more frequent and less pointed than before. When Crow left Alkon's lab in the early eighties, the references resumed their somewhat disparaging tone.

Kandel and his colleagues, for their part, did not cite Alkon before the end of 1979, when, as one of Kandel's co-workers has said, it was pointed out to them that they "had been remiss." Although the lack of citations before then could be justified, since it wasn't until 1978 that the New York lab accepted Alkon's claims for associative learning, Kandel's treatment of Alkon's work after 1978 and until the mid-1980s could also be seen as less than fair. Kandel's group mentions the *Hermissenda* research merely as one of several invertebrate preparations being used to study learning and never refers to Alkon's specific contributions or the significant headway that he has made in understanding the basis of associative learning in his chosen snail. Without such specific references, Alkon feels,

Kandel is just damning him "with faint praise." The reason Kandel and his colleagues don't refer to his work more, Alkon would argue, is that an acknowledgment of progress in other preparations might take the spotlight off of Kandel and the *Aplysia* work to some extent.

Over the years, both Kandel and Alkon have made periodic attempts to improve their relationship, in print and in person. Kandel, reportedly, has called Alkon more than once to ask him what he can do to smooth things out ("Cite our papers more," Alkon says he replied). Alkon started citing Kandel more frequently and less disparagingly, especially in papers of which Terry Crow is the first author; also, during a period when Kandel's application to the MBL for laboratory space to use for the mariculture of *Aplysia* was pending, Alkon offered Kandel the use of one-quarter of his lab. Kandel took him up on the offer in 1978; in return for the favor, Alkon later got a gracious letter from Kandel and an invitation to give a seminar at Kandel's Columbia lab. Normally, these seminars are informal talks that last about an hour and are followed by ten minutes or so of questions. When Alkon spoke before Kandel and his colleagues, he says, he was so frequently interrupted by questions that it took him four and a half hours to finish. Most speakers, if they had been bothered by so many interruptions, would have had the presence of mind to ask the audience to hold its questions until the talk was over. Most audiences, moreover, would have let up on noting that a guest speaker was getting flustered. Kandel's group didn't let up, though, nor was Alkon able to take charge of the situation. He played according to the rules of Kandel's lab and left feeling, he says, "I was silly in making overtures to this man. I was dealing with an enemy."

"I don't think Alkon was treated differently than our own speakers," Bob Hawkins, an investigator in Kandel's lab, says now. "Well, yes, maybe four and a half hours was a little extreme, but that's because he's so close to what we're thinking about all the time."

Like most unfriendly relationships, that between Kandel and Alkon has been a two-way street; Alkon's habit of continually pushing the merits of his research while criticizing the work of others does not inspire the most generous or accommodating behavior, but Kandel's early success with *Aplysia* made him less than eager to share center stage with newcomers. Given the widespread enthusiasm over Kandel's work with *Aplysia,* it's easy to forget that before Kandel even found associative conditioning in *Aplysia,* Alkon had established in *Hermissenda* both associative learning and a well-defined circuit in which to look for the changes accompany learning. He might have been as irritating as a hairshirt, but he was also Kandel's chief competitor and the first to claim that he had found an engram—a memory trace, the site where a particular form of learning was stored.

Alkon had started looking for his memory trace in about 1975, some three years before he and Terry Crow published their exhaustive paper on associative conditioning in *Hermissenda,* a paper that laid to rest any doubts that these snails could learn, that they could change their normal reaction to light as a result of having received paired presentations of light and rotation. Before Alkon's schooling, these colorful, sylphlike snails were attracted to light but "hunkered down" in response to rotation; after training, they hunkered down in response to light as well. It took an "educated" snail two to three times as long as its untrained counterpart to approach a brightly lit spot.

Convinced that he had real associative learning long before others in the field were ready to believe it, Alkon wanted to know which of the cells in his previously described circuit of statocyst, photoreceptor, and optic ganglion cells and changed as a result of the learning—and how. How did the changes translate into the change in behavior?

"I was lucky," he says. "It could have been that I never found any changes, but I did. The way you think about your experiment—the whole gestalt that you bring to bear—has a lot to do with what kind of data you are going to find. The process is extremely self-centered—like writing a poem; you have to be able to listen to what your feelings and intuitions are. I had always thought that the convergence points between two distinct sensory inputs would be an important place to look for changes, and this had a great deal to do with the way I designed my conditioning paradigm. The fact that I was thinking in terms of existing circuits suggested that I should be looking for biophysical changes."

Alkon didn't know in which cells to begin his search, but he decided that, ideally, he would like to look for the changes as they took place, to actually have microelectrodes in the hair cells, for example, as light was paired with rotation. This was the ideal way, but was it possible? Microelectrodes tend to fall out of a cell if someone slams the laboratory door too hard. What were they going to do when Alkon, who now spun his snails around on a turntable rather than shaking them up, turned the record player on?

"This proved to be the most difficult problem that I've ever had to work on," Alkon told me one day as we ate lunch in the Black Duck, an informal restaurant perched over Woods Hole's Eel Pond and one of two restaurants where many of MBL's scientists eat, rubbing elbows with tourists as well as members of Woods Hole's other communities—researchers from the Woods Hole Oceanographic Institute (WHOI, or Whooee, as it's pronounced), summer residents, and townspeople.

"I had been musing on this problem for six or seven months and was just about ready to give up when I realized that I was, in fact, dealing with several sources of movement. Rotation I had to put up with, but torque in the mechanical devices, the sloshing around of seawater, and the movement of the preparation itself were all things that could be minimized, if not eliminated." The solution he finally arrived at was to immobilize the snail's nervous system—its ganglia and sensory organs—inside an inverted plastic jar that was filled with seawater (so that there was no air/water interface) and sealed with Vaseline to the turntable. The jar was solid except for several tiny holes through which Alkon inserted his microelectrodes.

The first cells that Alkon examined were the hair cells of the statocyst, cells that get excitatory synaptic input from the Type A photoreceptors and that themselves inhibit the Type B photoreceptors during rotation. When Alkon gave these cells paired presentations of light and rotation, he almost immediately found a change. As training took place, the hair cells fired less and less. Further experimentation, though, showed that it wasn't that the hair cells themselves were changing but rather that the input to the hair cells had changed. Alkon realized at that point that since hair cells received excitatory input from the Type A photoreceptors, he should be looking at the photoreceptors. He put microelectrodes into the Type A photoreceptors and recorded from them. Sure enough, after training, the Type A photoreceptors sent many fewer excitatory impulses to the cells that they synapsed on. These cells included the hair cells as well as some interneurons in the snail's large, cerebropleural ganglion. According to what Alkon knew about how *Hermissenda* was wired, it was these interneurons that connected with motor neurons, the cells that drive the muscle contractions of the foot and move the snail toward light. Fewer excitatory signals from the Type A cells meant that the snail's foot would contract less and that the animal would be less attracted to light.

The next question for Alkon was whether the change in the firing pattern of the Type A cells resulted from an intrinsic change in those cells or from a change in their synaptic input. Since he already knew that Type A photoreceptors received inhibitory input from the Type B photoreceptors, Alkon suspected the latter. On putting electrodes in Type B cells, he found that even a single pairing of light and rotation was followed by a prolonged increase in their firing. Increased firing of Type B cells meant increased inhibition of the Type A cells and, therefore, a decrease in the Type A's excitatory signals to the hair cells, interneurons, motor neurons, and so on. The change in the Type B cells looked as if it might be responsible for all the others and as if, as Alkon would later show, it was intrinsic to the Type B cells themselves. It arises during the pairing of light and rotation because of very complex and precise interactions between the Type B cells' normal response to light and the combined synaptic input from the hair cells and optic ganglion cells. The net effect is that the Type B cell's normal depolarization to light (the fact that the inside of the cell becomes more positive when a light is flashed) is greatly enhanced as a result of training, and therefore the B cell is much more excitable: it fires many more action potentials. That this excitability is intrinsic to the Type B cell, Alkon showed when he removed all synaptic input to the B cell and found that the B cell was still more excitable.

A slightly enhanced depolarization is noticeable even after one pairing of light and rotation; after many such pairings, it is more evident still. Then, after training is stopped, the Type B cells remain more excitable to light. In some manner, these cells have stored within them the memory of the paired presentations of light and rotation. Somehow, they now react to light alone as if they were receiving the complex synaptic inputs (from the hair and optic ganglion cells) that they got when light was paired with rotation.

But how? How was this information stored in the Type B photoreceptor? Alkon began to examine this question by looking for biophysical differences in the B cells of naive (untrained) and trained animals. The first difference he found was in input resistance, a difference that translates directly into a change in excitability. With a voltage and current electrode in Type B photoreceptors and a reference electrode in the bath, Alkon injected known amounts of current (positive ions) into the cell, then observed the change in voltage across the membrane. Since Ohm's law predicts that the voltage across a circuit (in this case the membrane) is equal to the current times the resistance of the circuit, Alkon was using this method to see if the membrane resistance of the Type B cells in trained animals had changed. He found that the same amount of current injected into the B cells produced a much greater voltage change in trained animals than in untrained animals. The current input was the same in both cases. What had to have changed was the resistance of the Type B cell membrane. It had increased, Alkon calculated, by about 30 to 40 percent; that is, it was now 30 to 40 percent more resistant—or less leaky—to the passage of current (ions) than the membrane of Type B photoreceptors in untrained animals. Again according to Ohm's law, this meant that it was now much more excitable. The same amount of depolarizing synaptic current now produced much greater voltage changes across the Type B cell membrane. The B cell responded to these greater changes in voltage in the only way that it could (remember, action potentials vary in frequency, not in size; the intensity of a stimulus is conveyed only by the frequency of the potentials it elicits)— by firing more action potentials.

Interestingly enough, given that most theories on learning had held that the changes associated with learning took place at the synapse, this change in resistance was associated with the cell body of the B cell and not just its synapses. When Alkon cut the axon of the B cell at the point at which it joins the cell body (a procedure that sounds drastic but from which the cell quickly recovers, minus its ability to fire action potentials), he found the same change in resistance. "We didn't know where to look for the changes," says Alkon, "and like everybody else, I guess, I thought they would be at the synapses; but I had to follow my experimental results."

Potassium channels, the source of the resting potential in cells and, therefore, the basis of all bioelectricity, are—as Alkon was well aware—the main contributors to the resistance of the cell membrane. So when he found such a large change in the resistance of the Type B cell membrane, he immediately thought of them. He reasoned then that such an increase in resistance could be explained by a decrease in the number of open potassium channels. Alkon, in a 1978 paper, was not the first to suggest that potassium channels—through some sort of a change that affected their ability to open—could be the storage sites of learning. (At a neuroscience meeting in 1976, Graham Hoyle and a colleague had suggested that a change in potassium conductance could explain a change of impulse frequency in their operant conditioning paradigm in the locust. But because of the disadvantages of working with the locust's nervous system, they had little evidence to support the idea. "It was," as one neurobiologist says, "something between a derived experimental result and a guess." When Hoyle tried to publish his findings, his paper was rejected.) But Alkon was the first to have a system in which it was possible thoroughly to study the role that potassium conductances play. Kandel, at the time, was still thinking in terms of calcium channels in his model of sensitization in *Aplysia* (according to Alkon, he laughed at the idea of potassium channels when Alkon presented his findings to a meeting of the Columbia faculty club), yet less than two years later he, too, would be jumping on the potassium channel bandwagon. Alkon did not mention Hoyle's hunch about potassium channels in his papers on the subject; Kandel, with less apparent justification since Alkon had published evidence to support the role of potassium channels in learning, failed either to mention Hoyle or to cite Alkon.

How do potassium channels affect a nerve cell's behavior? Hoyle described the process to me in a wonderful imitation he gave of a spontaneously firing cell. "You have to think of these things in terms of dynamic processes in intrinsically active cells," he told me. "If a cell that is firing away, pop . . pop . . pop . . pop, has an increase in its conductance to potassium—i.e., more channels are open—it goes slower, pop . . . . pop . . . . pop . . . . pop. If channels are closed, thereby decreasing potassium conductance, poppoppoppop; it fires faster."

Basically, when fewer potassium channels are open, the cell's resistance and, therefore, its excitability go up. The cell fires more action potentials for the same amount of synaptic input. This, however, is a very general picture of the relation between potassium channels and nerve cell activity. A more complete picture of the effect of a decreased conductance depends on the type of potassium channel that is closed. Closing potassium channels that are important in producing the cell's normal resting potential, for instance, increases the resistance and the cell's excitability. Closing a potassium channel that is involved in repolarizing a cell during an action potential doesn't increase a cell's excitability, but it does make an action potential last longer.

These two changes, though, have one important side effect

in common, namely that they indirectly increase calcium influx into the cell. Calcium, remember, enters the cell at the tail end of an action potential; in many cells, though, it also contributes to the primarily sodium-mediated upswing of the action potential. More action potentials mean that more calcium enters; longer action potentials mean that calcium has more time to enter. At the synaptic terminals, a greater concentration of intracellular calcium means that more neurotransmitter is released; at the cell body, calcium may have far subtler and more diverse effects, which scientists are only beginning to fathom.

Like cyclic AMP, calcium is a potent regulatory molecule, a second messenger. It plays a key role in so many processes that it has even been nicknamed the universal second messenger. A quick burst of calcium into a cell, it is now known, triggers such diverse cellular functions as muscle contraction, fertilization, sperm motility, inflammation reaction, nerve transmission, and, as both Alkon and Kandel now suspect, learning. Calcium is known to activate enzymes that close potassium channels. Calcium can also "talk" directly to the genome, the cell's DNA, and effect the genes that a cell is expressing and, ultimately, the proteins that the cell makes. "Calcium is one of the few elements capable of transforming electrical events into memory," notes Llinás. Calcium lets the genome know that the cell has been active. In doing so, it may direct the genome to produce different proteins—a new type of channel protein, perhaps, one that may make a cell permanently more excitable.

In 1978, Alkon published a paper in which he noted that the resistance of the Type B photoreceptors had changed as a function of learning. In 1979, he thought he had found the potassium conductance that decreased in Type B cells during learning and was responsible for the change. That conductance is an early-activating potassium conductance, and one of at least four different potassium channel types observed in invertebrate neurons and one of six different ionic conductances (sodium, calcium, as well as potassium) that Alkon would find in the Type B cells. Unlike the potassium channel that is so important in Hodgkin and Huxley's model of the action potential, Alkon's potassium channel is early activating. It opens and closes in response to small voltage changes across the membrane. It plays a role not in the action potential itself but in the Type B cells' normal, long-lasting depolarization to light, a depolarization that in turn triggers action potentials. Closing those channels has the effect of enhancing that depolarization.

During the same period, Alkon began to suspect that calcium might play an important role in initiating the Type B cell changes when he found that during training the calcium current into the Type B cell is greatly enhanced and the intracellular level of calcium temporarily rises (later, it falls back down to normal). At the time, there was a theory that ionic channels might be closed if an enzyme attached to the channel protein a specific chemical grouping, a small cluster of atoms called a phosphate group, because it contains an atom of phosphorus as well as atoms of oxygen and hydrogen. If the electrically charged phosphate group was bonded to the channel protein, it was hypothesized, the shape of the protein might change in such a way that the channel would now be closed to the passage of ions. Because it was known that the enzymes that carry out the phosphorylation of proteins are activated by cyclic AMP and sometimes calcium, Alkon began to think in terms of a calcium-triggered closing of potassium channels as a mechanism for the changes produced in the Type B cells.

As light and rotation are paired during training, he proposed, input to the Type B cell converges in such a way that the B cell undergoes an enhanced depolarization and increase in activity. As a result, the calcium level in the cell rises, triggering the closing of potassium channels (via phosphorylating enzymes). This, in turn, produces an increase in the resistance of the cell that further enhances depolarization and the B cell's activity. In a postive-feedback cycle, more calcium enters the cell, more enzymes are activated, and more channels are closed. After training, the closed channels represent the memory of the pairing, the engram. Alkon doesn't talk in terms of short-term and long-term memory (he would rather have that distinction arise out of his experimental results than be superimposed on them), but says that phosphorylation "represents a reasonable basis for a fairly long-lasting change." Whether or not the genome is involved is pure speculation at this point, but it is evident that Alkon's cycle, which has been increasingly substantiated in the years since it was first proposed, provides an elegant mechanism by which the same increase in calcium could effect both short-term and long-term changes in a cell's activity: short-term changes through the activation of enzymes that phosphorylate and close potassium channels; long-term changes by "talking" to the genome and, perhaps, calling for cutbacks in the manufacture of a particular type of channel protein or the production of an altogether new type.

Alkon's findings on "the neural correlates of conditioning" began to appear in 1975 as a somewhat confusing series of papers in which the focus was first on the hair cells, then on the Type A photoreceptors, and finally on the B cells. At one point, cyclic AMP seemed to be important to the change in the B cells; then, the next year, cyclic AMP wasn't so important, but calcium was. At first the change in B cell excitability and resistance was brought about by just one type of potassium channel, but by the early eighties Alkon had evidence to suggest that two types of potassium channels were involved. It was a difficult story to follow, partly because of the way in which Alkon presented it and partly because of the enormous complexity of the system with which he was working—the intrinsic messiness of that thin slice of life that he had chosen to study. And though changes in a scientist's story or model are to a certain extent inevitable and to be expected, some think Alkon might have made more converts by withholding publication until his story was a little more complete. Joe Farley, one of Alkon's current colleagues, says, "He tried to sell the story before it was in. He jumped the gun, and he's aware of that. He has a record of making claims prematurely, and that's something he'll have to live down. But I don't think it in any way detracts from the importance of his work. His mistakes were honest ones, given what was known about the circuit at the time."

As it was, Alkon's powerful, calcium-triggered, positive-feedback cycle—which in the words of Chip Quinn, a neurobiologist then at Princeton University, "is not only clever but has a simplicity and elegance that suggests that it's true"—tended to get lost in his complicated wiring diagrams, biophysical analyses, and tight, defensive, and not always clear writing style. It was a story that some could not readily understand and that others, perhaps, given Alkon's personality and / or their own interest in the mechanisms of learning, chose not to.

When Alkon began to think that rising calcium and a changing potassium conductance were the means by which his snails "remembered" that light had been followed by rotation, the scientist from whom he borrowed the theory on how a cell might change its ionic conductances was Paul Greengard, a biochemist at Rockefeller University. In 1976, Greengard, an authority on the action of cyclic AMP in cells and on the relation between cyclic AMP and intracellular proteins, hypothesized that ionic channels could be modified by the attachment of a phosphate group. Phosphorylation is just one of the ways that proteins can be modified after they are made, but it is the only known role of cyclic AMP in the cells of all multicelled animals. Cyclic AMP regulates a group of enzymes called protein kinases, which attach phosphate groups to proteins. In that one way cyclic AMP carries out all of its many diverse functions. Calcium, it was known at the time, was also involved in the regulation of protein phosphorylation, but it was not known exactly how. Several examples of cyclic AMP-dependent protein kinases had been isolated, and there was evidence that some of these kinases were regulated by calcium as well. It was only later that kinases dependent on calcium were also found. They came to be called calcium-calmodulin-dependent kinases because calmodulin—a protein shaped like a four-leaf clover—is the protein to which any calcium inside a cell is usually bound.

In 1976, Greengard had a hypothesis about how the phosphorylation of ionic channels could bring about fairly long-lasting changes in the activity of nerve cells. He also had plenty of purified, active cyclic AMP–dependent protein kinase that was able to catalyze the phosphorylation of proteins in the absence of cyclic AMP. What he didn't have was a system to test his hypothesis. Then, in the fall of 1978, Greengard happened to run into Felix Strumwasser at the annual neuroscience meeting. Strumwasser, who had, as he had once predicted, devoted his research career to *Aplysia,* was now studying the nerve cells that trigger egg laying in *Aplysia.* He told Greengard in great detail about the curious change in the electrical properties of these cells that happened just before egg laying commenced. Then he told him that this change was associated with a rise in intracellular cyclic AMP. Greengard became very excited and told Strumwasser about his theory that the link between cyclic AMP and the biophysical changes might be protein phosphorylation. He promised to supply Strumwasser with the cyclic AMP–dependent protein kinase. Strumwasser, in turn, said he would inject the kinase into the cells and see if the kinase could by itself simulate the biophysical changes associated with the onset of egg laying, therefore bypassing the cyclic AMP step.

Unbeknownst to Strumwasser, at about the same time Greengard also heard about Kandel's work with sensitization, specifically that the injection of cyclic AMP into a sensory neuron could mimic the effect of a sensitizing stimulus and cause enhanced postsynaptic potentials in a gill motor neuron. Greengard supplied the same enzyme to Kandel, and both Strumwasser and Kandel soon had evidence to support Greengard's hypothesis. In both systems, the kinase by itself was able to produce the changes previously associated with cyclic AMP and linked to egg laying in Strumwasser's system and to sensitization of the gill withdrawal reflex in Kandel's. In both systems, moreover, the changes produced by the kinase were associated with an increase in the membrane resistance of the cells.

Greengard arranged for the simultaneous publication of papers from the two labs in a 1980 issue of the *Proceedings of the National Academy of Sciences;* Kandel and Strumwasser then went on to find potassium channels that accounted for the resistance changes they had observed. The potassium channel described by Kandel and his colleagues was one that had not previously been described. Relatively voltage independent, it is not activated by depolarization, but it is sensitive to serotonin and cyclic AMP, two compounds that the Columbia lab already knew could simulate sensitization. Decreasing this conductance (via cyclic AMP–dependent protein phosphorylation) has the effect of slowing down repolarization during action potentials and, thereby, enhancing the influx of calcium. Increased calcium, in turn, increases neurotransmitter release from the sensory neurons and, finally, causes the gill to contract more. Several years later, Alkon's story also advanced with the help of Greengard when he supplied Alkon with a cyclic AMP–dependent protein kinase to inject into Type B photoreceptors. When the kinase had very little effect on the potassium channel that Alkon believed was responsible for changes associated with learning (though it did have an effect on another potassium channel in the Type B cell), Greengard gave him a sample of a recently purified, calcium-calmodulin-dependent protein kinase. The second enzyme did the trick. It changed the right potassium conductance and changed it in the right direction.

The story Kandel was piecing together on sensitization was exciting, but sensitization was not associative learning, and he was under increasing pressure to show that his studies of habituation and sensitization had some relevance to the higher forms of learning. At the same time, many of those in Kandel's group had all but given up on conditioning in *Aplysia*. It was a dumb animal, they had decided after years of failed attempts at conditioning; they were going to be able to go only so far with it. So in 1974, when an undergraduate student at Reed College wrote to Kandel about some very encouraging results he had gotten in attempts to condition tentacle withdrawal in *Aplysia,* there was great skepticism in Kandel's lab, especially on the part of Irving Kupfermann and Tom Carew, the learning psychologists who had spent much time trying to teach *Aplysia* tricks. However, Kandel, who is admired by colleagues for his excellent scientific intuition and his knack for knowing what's doable, wrote back, encouraging Terry ("Edgar T." or "E.T.") Walters to come and try his experiments at Columbia.

Walters, a tall, lanky man with sandy hair, arrived at

Columbia that same year and set to work immediately. He soon found that nearly all of the experiments he had done before graduating from Reed were worthless because he hadn't been conducting them "blind." In other words, when he was testing his animals for evidence of learning, he hadn't kept himself ignorant as to which of his animals were in the experimental group (those he hoped would show learning) and which were in the control group. The results, therefore, could have been the results of investigator bias rather than real learning. "Like other biologists," he says now, "I was incredibly naive about learning. I didn't realize how many ways there were to fool yourself."

When Walters tried to repeat his conditioning experiments, in which he paired a mild stimulus to the tentacle with a shock to the head, but now using the rigorous criteria and experimental methods of the New York group, the results were as Tom Carew and Irving Kupfermann expected. Most of the previous effects he had reported disappeared. Kandel, according to Walters, was still unfailingly supportive of his efforts, but he then persuaded Walters that if he was going to continue looking for associative learning in *Aplysia,* he might as well be looking at the gill withdrawal reflex. At least they had the circuitry all worked out for that behavior if and when he was successful.

Walters tried one pairing procedure after another, and thousands of hours, dozens of pairing paradigms, and hundreds upon hundreds of *Aplysia* (at ten dollars apiece) later, he still hadn't found a training procedure that Kandel and his group could work with, one that produced reliable and robust learning. "I got results," Walters says, "but they didn't jump off the lab bench. I saw what a lot of people had seen before me: some evidence of learning, but it was extremely variable. One animal would show positive results; the next one wouldn't.

Everyone said it was just noise, but I don't think so. Learning is affected by many, many things—seasonal, climatic, and hormonal factors, et cetera, and I just think we didn't know—and therefore couldn't control for—all the things that were influencing learning in these snails."

Walters was far from ready to give up, though. He may have had his moments of discouragement, but he was buoyed up by the atmosphere in the Columbia laboratory and, especially, by Friday afternoon rap sessions with Tom Carew and Kandel, who unlike the heads of many large labs remains accessible—if only by telephone—even to fledgling colleagues. In these sessions, the imaginative Walters and Kandel used to speculate just how far they could "stretch *Aplysia*'s cognitive universe and apply it to humans," while the more conservative Carew played the straight guy to their ideas.

Many of these dialogues were about whether there was a relation between long-term sensitization, the state of constant arousal produced in *Aplysia* as a result of repeated shocks to the head, and "chronic anxiety," a human condition defined by psychiatrists as a persistent feeling of tension that cannot be related to obvious external threats. Although anxiety is usually thought of as being uniquely human, it struck these neurophysiologists that there was a great deal of similarity between long-term sensitization and chronic anxiety, as well as between adversive conditioning (in which a neutral stimulus like a tone is paired with an aversive stimulus—an electric shock) and what psychiatrists call signal anxiety, an acquired fear response triggered by a signal—a dentist, a fire engine's siren, and so on—that has come to be associated with danger. In a 1983 paper that came out of these sessions, "From Metapsychology to Molecular Biology: Explorations into the Nature of Anxiety," Kandel discussed the adaptive significance of most anxiety and the usefulness of signal anxiety in warning and preparing us for danger. He also argued that anxiety is not uniquely human, that signal anxiety is what an animal feels when it hears a bell that in the past reliably preceded an electric shock. And if the anxious state is common to animals and humans, the underlying mechanisms of anxiety are also probably the same. *Aplysia*'s simple nervous system, Kandel went on to suggest, allows scientists to study anxiety at the cellular and molecular level, and thanks to his lab's work on sensitization, "a simple form of chronic anxiety can now be understood in terms of its cell-biological mechanisms." Many biologists are still taken aback by Kandel's leaps from sensitization to anxiety, from snails to humans, but psychiatrists were enthusiastic. Finally, here was someone willing to express the complexities of cell biology and neurophysiology in terms they appreciated and understood. At one lecture to a group of psychiatrists, Kandel was so well received that he spoke for three hours before his audience allowed him to quit and go home.

Back at his laboratory bench, Terry Walters (like Alan Gelperin and Jack Davis before him) finally decided to take an ethological approach to the problem of learning in *Aplysia*. "At the time," he says, "much of the psychological and ethological literature indicated that learning often involves sound or visual stimuli—the distance receptors—rather than touch. This makes sense because by the time you touch something, it's often too late to do anything about it. An animal needs to be able to predict a harmful event before it happens. Therefore, it's going to associate a harmful event with the first stimuli with which it detects it."

For vertebrates, that is usually the sight or sound of something, but what are the distance receptors for a snail? "They don't see very well, and there's no evidence that they can hear," says Walters, "but they do smell. Moreover, Gelperin and David had already shown that snails can use smells to learn."

So Walters tried teaching *Aplysia* that shrimp were out to get them by pairing the smell of shrimp with a shock to the head, then looking for the effect that the smell of shrimp by itself had on the snail's locomotive behavior. It came as a surprise to just about everyone when Walters found that *Aplysia* after *Aplysia* could learn to associate the smell of shrimp with head shock quickly and easily. Give a trained *Aplysia* a whiff of shrimp, touch it, and it will flee as quickly as a snail can. Its locomotive response has been greatly and reliably enhanced by the previously innocuous smell.

The Columbia group was thrilled. When the shrimp-conditioning paper came out in the *Proceedings of the National Academy of Sciences* in 1979, it had been fourteen years since Kandel and his colleagues started looking for associative conditioning in the snail and an expensive three and a half years since Terry Walters took over the search. Only one thing dampened their excitement. Little was known about the neural circuits underlying either locomotion or smell, but they promised to be extremely complicated. "We're very happy," Chip Quinn recalls Kandel as saying at that time, "but if we have to go with this learning it's going to be years before we can get to the cellular mechanisms—ten years."

Kandel was spared the fulfillment of this depressing prospectus by a chance observation made almost simultaneously by three of his investigators—Walters and Carew, who were working on the shrimp-conditioning paradigm, and Robert Hawkins, who was involved in the sensitization project. While Walters and Carew were doing some follow-up work on conditioning and Hawkins was poking around the abdominal ganglion looking for the interneurons that mediate sensitization of the gill withdrawal reflex, all three happened to notice at about the same time that some of the cells in the abdominal ganglion seemed to be exquisitely sensitive to tactile input from the tail.

Until then, most of the attempts to condition the gill with-drawal reflex had paired a mild tactile stimulus to the siphon (which produces a weak withdrawal of the gill) with a strong shock to the head (which produces a massive withdrawal of the gill) and had failed. Now, after this observation, Walters and Carew tried basically the same paradigm, only now they substituted tail shock for head shock. Suddenly, the snails were "A students." After just a few pairings, they responded to the squirt from the Water-Pic with the same massive withdrawal of the gill and siphon that they had previously reserved for just the shock.

Carew and Walters's discovery was published in Decem-ber of 1981. Typical of the way in which the conventions of scientific writing ignore the human elements of science (in this case, the fourteen years in which Kandel's group had tried to find associative learning in this reflex and the chance obser-vation that finally led them to it), their paper begins, "The ability of *Aplysia* and other gastropod molluscs to exhibit com-plex behaviors that can be modified by associative learning has encourged us to search for an elementary behavior controlled by a simple and well analyzed neural circuit that also can be modified by this type of learning. Toward that end, we have now produced classical conditioning in the defensive siphon and gill withdrawal reflex of *Aplysia*."

"Why did a shock to the tail work when one to the head hadn't?" I asked Terry.

"This is just speculation, but I really enjoy speculating on the biological significance of these things," he replied. "Besides, you have a million different learning paradigms to choose from (I've looked at a lot of them), and the only ones that work, I've found, are those for which I've been able to come up with some pseudoethological explanation. Anyway, all this is speculation because *Aplysia* isn't known to have any natural predators; however, some relatives of *Aplysia* are preyed upon by other carnivorous mollusks, and these mollusks locate their prey by following the slime trail that the snails leave behind. It's quite likely, therefore, that in the wild, an animal like *Aplysia* is contacted, then attacked from the rear. As a result, it might be especially sensitive to input from that part of its body.''

Whether or not this rationale is biologically sound, the discovery of classical conditioning in the gill withdrawal reflex meant that now Kandel and his colleagues would be able to look for the cellular mechanisms of learning in the same circuit that they had traced all along and that for fourteen years had looked so resistant to learning. It was also the same circuit in which they had already gained powerful insights into habituation and sensitization. So, in addition to representing a tremendous savings of time and scientific effort, the new paradigm meant that they might now be able to compare the cellular mechanisms of nonassociative learning (habituation and sensitization) with those for associative conditioning. Are these mechanisms fundamentally different, as some researchers, including Alkon, maintain? Or are habituation and sensitization perhaps building blocks for associative learning? In that case, learning is much more of a continuous process than the old divisions between associative and nonassociative learning imply; also, associative learning might, in turn, prove to be a building block of even more complicated forms of learning— insight or ''Aha!'' learning, for instance: kinds of learning most developed in higher vertebrates.

The discovery that the gill withdrawal reflex could undergo classical conditioning was a stroke of luck for the Kandel group, but of luck that could happen only because Kandel's enormous resources allowed him to put so much time and money into the same, stubborn reflex. Why did it take Kandel's group so long to find associative conditioning? Chris Sahley, who likes to tease Kandel about the fact that she wrote a paper on learning in the gill withdrawal reflex that came out before his, says, "The Columbia lab was slow because they had habituation and sensitization and didn't really feel any competition. When that group feels competition, they can really move."

EIGHT

The Flip Side of Science

"EVEN IF IT'S NOT formally recognized, you're always in a race," Vincent Castellucci, the Canadian-born neurophysiologist who joined Kandel's lab in the late sixties, told me as we talked in Kandel's modern office on the seventh floor (he and his colleagues occupy two floors) of the new research annex of the New York State Psychiatric Institute, just a block away from Columbia University's College of Physicians and Surgeons. Kandel was out of town, and we had borrowed his office with its splendid view of the Hudson River for this interview. As we talked, we sat on low, beige couches in one corner of the large room. One of the walls was lined with bookcases filled with reprints of Kandel's 150-odd scientific publications. Another was covered with *Aplysia* memorabilia: photographs and statues of the now-famous marine snail. The easel (and its thick pad of white paper) that stood in the center of the room, Castellucci explained, was used during the lab's informal brainstorming sessions, which Castellucci described as "free-for-alls" where all interrupt each other and everyone is continuously on the spot.

"In a given time, there is a limited set of problems that can be solved," Castellucci continued. "Since originality is the only thing in science, you have a race to see who can solve those problems first. It's part of the fun. The second trip to the moon might have been more profound, but who wouldn't want to be on the first?'' There is nothing new about competition in science. Anyone who has ever read *The Double Helix* will remember the lengths to which Watson and Crick went to make sure that they came up with the structure of DNA first. According to many scientists, competition actually benefits research. It keeps scientists on their toes. It speeds up the pace of research and sharpens the criticism of experiments, so erroneous data and false assumptions are less likely to slip by. Competitiveness may be the natural result of the reality that the structure of science awards only originality, but competition—and the high level of criticism it inspires—may also be an essential part of the scientific endeavor, a hard edge against which scientists can hone their experiments.

Competition is also a reflection of the human side of science, a by-product of the fact that science is a system devised by human beings with all the usual foibles and emotional needs of human beings. This is a side that some scientists would prefer not to dwell on—at least not in talking to a layman.

"Competition is just one of the things that keeps scientists going," Rodolpho Llinás told me. "It is not in itself important."

Or as Terry Crow, the learning psychologist who went to work with Dan Alkon in the mid-seventies but after an acrimonious split established his own lab at the University of Pittsburgh, once advised me, "I don't think people would be interested in reading about the competition and the personalities in this field. You should stick to the science. That's what's interesting."

"Competition and personalities—that's the trivial side of science, the episcience," says Kandel. "I'm just not interested in it."

At first, this attitude of scientists toward the more human elements of their work gives the impression that these researchers are far too absorbed in the business of revealing nature to be bothered with the intricacies of human nature. Later, after the same kinds of dismissive comments have been heard again and again, one begins to suspect that the reason for them is not so simple, that it might in fact be rooted in the nature and structure of science itself. This attitude, it seems, might derive from an essential duality of science, the fact that although scientific experimentation is an immediate endeavor carried out by the normally fallible run of human beings, the advancement of scientific knowledge is really a historical process. It takes years and sometimes decades to sort out useful from useless data, the good approaches from the bad, to begin to understand the erroneous assumptions that led a scientist astray.

Science is a process that works (a very good way of finding out about the world) but usually in the long run. In the short run, it is an intensely human affair in which rational and nonrational processes, data, and personalities all play important parts. Over time, the useless data, along with all the human wrinkles of personality, propaganda, ambition, and eccentricity, will be ironed out. Today's investigators exist, wonder, experiment, squabble, and cooperate in the here and now, but the history of science tells them that only future generations of scientists will know if they have made a real and lasting contribution. On the one hand, they must continue to fight for recognition and advance their "piece of the elephant"; on the other, they must be deeply humble—both before the enormous complexity of life and before the historical process of science, with its clear demonstration that many equally certain scientists before them have been proved very wrong.

Somewhere in between these conflicting perspectives, the humanity of scientists tends to get lost. Since in the long run human elements play only a small role in science, it might be that scientists are somewhat uncomfortable with them in the present. They flip-flop between an awareness of science's long-term and short-term perspective, and they do this to their convenience and advantage. They tend to take a long-term view of the human elements in science—no, in a hundred years the competition between two scientists won't matter very much—while continuing to compete and vigorously promote the importance of their research in the present.

Although scientists have little control over their professional immortality—whether or not their names and ideas will be remembered a hundred years from now—their immediate survival depends on their doing original research, "being first." That is the badge that lets a scientist and his colleagues know that at least in today's terms—under the assumptions and philosophical constraints of at least one generation of investigators—they are good scientists. Their conversations are full of acknowledgments of these badges with comments like "His contribution was to . . ." or "We were the first to . . . ," a continual intellectual credit assigning and credit taking that sounds strangely self-conscious and pedantic until you recognize just how temporal and easily appropriated most scientific contributions really are. Being first is also part of a positive-feedback cycle. "When you're the first," as Vincent Castellucci puts it, "you get recognition. The more recognition you get, the more money and resources you receive. More money, in turn, makes it more likely that you'll be first again."

That cycle was dubbed by Robert Merton, the father of the sociology of science, the "Matthew effect," after a passage in the Gospel of Matthew. "For unto everyone that hath shall be given," the passage goes, "and he shall have abundance: but from him that hath not shall be taken away even that which he hath." Or, as Billie Holiday sang, "Them's that got shall get / Them's that not shall lose. So the Bible says and it still is news.''

The Matthew effect is a reasonable answer to the immense difficulties of dividing up limited resources among the country's fifty thousand basic-research scientists. The funding agencies that finance research need some way to decide how to allocate their money, and a good record is a better criterion than most. What's more, by and large, Merton's Matthew effect is largely meritocratic; according to the Mertonian model (whose validity has been largely borne out by empirical research), the five independent but interrelated variables that contribute to the accumulation of advantage in science are age, prestige of Ph.D., prestige of academic affiliation, quantity of publications, and quality of publications. But the Matthew effect is also somewhat of a self-fulfilling prophecy. Scientists who are earmarked as having promise early on in their careers are given better conditions for work—good facilities, more money for equipment, assistants, and so on. These in turn facilitate research, which can then help confirm the initial prediction.

There are many advantages in assigning large amounts of resources to the work of one scientist—as Merton once observed, it makes a difference, and often a decisive difference, for the advancement of science whether a composite of ideas and findings is heavily concentrated in the work of one scientist or is thinly dispersed among a great number of scientists—but there are disadvantages as well. The concentration of resources may put too many eggs in one basket, a basket that may not stand the test of time. ''When you see someone who's doing well in terms of funding and listen to him speak,'' notes one California neurobiologist, ''there's always the same tone, a tone that implies that he's on the frontier of research. Actually, he's usually pushing research backwards. In five or ten years, he will usually be found wrong. Some of his research or assumptions will be discovered to be sloppy.''

"You never know where the answer is going to come from,'' several neurobiologists have remarked to me during discussions about the effect that Kandel's considerable resources might have on developments in the field.

"People don't like to admit it,'' says Robin Forman, a postdoc in Alkon's lab, "but frequently you just stumble on things.''

One thing that many neurobiologists are able to agree on is that, for the big scientific problems, no one lab ever has the whole story. As Stanley Kater, a biologist at the University of Iowa, has remarked, "There isn't just one truth. There are many truths. Some people are just more adept at pushing their truths than others.''

"Real answers never lie in just one person's experiments,'' observes Izja Lederhendler, a psychologist who works with Dan Alkon.

Another disadvantage in the focusing of resources, and the scientific power that resources generate, on a scientific elite is that it tends to ignore the fact that the "objective'' side of science has its nonobjective flip side, one created by the fallibility of its participants.

Scientists police science: they referee journals, review grants, recommend appointments, and nominate each other for awards —all supposedly according to universalistic and meritocratic criteria. In fact, scientists are just as biased and susceptible to rhetoric as are politicians, artists, and businessmen. Those who wield a great deal of power—through the resources they command or their positions on grant review panels, on editorial boards, or in learned societies—are not more immune to bias than the rest, but their biases can become very important. They serve, in effect, as the gatekeepers of science, and their beliefs as to which directions in research are important and which are not will shape the way in which science advances for some time to come. Most of their decisions on which projects to fund, which papers to publish, which careers to boost derive from scientific insight and that very intangible but real knack for spotting the significant problem that many notable scientists possess. Yet, other decisions stem from the nearsightedness that focusing on one problem for many years sometimes brings on, or from friendship, or from a long-standing grudge.

The English biologist Thomas Henry Huxley wrote, "You have no idea of the intrigues that go on in this blessed world of science. Science is, I fear, no purer than any other region of human activity; though it should be. Merit alone is very little good; it must be backed by tact and knowledge of the world to do very much. For instance, I know that the paper I have just sent in [to the Royal Society] is very original and of some importance, and I am equally sure that if it is referred to the judgement of my 'particular friend' ——— that it will not be published. He won't be able to say a word against it, but he will pooh-pooh it to a dead certainty.

"Why? Because for the last twenty years ——— has been regarded as the great authority on these matters, and has no one to tread on his heels, until at last, I think, he has come to look upon the Natural World as his special preserve, and 'no poachers allowed.' So I must manoeuver a little to get my poor memoir kept out of his hands."

Today's neurobiologists in the field of invertebrate learning have similar concerns, and because of the size and reputation of Kandel's lab, as well as the numerous gatekeeping positions that Kandel and his colleagues fill, many of them are focused on the Columbia researcher. Several investigators have spoken enthusiastically of Kandel's support for young researchers and of the interest and support for this type of research that his personal style and success with *Aplysia* have generated, but others worry about possible negative effects of Kandel's burgeoning resources. Some think that the existence of a large lab like Kandel's actually discourages young investigators from independently pursuing their own questions regarding learning and that Kandel's enormous resources appear to make his star appear to shine brighter in the scientific heavens, his research to appear to be much more valid than that of the rest of the investigators in the field. Others also fear that Kandel and his colleagues actually use their position on grant and editorial review boards to make it harder for them to get funding and to publish papers. Izja Lederhendler, Dan Alkon, Harold Pinsker, and Graham Hoyle have all mentioned difficulties they've had in getting their scientific papers published in certain journals. Alkon says that in 1977 and 1978 he had trouble getting papers published in one journal and that he couldn't figure out why. He decided to put on the papers he was submitting to that journal the comment ''Please do not send to Eric Kandel and his colleagues for review'' and says he hasn't had any trouble since. Alternatively, of course, the quality of Alkon's papers may have improved; the policy of confidentiality that surrounds the peer review system makes it impossible to rule this out. Graham Hoyle, who before he died of a heart attack in 1985, had found that changes in motor cells rather than in sensory cells were important to learning in the insect system he was studying, complained that his lab was operating in the red and blamed his lack of funding on the ''collective opinion that emanates from Eric Kandel.'' Others, though, suggest that Hoyle's lack of success with grants stemmed from the tone of his applications, a tone that implied that Hoyle could do everything. Kandel's colleagues contend that the charges leveled by their competitors are the result of nothing more than a sour-grapes attitude, the understandable jealousy they see as stemming from Kandel's great success.

One thing that can be said for certain about the field in which Kandel, Alkon, Gelperin, Davis, Hoyle, and Sahley, among others, work, is that despite all the talk of a race for a Nobel Prize and of scientists "tasting the finish line" the search for the cellular mechanisms of learning and memory is still very much in its infancy. No one knows how much of this research will actually survive and which, if any, of the mechanisms of learning found in snails will be of importance to the rest of the animal world. The mechanisms themselves are intriguing and point to countless avenues of research; there is also some evidence that they might be operating in vertebrate brains. Yet, with a phenomenon as important as learning in an organ as complex as the brain, it is certain that there will be other mechanisms as well. Learning and memory in humans, the study of amnesiacs has clearly shown, involves many different structures in the brain and the parallel processing of information by many different pathways. Whether the relatively simple and linear mechanisms that have now been found in snails will play an important part in this is very much in question. Nor has anyone even begun to address in invertebrates such aspects of memory as recall or forgetting.

While Kandel was at Arcachon with Tauc, three neurobiologists—Alan Hodgkin, Andrew Huxley, and John Eccles—were awarded the 1963 Nobel Prize in physiology or medicine for their studies on the action potential and synaptic transmission. Kandel predicted then that the next Nobel Prize in neurobiology would be given in about ten years and would go to the scientist who solved the cellular basis of learning and memory, a problem that had recently become tractable because of new electrophysiological techniques and the reemergence of a localizationist view of the brain. Kandel's time scale was off by at least a decade (the prediction was made in 1963; as of 1986, no one has won a Nobel Prize for work in this area). Any initial premise on his part, that there might be *a* solution to the cellular basis of learning and memory, probably derived from his medical training (physicians tend to be less aware than biologists of the great diversity of solutions that animals have evolved for most problems; they're most interested in the solutions found in humans), as well as from the strong impression that molecular genetics and the conservation of DNA made upon him. If the genetic code was the same in the nucleus of the cells of worms and chimpanzees, why not the mechanism behind learning, behind the association of two events? If nature finds a good solution to a problem, the argument runs, she doesn't chuck it and start over. This is the philosophy behind the "simple systems" approach, the reason Kandel felt confident in spending twenty years studying learning in a sea slug. The approach worked in genetics and in much of neurophysiology. That it will also work with learning and memory—processes more developed in mammals—requires a somewhat greater leap of faith.

"From my point of view," says Richard Thompson, a vertebrate neurophysiologist at Stanford University who is attempting the difficult task of studying the localization of memory in vertebrates, "it is more interesting to know how humans store memories than how *Aplysia* store memories. I have the feeling that in the end we will only know that by working on mammals."

No one says that Kandel's and other scientists' "simple systems" approach to learning isn't important and necessary, but many researchers do feel that the work is being overtouted, and most blame Kandel.

"Kandel talks as if he's got memory and learning all sewn up," Robin Forman once said. "Really, we haven't made a dent in these problems."

"The only thing I get mad at Eric for is that he presents his science as if he's answered all the questions," Chris Sahley told me.

"Because Eric's such a good salesman for the invertebrate learning work and the 'simple systems' approach, in some ways he's made it a lot easier for the rest of us," observes Ken Lukowiak. "But what's going to happen to us when the people who fund this work start asking questions about what we really know? In a way, we know less now than we did ten years ago."

What seems to be missing from many of Kandel's papers is the recognition that he is looking at just one mechanism of habituation, sensitization, or associative conditioning in one reflex in one invertebrate, and that the mechanism he has found may or may not be relevant to other animals and other reflexes. Kandel likes to use the argument that because nerve cells are basically the same in sea snails and humans, the mechanisms for modifying the behavior of those cells may also be the same. That argument is sound, but it neglects to mention the great diversity of nerve cell types in *both* sea snails and humans, a diversity sure to be the basis of alternative mechanisms for even the simplest kinds of learning-associated changes. These days, no one would be so scientifically naive as to suggest that there may be just one mechanism for each of the different types of learning and memory, yet the tone of some of his papers implies this, a tone absent in the papers of other investigators in the field.

For example, Castellucci, Carew, and Kandel begin a 1978 *Science* paper as follows: "An unresolved question in the study of learning is the relation between short-term and long-term memory. Some behavioral and pharmacological studies suggest that short- and long-term memory are two different processes having different loci and different neural mechanisms. Others suggest that memory consists of a single trace which changes in character with time and with processing. This question can be directly approached by examining the loci and cellular mechanisms of both short- and long-term memory in a given behavioral system and by determining the interrelation between them. To accomplish this end, we have studied the retention of habituation of the gill-withdrawal-reflex in Aplysia californica; this reflex involves both short- and long-term memory in habituation training.''

By contrast, Alkon is less optimistic. ''Cellular analysis of long-term behavioral modifications in invertebrates,'' Alkon begins a 1980 *Science* paper, ''may elucidate neural mechanisms of learning.''

And Jack Davis is far less general. ''The purpose of this paper,'' he says in a 1982 review of his work, ''is to briefly review one case in which we are beginning to understand how both non-associative and associative experiences alter the neural circuits underlying a particular behavior, namely feeding in the carnivorous marine gastropod *Pleurobranchaea*.''

At the same time that Kandel tends to present his work as a carefully plotted story line with only a few remaining chapters left to be written, the researchers in this field are, in fact, still in the process of battling it out, challenging each other on the general significance of their work, as well as on their assumptions, methods, and conclusions. At the center of this field of science, there is very little consensus as to the importance of a researcher's findings or the validity of his approach.

''Eric Kandel's bumptiousness notwithstanding, we know nothing about the cellular basis of learning and memory,'' Graham Hoyle, who is known for his outspokenness, has said.

"Real learning doesn't begin with associative conditioning—a simple obligatory event in which the animal has to learn—but with B. F. Skinner and operant conditioning, the kind of learning where an animal has to discover for himself the association between two events." (His implication: Kandel is studying a process that will be of little importance to the kinds of learning we are interested in as humans. Not surprisingly, Hoyle studied operant conditioning in insects.)

"I don't know that the associative behavior that Alkon is studying in *Hermissenda* is of any adaptive value," says the ethologically inclined Alan Gelperin. "The connections between the photoreceptors and the statocysts could just be fortuitous, which could explain why you have to drive the hell out of it to get conditioning." (The implication here is that if the connections are fortuitous, the mechanism that Alkon has found may also be fortuitous, that is, somehow artificial.)

"Kandel still doesn't have a system that learns" is one of the very important criticisms that Alkon, Davis, and others level at the work of the Columbia laboratory. "All Kandel has is an analogue of learning,'" Alkon once told me. "He has never shown that he can take an *Aplysia*, train it, then go inside its nervous system and find changes associated with learning. He does his behavioral experiments with one group of animals, and his neurophysiological experiments with another. In that group, learning is simulated through the zapping of connectives or dumping on serotonin. He has never directly shown that this has anything to do with learning." Most investigators, though, are willing to accept that it does and that Kandel's neurophysiological parameters closely mimic the behavioral ones, but the implication is that if Kandel trained animals, then opened them up (as Alkon and David do), he might not find the same changes that he does when he simulates learning in an animal that is opened up and restrained.

The investigators at the center of this field can also be casually dismissive of each other's work.

"It's hard to know exactly what Alkon's model is, it changes so often," one of Kandel's colleagues told me.

"Alkon's papers are written in something other than English," says another scientist.

And some of them engage in outright personal attacks.

"A lot of us wonder how high Kandel can build his house of cards. To the Lasker Award? To the Nobel Prize?" says Alkon. "It is beginning to fall. The only question now is one of kinetics. How fast will it fall versus how fast he can build it up."

"Alkon and Kandel are like carpet salesmen," another neuroscientist has observed. "Kandel's a little better than Alkon, but neither of them like to admit to holes in their research. After being with either of them, I always have to pat myself mentally to make sure I'm all there."

"In spite of the fact that he has won all those wonderful prizes, Eric Kandel is a colossal, impudent jerk," Graham Hoyle told me. "How has he won them? People like to think that there are scientists around solving all kinds of important problems. There's such a potential market for that, and Eric jumped right into it. He totally overstates his case. I'm not knocking his physiological work—that's excellent; it just doesn't have anything to do with learning and memory."

"Alkon is so competitive that it's sick," notes one neuroscientist.

"Scientists are so mean," Rudolpho Llinás once said, "because the stakes are so low: a pat on the back, a little recognition."

That may be one reason, but scientists are also "mean" because criticism, "trying to shoot down what another scientists says," is an essential ingredient of the scientific process.

And they're mean because they're human. Most of them cannot invest twenty years of their life in a particular preparation, a particular way of looking at things, without becoming somewhat blind to the advantages of other preparations, without coming to think of at least a small part of the "Natural World" as their own special preserve.

In 1981, after he and Tom Carew put the finishing touches on their associative-learning paradigm, Terry Walters left Kandel's lab, in which he had completed his Ph.D. training as well as a one-year postdoctoral fellowship, to start another fellowship with Jack Byrne at the University of Pittsburgh. Five years earlier, Byrne himself had left the Columbia group; he now was a professor with his own laboratory. Walters went there to learn more biophysics, but he also had it in his mind to continue working on *Aplysia*'s sensory neurons, those neurons that Kandel and his colleagues had found to be the site of the learning-associated changes of habituation and sensitization. When Byrne learned of Walters's plans, he was reluctant to let him go ahead with them, Walters says now. Learning was Kandel's territory, and none of those who had left Kandel's lab had ever competed with him head on. Harold Pinsker, who was now at the University of Texas, was concentrating on neuronal activity in behaving, intact animals; Byrne had focused on *Aplysia*'s inking reflex and the ink motor neurons; and when Tom Carew would leave Kandel's lab a few years later, he would concentrate on development. Walters argued, though, that it was within his rights to continue working on sensory cells if he worked on cells he himself had located while still at Columbia—a group of sensory neurons that mediate input to an *Aplysia*'s tail. Though it represented what Walters calls "an unprecedented situation," he managed to convince Byrne.

The reason Walters couldn't walk away from these neurons and from learning was that associative conditioning had him deeply puzzled. How did it work? How could nerve cells learn that signals following each other closely in time meant something different from signals separated by a minute or more? By what mechanism did they respond differently to these paired and unpaired stimuli, and did this mechanism have anything to do with the one that Kandel and his group had discovered to be the basis of sensitization—presynaptic facilitation involving the cyclic AMP cascade and the closing of potassium channels? Even before he had succeeded in finding associative conditioning in *Aplysia,* Walters had spent a lot of time pondering these questions. Now that there was a way of addressing them, he wasn't about to give up.

Back at Columbia, Kandel, Bob Hawkins, and Tom Carew were also puzzling over the same questions with their newly discovered associative-conditioning paradigm as their framework. If they gave a weak stimulus to an *Aplysia*'s siphon (they had recently switched from squirting the siphon with water to touching it lightly with a hair bristle), then shocked its tail, the snail learned after a number of these pairings that the light touch to its siphon predicts shock. It now reacted to just the touch alone with a massive withdrawal of the gill and siphon. If the shock was delivered a minute or two after the touch, on the other hand, the association wasn't made. Kandel, Hawkins, and Carew already understood much of the neural circuitry involved in this learned association. From their studies with habituation and sensitization, they knew that touching *Aplysia*'s siphon stimulated twenty-four sensory neurons in its abdominal ganglion and that these neurons made direct connections onto six motor neurons controlling gill withdrawal. The sensory neurons, they also knew, made and received connections from identified facilitatory interneurons, those nerve cells that mediated sensitization by releasing a serotoninlike substance on the presynaptic terminals of the sensory cells. They were also aware, from Terry Walters's work before he left Columbia, that input to an *Aplysia*'s tail stimulated a group of sensory cells in its pleural ganglion, one of several ganglia that form a lumpy ring around the snail's esophagus and which is connected to the abdominal ganglion via a long bundle of nerve fibers. These tail sensory neurons feed indirectly into both the gill motor neurons and the facilitatory interneurons that mediate sensitization of the gill withdrawal reflex; that is, the tail sensory neurons are connected to these other cells via one or more unidentified interneurons.

On the basis of this knowledge of the neural circuit, Kandel and his colleagues hypothesized that pairing siphon stimulation with tail shock produced associative learning through the excitation of an unidentified facilitatory interneuron, one that would be excited not if it received input from either the tail or the siphon alone but only if input came from both the tail and the siphon together. The model was a summation or convergence model. Their hypothetical interneuron had a high resting potential (it required a lot of stimulation or depolarization in order to fire), and it received input from both the siphon and the tail. Neither pathway by itself was strong enough to excite it. Only when both pathways were active would the cell fire, releasing serotonin on the presynaptic terminals of the sensory neurons and, thereby, causing presynaptic facilitation and enchanced gill withdrawal.

How the cell would "remember" that the two inputs had been paired (in such a way that, after training, it now reacted to input from the siphon alone as if it were getting input from both the tail and the siphon was not very well formulated in this hypothesis, but the idea was that repeated pairing somehow leads to more "profound and prolonged facilitation" so that the siphon pathway is sufficiently strenghtened to drive "motor pathways over which it had previously little or no control."

The model wasn't a bad one, but it had the great disadvantage of being extremely difficult to test. Proof for it depended on the Columbia group's being lucky enough to find the hypothesized facilitatory interneuron. The fact that the interneurons they knew about and could test didn't behave in the manner they had hypothesized didn't mean much. Among *Aplysia*'s one thousand abdominal ganglion cells, there still could be an as yet undiscovered neuron that behaved exactly as they had said it would.

Not all neurobiologists in the field thought highly of the model. "It looked like a mess to me," said Chip Quinn, who with the benefit of hindsight discussed some of the events surrounding the Columbia laboratory's switch to a new model of associative conditioning, "but Eric, who thrives on complexity at times, liked it quite a bit. He'd present this model at seminars, then ask, 'Is it foolish?' 'I'd say, "No. Wrong ideas are better than no ideas.' "

Since Kandel's group held the same model of associative conditioning for several years, it's little wonder that many scientists were taken by surprise when in January of 1983 Kandel and three of his colleagues published two papers back-to-back in the journal *Science,* papers that presented evidence for a stunning new biochemical mechanism of associative learning, a mechanism that was an elaboration of the mechanism for sensitization and that members of Kandel's lab were ready to say they had been entertaining all along on the basis of Kandel's experiments with Tauc at Arcachon.

There are several different accounts of how those papers— and the new model—came about. The way Bob Hawkins, the first author on one of the papers, tells it, he had been trying to get evidence for the convergence model, but it hadn't been going well. The interneurons that he had identified and that were known to mediate sensitization didn't fire any better when he paired siphon and tail input (as the model predicted at least some would) than when he stimulated either the siphon or the tail alone. What happened next, he says, is that he, Carew, and Kandel decided to look for differential conditioning in *Aplysia*, to see if they could take two different stimuli—a squirt of water on the siphon and a weak electrical stimulus to the mantle of the snail and pair just one of them with tail shock— then get a differential response to the stimuli presented alone. They could. The stimulus that had been paired with tail shock produced by itself a massive withdrawal of the gill and siphon; the stimulus that hadn't, did not.

This finding, according to Hawkins, a boyish-looking investigator in his thirties who likes to listen to classical music when he's poking around in an *Aplysia* ganglion and takes his time answering questions, led the group to examine whether they might be able to produce differential conditioning within subpopulations of a single cluster of sensory neurons—the twenty-four sensory neurons stimulated by tactile input to the siphon. They stimulated two separate sites on the siphon skin (one toward the back of the animal, the other toward the belly) but paired the stimulation of just one site with tail shock. After training, stimulation of the site that had been paired with tail shock produced a massive withdrawal of the gill and siphon; stimulation of the site that had not been paired produced the usual modest withdrawal.

It was this experiment, Hawkins told me, that convinced Kandel and his colleagues that their convergence model for associative learning was wrong. As they had envisioned it, all the sensory neurons for the siphon were served by the same, small group of facilitatory interneurons, so it should be impossible to produce facilitation of one sensory neuron without producing facilitation of all the others. The results of this experiment, though, indicated that sensory neurons could be individually facilitated. That meant either that each sensory neuron had its own private facilitatory network—"And from what we knew about facilitating neurons, that didn't seem likely," says Hawkins; "our evidence was that facilitating neurons do go to all the sensory neurons"—or that associative learning was produced by a different mechanism, one that resided in each individual sensory neuron and that was not entirely dependent upon the properties of the circuit. "These findings forced us to think in terms of biochemical mechanism," says Hawkins, "some sort of internal biochemistry that allows a cell to associate only those stimuli that are presented in close temporal proximity."

The next step, according to Hawkins, was to see if they could simulate conditioning in single sensory neurons in a preparation in which all that remained of the animal was its desheathed nervous system connected by intact nerves to the animal's tail.

"Jumping into the nervous system was a radical thing to do, but it was the most direct way to test this new hypothesis," notes Hawkins. "We had been trying to take the same systematic approach for associative learning that we had used for habituation and sensitization—going step by step from the behavior in intact animals to the neural mechanisms in the dissected nervous system—but it hadn't worked."

In an experiment that greatly resembled those Kandel and Tauc conducted at Arcachon (experiments in which they tried to change the response of a nerve cell to a small "test" stimulus after pairing that test stimulus with a strong zap to the cell from another pathway), Hawkins, Carew, and a young postdoctoral student named Tom Abrams injected depolarizing current into one sensory cell (through a microelectrode in that cell), then immediately shocked the tail: buzz / zap to the tail. buzz / zap to the tail. Another siphon sensory neuron received the same injection of current (an amount adjusted to stimulate the firing of exactly five action potentials) but followed by tail shock two and one half minutes later. Buzz / long pause / zap to the tail. Buzz / long pause / zap to the tail.

Fifteen minutes after five of these training trials, the two sensory neurons were tested for their response to injections of current alone. As a measure of their response, the Columbia investigators used the size of the postsynaptic potentials (the depolarizing currents that push a cell toward the threshold at which it starts firing action potentials) that these sensory neurons produce in a gill motor neuron. As expected, the postsynaptic potentials produced by both sensory cells were enhanced as a result of training (both cells were being "sensitized" by this procedure), but the potentials from the cell that had received the paired input were much more enhanced. Something about the fact that that sensory neuron had been firing action potentials just before the arrival of the facilitating stimulus from the tail resulted in this enhancement.

"What our experiments showed," explains Hawkins, "is that if there's spike activity in the sensory neuron just before the facilitator transmitter arrives, then something about the events of presynaptic facilitation is enhanced or amplified."

"Put another way," Kandel told a group at Princeton University, "if an action potential has just occurred in the sensory neuron, that neuron will respond to the same activity of the facilitatory neuron in a much more dramatic way. The action potential somehow primes the sensory neuron."

Kandel and his colleagues called this pairing-specific enhancement in the activity of the sensory cell "activity-dependent amplification" of presynaptic facilitation. In presynaptic facilitation, they knew, release of neurotransmitter from the sensitizing pathway (a shock to the tail or a blow to the head) triggered the cyclic AMP cascade in the sensory neurons, thereby initiating the production of cyclic AMP molecules, the activation of protein kinases, and the phosphorylation of special potassium channel proteins. The result, after training, was slower repolarization during an action potential, more calcium influx, and a stronger signal to the gill motor neurons.

Since pairing current injection and tail shock has the effect of further strengthening the signal that the sensory neurons send to gill motor neurons, the first thing Kandel and his colleagues looked at when they began to seek the mechanism behind this amplification was the shape of the action potential in the sensory neurons. Sure enough, action potentials were broader (repolarization occurred more slowly) in those cells that had received paired input than in those that hadn't. Here, then, was some indirect evidence that a potassium conductance might be playing a role. Here was also evidence that the changes involved in sensitization had been enhanced to produce associative conditioning.

Many questions remained to be answered, but Kandel and his colleagues had enough to generate a working hypothesis for the mechanism of associative conditioning in the gill withdrawal reflex. Calcium is the signal that amplified presynaptic facilitation, they proposed. If calcium enters the cell (as the result of an action potential fired by that cell) just before the neurotransmitter from the sensitizing pathway triggers the cyclic AMP cascade, it somehow enhances that cascade, causing more cyclic AMP molecules to be manufactured and, eventually, more potassium channels to be closed. "We didn't get this hypothesis out of the blue," notes Hawkins. "There was some evidence from other systems that calcium can interact with the cyclic AMP cascade to magnify it." Exactly how they interact is still a puzzle, but if the Columbia group's hypothesis proves true (and experiments, so far, have borne it out), the mechanism they've proposed would be an extremely attractive one; one that might be very general throughout the animal kingdom, since it requires very little special circuitry (just a T-joint, one neurobiologist has observed) and uses a biochemical cascade common to practically all cells.

That was one account of how this new and provocative model came about. According to Tom Abrams, the young investigator who was the second author on one of these important papers, Hawkins's version—the version presented in the *Science* papers—has it backward: the reason they started looking for differential conditioning in the first place was that he (Abrams) had an idea that associative conditioning could work through calcium-mediated amplification of presynaptic facilitation. He had come to that idea while performing some experiments for his postdoctoral proposal and because of the reports emerging from a number of different laboratories at the time on calcium's capacity to act as a second messenger in cells and on the effect that calcium can have on the cyclic AMP cascade. An indirect test of Abrams's idea was whether they could get differential conditioning (his idea predicted that you could; the convergence model, that you couldn't). A more direct test was the training of individual sensory neurons and the subsequent examination of their biophysical and biochemical changes.

Regardless of which story is the right one (and there is yet another), when the Columbia lab got these findings, Kandel and his colleagues were, in the words of a visitor to the lab at the time, "on the ceiling for about a week." "We were elated at finding associative learning in *Aplysia*," says Hawkins, "but it was nothing like the elation at getting at the neural mechanisms."

This was the culmination of two decades of research on

this simple marine slug. Kandel's persistence in sticking with *Aplysia* had paid off, and the years he had spent analyzing the mechanisms of such rudimentary forms of learning as habituation and sensitization now seemed to be the result of extraordinary scientific insight. At last, he had a mechanism for a higher form of learning, a mechanism that—as an elaboration of sensitization—had important implications about the nature of learning and that could readily be tested for in other nervous systems.

Moreover, this new development out of the Columbia lab didn't go unrecognized in the scientific community. The year in which Kandel introduced evidence for "activity-dependent amplification of presynaptic facilitation," he was awarded an honorary doctorate of humane letters by the Jewish Theological Seminary of America, as well as the prestigious Albert Lasker Basic Research Award. When he arrived to accept the Lasker award, Kandel brought with him juvenile *Aplysia* in plastic cups for the press to hold during the ceremonies. The size of the award—$15,000 ($7,500 for Kandel, because he shared the award with Vernon Mountcastle, another neurobiologist)—was small, given the amount of the research funds available to Kandel. What was significant was the reward's reputation as being the New Hampshire primary of the scientific world. Among the winners of the Lasker Award in the thirty-nine years that it has been given out have been thirty-seven scientists who later went on to win the Nobel Prize.

In the same year, Kandel was made a University Professor at Columbia University, the highest-ranking academic position at Columbia. He is now in even greater demand as a lecturer, and during his lectures he mentions the research of other investigators in the field. Often, he concludes with a ten-minute synopsis of where his and Alkon's models of associative learning stand, what each model tells the other, their parallels and divergences; he also points out that, working independently, Terry Walters and Jack Byrne found the same phenomenon of activity-dependent amplification in the system they were working on.

NINE

Setting Priorities Straight

"NOT EVERYONE IN this field is competitive," said Tom Carew, a learning psychologist who worked in Kandel's lab until the middle of 1983. We had just been talking about a MBL symposium on learning and memory that Dan Alkon sponsored in the fall of 1983 and that neither Kandel nor any of his colleagues had attended, though most had been invited. Carew complained that Alkon had structured the meeting so as to "sell his product" and said that many researchers in the field felt that this was not healthy, that there were other ways to do science.

"It doesn't have to be like that," Carew went on. "It's a big mistake for anyone to say that they've got the preparation where truth is going to be found. This problem is so complex and exciting that there's room for anybody that's creative and works hard. Most of us feel that way. Look at the papers in *Science*."

Carew was referring to the January 28, 1983, issue of *Science*, in which Kandel and his colleagues had recently published evidence for their new model of associative learning. In the same issue, immediately following the Columbia lab's two papers, is a paper by Terry Walters and Jack Byrne that presents evidence for the same mechanism.

"Independent of us," Carew continued, "Byrne and Walters found the same mechanism in a different system. We could have put our papers out first, but we knew that they had these findings, and we thought it was important to cross the finish line together."

I had seen the three back-to-back papers and had wondered about their genesis. The history of science offers many instances of simultaneous discoveries, two labs independently coming out with the same findings at the same time, but because of the close associations between the laboratories of Kandel and Byrne, the fact that both Byrne and Walters spent many years at Columbia, it was possible that in this case there had been some cross-fertilization of ideas. Alternatively, perhaps Kandel had asked Walters and Byrne to replicate the experiments in which his group had found evidence for a new biochemical mechanism of associative learning in their system—the tail sensory neurons in the pleural ganglion. This would add to the generality of the findings of the Columbia group and, therefore, to their importance.

In May of 1984, when I called Terry Walters, by then a assistant professor at the University of Texas in Houston, to talk about the years he had spent trying to get *Aplysia* to show associative conditioning, I also asked him how it came about that both labs were working with differential conditioning at the same time and whether it was coincidental that they both arrived at the same mechanism.

"No," he said after a moment's hesitation. "When is this book going to come out?"

"In late 1985," I answered optimistically. "Why?"

"I have to be careful. People have different investments in the way things happen. If I'm completely frank with you, it's conceivable that it could rebound on me." Walters then began to tell me how he believed Kandel's new model of associative conditioning originated; his version of the events differs from both Hawkins's and Abrams's and provides a revealing account of interactions between science's two dissimilar sides.

When Walters left Kandel's lab in 1981 to do a fellowship with Jack Byrne at the University of Pittsburgh, he said, the only model of associative conditioning that Kandel and his colleagues were considering was the "temporal summation on an interneuron" or convergence model. That was the only model Walters had heard discussed in his six years at Columbia; it was also the only one presented at seminars. Walters says now, though, that he never liked that model. It wasn't at all parsimonious, and it couldn't account for some aspects of associative conditioning (that is, why backward conditioning— presentation of the conditioned stimulus after the unconditioned stimulus—doesn't produce learning) that he considered extremely important.

Then, as Walters, who was being supported in Byrne's lab by a NIH postdoctoral fellowship for about $18,000 a year, went to work on sensory cells in *Aplysia*'s pleural ganglion, he noticed that these cells were capable of undergoing a certain phenomenon of which Kandel and his colleagues had long thought *Aplysia*'s sensory cells to be incapable, and, more important, a phenomenon that in other nerve cells had been linked to an influx of calcium. Walters was well aware of the Yale researcher Howard Rasmussen's work on how calcium can act as a second messenger in cells and on the effects calcium can have on the cyclic AMP cascade, and he suddenly realized that there was a much simpler way to explain associative conditioning. Wouldn't it be neat, he thought, if the specificity of associative conditioning was brought about not by converging signals on a facilitatory interneuron but by calcium priming of the cyclic AMP cascade. If calcium entered a sensory neuron as a result of activity in that cell just before the sensitizing stimulus, it might somehow amplify the cascade, causing an even greater facilitation.

Walters was able to examine this idea in a group of sensory neurons that mediate input to the tail and whose output could be turned up or facilitated following a strong, "sensitizing" electric shock to the tail. He hadn't yet found the interneurons that produce this facilitated response, but he was assuming that, like the interneurons that mediate presynaptic facilitation of the sensory neurons involved in gill withdrawal, his interneurons in the tail—which are activated by shock to the tail—contact the sensory neurons at their synaptic terminals. There they would release a neurotransmitter that activates the cyclic AMP second-messenger system in the sensory neurons, producing facilitation.

Once Walters had the idea for this new mechanism, he wanted to test it as quickly and as directly as possible, to go right for the cellular mechanisms. If the basis of the temporal specificity of associative conditioning was that a short-lived increase in intracellular calcium primed the cyclic AMP cascade, he should be able to condition sensory neurons individually by pairing an injection of current into a sensory cell with a shock to the animal's tail. In the summer of 1981, Walters began trying to do just that; by December, he had completed twelve pilot experiments, most of which looked very promising for his theory.

In January of 1982, he began a full-time, formal study of the theory, ten difficult experiments in which he intended to expose the pleural ganglion of an *Aplysia,* insert three microelectrodes into three different sensory cells (one cell would receive unpaired injections of current and input from the sensitizing pathway—the shocked tail; one, input from the sensitizing pathway alone; the third, paired input), as well as a fourth microelectrode into a common motor neuron, then train the cells and measure the results. Walters hadn't told any of his former colleagues at Columbia about his plans or his preliminary, promising results ("That," he says, "would have been suicide"), but on completing all ten experiments, he intended to call Kandel.

On February 15, 1982, though, his work was interrupted by a call from Tom Abrams, a postdoc in Kandel's lab whom Walters had met just before leaving Columbia. Abrams was calling for political advice, he told Walters. He had this idea for how associative conditioning could work, but, he said, Tom Carew thought it was unlikely, and because Tom thought it was unlikely Eric wasn't as enthusiastic about it as he might be. Abrams was calling Walters because Walters knew Carew and Kandel and could perhaps give him advice on how best to get where he wanted to be: in the position to test his idea in the best way possible. "Abrams had been thrown a bone," Walters said. "They had told him that he could test his idea using extracellular stimulation of sensory neurons, but that wasn't going well." Even if successful, those experiments would provide only very indirect evidence for Abrams's idea.

Instead of advice, Abrams got the news that, yes, his idea was a good one—and it was right. Walters had the data to support it. At that point, he had completed six of the ten experiments, and just those six made his results significant. Walters told Abrams about his data and some of his techniques; the conversation ended with Abrams giving Walters his congratulations.

That was far from the end of the matter, though. Kandel was in Europe at the time, but others in Kandel's lab told Walters he had been very disloyal. Much of the preparation and theoretical framework for Walters's experiments had been developed in Kandel's lab over the years, but Walters didn't feel in the least disloyal, because all of that information was in the literature and, therefore, available for any scientist's use. "They asked me how I could go and do something like that without telling them," Terry said. "If I had told them, I knew that they would have done the same thing, only faster. They had the manpower and I didn't. I was the only one doing these experiments, but I knew that they could put three people on them."

That is exactly what happened. In about a week, Carew, Hawkins, and Abrams set about performing experiments similar to Walters's in their system—the cells that mediate the gill withdrawal reflex. When Kandel returned from his trip abroad, Walters called him, but Kandel wasn't about to acknowledge Walters's priority in the matter. They then began the negotiations that led to the joint publication in *Science*.

"But why negotiate?" I asked Terry. "You had the data before they did."

"There was no way to beat them to publication," he said. "Eric is a member of the National Academy of Science, and he could have had his results out in the *Proceedings of the National Academy of Sciences (PNAS)* while we were still waiting for our paper to be reviewed. We had no way of getting it in to *PNAS*. Friends of Eric's wouldn't have sponsored it knowing that he was in a hurry to get the same thing out. I actually asked Eric if he would sponsor our paper in *PNAS*— as he had the first paper on associative conditioning in *Aplysia*. 'I don't think I can do that,' he told me."

"Someone in Kandel's lab told me that they could have published before you." I said.

"That's ridiculous," Walters retorted. "We had to wait two months for them to finish their study. Our study was completed in early March of 1982. I believe that the testing of the mechanism at Columbia began in late February of 1982 and that their formal *Science* study did not end until about the beginning of May.''

Well, then, why didn't Walters call foul? "I didn't want to antagonize Kandel," he says. "One, because I like him. Two, I certainly don't want to have him as my enemy; three, I wouldn't want to lose him as my ally. As a young investigator, I've done very well with his support.'' Walters is full of admiration for Kandel, his former mentor. He also fears that an aggressive assertion of his priority in this matter might damage his career. At the same time, he would like recognition for the crucial part he played in the development of this new model of associative conditioning.

When I asked Walters how the incident had played out, where he thought the credit for the new mechanism had gone, he answered, ''I don't know. Probably most people assume it was Eric's discovery. A lot don't know that our paper came out at the same time. So far, citations have been fair, but I think most people assume that Kandel had these findings and wanted us to replicate them in our system in order to show generality. That's the way Eric talks about it now at meetings: 'Isn't it interesting that Byrne and Walters show the same thing in their system.' I certainly tell anyone who asks the way it really happened.''

A few days after this conversation, I talked with Tom Abrams, a small man of about thirty with curly, strawberry-blond hair, a full beard of the same color, a hooked nose, and large, blue eyes. Abrams and I talked in a coffee shop on 168th Street about two blocks from Kandel's lab. He had come up with the idea for a calcium-mediated amplification of presynaptic facilitation while doing experiments in which he had gotten some evidence for differential conditioning in a dissected preparation, he said. He presented the idea to Kandel and later wrote it up as a postdoctoral proposal that he submitted for funding.

"Eric didn't discourage me from testing the idea," came Abrams's heated answer to a question I posed. "He was excited about the idea both because it implicated calcium and because the circuitry was so minimal." There were, though, disagreements in the lab over the idea, Abrams admitted, and they prevented him from testing the idea directly.

The best way to test the hypothesis was to jump right in at the cellular level, as Terry Walters had done. "But," said Abrams, "Tom Carew is more conservative than that in his approach. Part of Carew's bias is that you should start with an intact preparation, then go step by step to a more reduced—or dissected—preparation. There is a conceptual tension in this work over whether to stick close to behavior or to go after the cellular mechanisms. Carew is for sticking close to behavior. Eric likes to go for the mechanisms, but he has to walk the line between the two camps. In the end, you have to make a bridge from these cellular mechanisms to a behavior to have them be important. You can find a lot of interesting mechanisms in cells in culture, but they're really only important if they relate to some behavior."

According to Abrams, then, Kandel was enthusiastic about the idea, but Tom Carew was reluctant to jump in and test it. At this point, Abrams admits, he called Walters, but he adds, "If I hadn't, the experiments would have only been delayed by a month or so. I think it's fair to say that conceptually we arrived at the model independently."

"Yes, they had the idea independently," agrees Walters, "but if Abrams hadn't called, they wouldn't have tested it for quite a while. First, there would have been a fight over whether they should put any effort into 'nailing down this hypothesis' et cetera. When they did decide to test it, they wouldn't have put three people on it."

But why not, if it was such a good idea? Why didn't Kandel, Carew, and Hawkins see its potential as soon as Abrams suggested it? Why did they have to wait until the pressure of Walters's experiments was upon them? Abrams gave one reason when he talked about the conceptual tension in the lab between sticking close to behavior and going after the cellular mechanisms. Another reason has to do with the fact that in the early sixties Kandel and Tauc had thought of a very similar mechanism as one of two possible explanations for their early findings in some unidentified cells in *Aplysia*'s abdominal ganglion. As time went on, though, Kandel and his later colleagues came to dismiss that explanation in favor of the convergence theory; to test it again would be a waste of time.

At Arcachon, Tauc and Kandel had found a few unidentified cells whose activity was enhanced when a weak input to one pathway was paired with a much stronger input to another, separate pathway. Kandel and Tauc proposed that this was due either to a kind of specific version of the presynaptic facilitation that they had observed in the abdominal ganglion's giant cell (a facilitation that would occur only when the axon terminals of the weak pathway had recently been invaded by a spike) or to "appropriate convergence and divergence in a complex neural circuitry." Back in Massachusetts and later on in New York, Kandel and several of his colleagues tried to replicate these experiments and extend the analysis of the first possibility. The results they got, though, were always ambiguous. They never produced any data for which they could completely rule out "appropriate convergence and divergence" as an alternative explanation, and finally came to the conclusion that if a mechanism for an activity-dependent gating of presynaptic facilitation did exist, it probably wasn't all that important. That mechanism had been replaced in their minds by a model for associative conditioning that depended on the temporal summation of converging inputs on a facilitating interneuron.

Today, not surprisingly, Kandel and Tauc's early papers are seen as proof of Kandel's priority for the idea of activity-dependent amplification of presynaptic facilitation and as evidence that this mechanism was always alive in Kandel's lab. There is, however, evidence that could lead to a different conclusion. First, there is the review of simple models of learning written in the late sixties by Irving Kupfermann and Harold Pinsker, two of Kandel's colleagues, in which the authors conclude that "data at the present do not support the hypothesis of specific presynaptic facilitation" but do support mechanisms based on nonspecific facilitation (that is, convergence on an interneuron leading to facilitation). Second, there is Kandel's treatment of the hypothesis of specific presynaptic facilitation in key grant proposals. At several points in a proposal to the Office of Naval Research for a grant for $763,000, Kandel diagrams and outlines their hypothesis for a mechanism based on convergence on a facilitating interneuron. He calls this hypothesis "particularly attractive." The alternative hypothesis of specific presynaptic facilitation is mentioned only very briefly. It is discussed as a type of facilitation that "has not thus far been described anywhere in the nervous system." This proposal was signed by Kandel on March 19, 1982, a week after Terry Walters had finished the experiments that eventually went into his *Science* article and over a month after Abrams called Walters.

I've met Eric Kandel only once—and just briefly. It was in February of 1984, during my first few months of research on this book. After an exchange of letters with Kandel, I had come into New York to interview Jimmy Schwartz, Kandel's close collaborator and friend of many years. We had a long and wide-ranging conversation, and when we were finished talking, Schwartz walked me down the hall to the elevator. On the way we bumped into Kandel, a short man with longish, graying hair and an immensely benign expression. He was wearing a white lab coat.

"Don't worry, Eric," Schwartz had called out to Kandel as we approached. "She's sweet and she's smart."

I was so flattered by the last part of Schwartz's statement (the adjectives were, in fact, the same ones that I would have used to describe Schwartz) that it was a while before I thought to be puzzled by the first. What did Kandel have to be worried about? Probably, it was just the idea of a layperson writing a book about a very complex and technical field of research. Or perhaps Kandel did not want the hostilities in the field—his well-known enmity with Alkon—to be made even more public.

Kandel didn't acknowledge Schwartz's comment. Instead, he gave me a quizzical look and asked to be reminded of who I was and what I was there for. I told him again about my intention of writing a book and requested time for an interview. He asked me to leave my name with his secretary; he would give me a call one weekend.

That was in the middle of February. I didn't hear from Kandel for three months. Then, on May 15, a day after I had spoken to Tom Abrams and a week after my conversation with Terry Walters, my phone rang sometime after ten in the evening. It was Kandel, and my first, naive thought was that I was finally going to get my interview even at this inconvenient hour. He soon made it clear, though, in his congenial, accented voice, that this was not the reason for his call. He had been "called into the fray" by his colleagues, he told me. Over the past few days, he said, he had received calls for help from several investigators who felt that I was a provocateur, a reporter who was interested only in the more prurient aspects of science.

It was obvious from what Kandel said that one of those he had talked with was Tom Abrams. Terry Walters was another. Dan Alkon, Kandel said, was a third. I interrupted Kandel's obloquy to say, "Dr. Kandel, I just can't believe that Dan Alkon called you about me."

"No," he admitted, "I initiated that one myself."

The conversation went on for about an hour and a half. Kandel repeated the charge that I was intentionally provoking scientists and interested only in the episcience. He went on to make some other observations:

"We all feel that you're not doing the field any good. . . . You're leaving divisiveness behind you. . . ."

"You aren't going to get anyone to cooperate with you. . . ."

"If you want to write about science, I'd be glad to help you, but if you want to write about scientists, you'll get no assistance. . . ."

"You're not doing science a service to talk about such trivial aspects of it as competition. . . ."

"What right did you have to come into my lab and interview my postdocs? How would you like it if I came into your home and interviewed your children? . . ."

"I didn't volunteer for this. I don't receive government funding which would make me participate. . . ." (Apparently, Kandel was referring to the fact that he is now funded by the Howard Hughes Medical Institute. At the time of our conversation, though, he was still receiving at least $250,000 a year from the government; during the time that his lab had been working on the research in question, he had been receiving some $650,000 in government support a year.)

"It's silly to talk about who had activity dependent facilitation first. It was a magnificient piece of research that was presented back-to-back. . . ."

I was stunned, but I reiterated that it wasn't my intention to write a gossipy treatment of the research in his field and pointed out that my questions about laboratory politics and competition represented only a very small part of any interview. Eventually, we hung up on an unresolved note. Kandel left me with the ultimatum that unless I agreed to write a book that was purely about science, he wouldn't give me any cooperation. I told him I would think about our conversation and get back to him. A little over a week later, I wrote him a letter stating my resolve to stick to my original intention—namely, to write a book in which both science and scientists would play a part—and expressing the hope that he would participate in it. I did not receive an answer. Later, I requested some reprints from his lab; they were never sent.

Though I was disturbed by Kandel's suggestion that none of the investigators in the field were going to cooperate with me, I didn't have long in which to ponder whether this extremely diverse group of investigators would indeed close ranks around Kandel. About a week after my late-night conversation with Kandel, I got a long letter from Terry Walters that confirmed and enlarged upon our previous talk (and the only letter I have ever received that contained a two-page bibliography).

Walters had gone back over his lab books and records to check the dates of the incidents and experiments he had told me about. He said he did not in any way want to diminish the contributions of Eric Kandel and his colleagues to the development of the activity-dependent neuromodulation model of associative learning. (The name of the mechanism is one of the issues in this priority dispute. Kandel's group calls this phenomenon activity-dependent amplification of presynaptic facilitation; Byrne and Walters, activity-dependent neuromodulation. The name that comes into general use will indicate in whose lab the idea is thought to have originated.) But Walters hoped it was clear that he and Byrne had obtained the first compelling experimental support for the model.

The first compelling evidence, yes, though it is impossible to say definitely who would have published that evidence first, barring Abrams's call to Walters. That, of course, would have depended on the pace at which Abrams would have proceeded in his work unprodded by any knowledge of Walters's data and on the speed with which Walters would have gotten his paper into print. All that can be said with near certainty is that the phone call prompted Kandel's lab to shift into high gear. At best, this resulted in the two labs' sharing credit for a discovery for which Walters *might* otherwise have had all or most of the credit. At worst, the size and reputation of the Columbia lab, as well as the fact that the two papers by Kandel's group in *Science* preceded the one by Walters and Byrne, has inevitably led to the perception that Kandel's lab deserves the lion's share of the credit.

The importance of this issue to Walters can be understood only in the context of the structure and norms of science. In one of his best-known essays, Robert Merton addressed the question of why priority disputes in science are so numerous and so heated. Is it, Merton wondered, because of an egotism in human nature or of one peculiar to scientists? Since the disputes often involve people whose dispositions are ordinarily modest, he thought not. A better explanation, he suggested, is that the norms of science exert pressure on investigators to promote their own claims. "On every side, a scientist is reminded that it is his role to advance knowledge, and his happiest fulfillment of that role is to advance knowledge greatly,"

Merton wrote. "Originality is at a premium in science for it is through originality in greater or smaller increments, that knowledge advances."

Walters talked and wrote to me, then, because as a scientist it was his job to assert his claim to priority and because it is only through original insights, large and small, that scientists build their reputation, gain recognition, and receive the resources necessary to continue their research. The investigators in the field of invertebrate learning find it important to remember whose idea it was to shock a snail on its tail rather than on its head and who was the first to use random control groups in testing snails for learning; next to these contributions, the discovery of the mechanism that lies behind the formation of a new association has the importance of the discovery of a new continent. It's little wonder that Walters would not want to let the credit for this discovery slip by. But he also talked to Kandel about our conversation because he was afraid that an attempt to press his claims might boomerang and because he still feels tremendous loyalty and affection for his former mentor.

"I want to make it absolutely clear that I love and respect Eric," Walters told me on the day we first talked. "He had an enormous stake in this. The idea had circulated around in his lab, but unfortunately, there were established interests that fought it. I don't want Eric to think I'm badmouthing him, but he knows me well enough to know that I have no compunction in telling the story as I see it. I don't see him as a villain, but I do see him as having a very large stake in this and not wanting what should be his finest hour and the culmination of a tremendous amount of investigation snatched out from under his nose by some whippersnapper who happened to have the idea first."

Merton's thesis enabled me to put Kandel's telephone call

in a better perspective, particularly in his description of the resistance of scientists to studies of multiple or simultaneous discoveries and priority disputes—studies that Merton viewed as important because of what they could reveal about the workings of social and cultural processes in the advancement of science. "Even to assemble the facts of the case," Merton wrote in a chapter on multiple discoveries and priority in his book *The Sociology of Science*, "is to be charged with blemishing the record of undeniably great men of science; as though one were a raker of muck that a gentleman would pass by in silence. Even more, to investigate the subject systematically is to be regarded not merely as a muckraker, but as a muckmaker."

Merton attributed this resistance (a recurrent pattern of denial characterized by scientists' constant attempts to dismiss as trivial matters of undeniable importance) to the fact that the social institution of science incorporates potentially incompatible values: that of originality, which leads scientists to want their priority to be recognized, and that of humility, which leads scientists to insist on how little they have in fact been able to accomplish. The tension between these values, he held, creates an inner conflict among those men and women of science who have internalized both of them, generating a distinct resistance to the systematic study of science. This tension may have been operating in Kandel, but I think it likely that he also resisted my inquiries about the simultaneous publications in *Science* because the discoveries in those papers were not, in fact, totally independent.

If Kandel did perceive Walters's work as a threat and acted accordingly, his reactions might be fairly typical of scientists. As Merton found, there are certainly many examples of questionably simultaneous discoveries; there are also numerous well-known incidents in which senior scientists received the credit for discoveries made by their postdocs. Part of the problem, then, is not that this kind of behavior exists but that its existence is not sufficiently recognized and, therefore, is not factored into the structure of science. One result of this is that when an incident like the one involving Walters and Kandel occurs, the "injured" party has no means of recourse that might not backfire on him, for the person he accuses of doing wrong may well be the same person who reviews his next grant application.

Not all scientists deny the existence of bias and proprietary feelings. Some cheerfully admit that scientists are no more objective than anybody else. An editor of a prominent scientific journal told me that he recognizes that referees may be biased in their opinions and, therefore, has the policy that a scientist submitting a paper may request that it not be reviewed by X, Y, or Z, no questions asked. More often, though, these less rational aspects of science are either trivialized or denied. On one level, of course, competition, priority disputes, rivalry, and animosities between labs *are* trivial; however, it would be disingenuous to deny that they can play an important role in what research gets funded, whose papers are published, who gets credit for a discovery, how research is disseminated, and whether or not it is readily accepted.

Since the joint publication in *Science,* Kandel's resources have continued to snowball, and in the beginning of 1984 the Howard Hughes Medical Institute formed the Columbia-based Institute of Molecular Biology, with Kandel as its senior investigator. Like the fourteen other Howard Hughes Medical Institutes around the country, this one is funded with dividends from the Hughes Aircraft Company (of which the Howard Hughes Medical Institute is the sole owner). Kandel's institute is estimated to receive more than $6 million a year, money that supports—besides Kandel—two full investigators, eleven

associate investigators, twenty-two technicians, and four oper-
ators of the mariculture facility in Woods Hole. To put this in
some perspective, the average NIH individual research grant
(which supports, typically, one senior investigator, a junior
investigator, one postdoc, and a technician) runs $100,000 a
year. Large project grants from NIH average about $600,000.
Kandel's level of funding is about one-fifth of the National
Institute of Mental Health's entire basic-neuroscience expen-
ditures in 1984. This level of support allows him to achieve an
incredibly detailed level of analysis; it also means that he can
send more postdocs to meetings, produce more results, publish
more papers, and impress more scientists, in and outside of
this growing tip of science, with his particular view of the
elephant.

TEN

A Scientific Melee

ON THE DAY BEFORE Jimmy Schwartz and I talked, Schwartz, a tall, skinny man, who wears black, thick-rimmed glasses that enhance the natural seriousness of his expression, had been interviewed for a television talk show. When I arrived at his lab, he was still upset by the experience; he thought he had done badly. "They asked me to justify myself," Schwartz told me. "They wanted to know how my work would help to improve human memory, but they didn't want me to use any technical terms—not even *molecules*. All I could say was 'I don't know.' "

Although the basic qualities of a good scientist—tenacity, originality, respect for the truth—are probably the same as they have always been, scientists today must also be good at grantsmanship, administration, giving lectures, and presenting their work simply and convincingly to the public so as to "justify" themselves. Given the inherent complexity of much biological research (two scientists in related fields, let alone a layperson and a scientist, may have trouble understanding each other), this isn't an enviable task. Scientists must bridge not only the gulfs in technical knowledge but also the wide gulf between the practice of science and the public's perception of the practice of science.

Scientists know that knowledge is in a state of constant flux, that basic research is a gamble, a real hit-and-miss, fumbling-about-in-the-dark affair that usually proceeds at a snail's pace, but somehow they haven't yet succeeded in getting this across to the public. Perhaps, for fear of alarming those who fund them, they haven't tried as hard as they might have. Instead, most have opted for two sets of explanations—one for scientists and another for laypersons. The one for a lay audience is their "story," a blurb about the importance and clinical relevance of their work that bears about as much resemblance to the actual research as an elephant to a flea. The same is usually true of the obligatory paragraph in grant proposals relating to human applications of the research.

"It's all part of grantsmanship," Paul O'Lague, a neurobiologist at UCLA, explained to me. "For government grants, you need to put in one paragraph about human applications; in a proposal to the American Cancer Institute, you would expand that paragraph to maybe two or three. You write it, but it has nothing to do with how you're thinking about your experiments or how you will go about your work. There's nothing terrible or deceptive about it; it's just above and beyond the practice of science, which is to reveal something about how the world works."

This is not to say that basic research cannot have clinical applications and potentially enormous benefits for mankind. It does. Basic research on the brain, for instance, led to the use of L-dopa in the treatment of Parkinson's disease, to an understanding of the cause of the devastating muscular disease myasthenia gravis, and to treatments for several kinds of mental depression. Given the current focus on the brain, many more such advances are certainly in the offing. These clinical spin-offs are pretty rare, though, considering the large number of labs doing basic research on the brain, and a fundamental reality of basic research is the unpredictability of its outcome. Some work will go nowhere; some will provide limited but accurate information about the natural world; a very small proportion will be of real importance either to scientists' view of the brain or in the treatment of human disease. According to at least some sociologists of science, though, that broad layer of inconsequential work is needed in part because a mass of scientists working on the problems that interest them (and in which they can interest funding agencies) helps attract the best students to research.

Furthermore, basic research doesn't operate in the kind of time frames that most of us are used to. Clinical applications from a particular field of research may seem decades away, then suddenly become practical overnight, or they may seem imminent yet never materialize. When insulin was finally isolated in 1922, for example, it looked like the cure for diabetes. Since then, daily injections of insulin have succeeded in controlling blood glucose levels in diabetic patients, but—sadly—such control had failed to prevent the terrible complications of diabetes that eventually lead to blindness and early death.

In the field of research into the cellular basis of learning and memory, applications for improving memory in humans could also be very far off or just around the corner. One treatment might be something as simple and inexpensive as one-a-day calcium tablets; others might be much more sophisticated. But while the discovery of ways to improve memory is of critical importance to the estimated three to four million Americans with memory impairment, it is not, of course, the only goal of this research—or even the most important goal of the researchers involved. Their main objective is to find out how animals learn and store memories (those things which, it can be argued, form the basis of our individuality) and to begin to address the question of how the brain generates mind. Along the way, their research might have clinical applications, as well as a profound effect on physicians and psychiatrists (not to mention laymen) who tend to think that some mental illnesses are due to actual, physical abnormalities in the brain while others are not.

Psychiatrists still make a distinction between mental illnesses that are "organic," ones with such obvious structural impairments as Alzheimer's disease, and illnesses that are "functional," or "nonorganic," the various depressive syndromes, neuroses, and schizophrenia, for example. But this distinction stems from studies in the nineteenth century, when physicians examined the brains of patients at autopsy and found a disturbance of the brain's architecture in some diseases and a lack of disturbance in others. Now it is clear that any such division is based on our ability to detect physical abnormalities in the brain—not on reality. It's pretty easy to link someone's mental condition to a physical abnormality when a large piece of brain is missing, but not so easy when all that has gone awry is one type of receptor in the nerve cell membrane or—as is strongly suspected to be the case for schizophrenia—one of the brain's many neurotransmitters.

As Kandel said in a lecture he gave to the Harvard Club of Boston in 1978, "Ultimately, all psychologic disturbances reflect specific alterations in neuronal and synaptic function." Or as he wrote in the *Principles of Neural Science,* a textbook he edited with Jimmy Schwartz, "Everything that occurs in the brain—from the most private to the most social thoughts—represents organic (biological) processes. We do not yet have the tools to demonstrate complex ideas and feelings on the cellular level, but the pace of neurobiological research is quickening."

He once explained this somewhat facetiously to a reporter for *Columbia,* the magazine of Columbia University. "As I talk to you and you listen to me," he said, "the cells in my brain are having a direct effect on the cells in your brain. What's more, the effect could be longlasting. So don't talk to strangers. It can produce entirely unwanted effects on your synapses."

Though there are continuing tensions between those who would give biological and those who would give psychological explanations of the brain (much the same tensions, in fact, that existed when Kandel made his switch from psychiatry to basic research in the 1960s), Kandel tries to stay in touch with the psychiatric community. His basic message is one that he outlined in his lecture to the Harvard Club: "The simplistic but perhaps useful idea that the ultimate level of resolution for understanding how psychotherapeutic intervention works is identical with the level at which we are currently seeking to understand how psychopharmacologic intervention works—the level of individual nerve cells and their synaptic connections."

"And insofar as psychotherapy works," Kandel said later in the same lecture, "it works by acting on brain functions, not on single synapses, but on synapses nevertheless."

Despite any talk about the possibility of a Nobel Prize in this field (and despite the open secret that Kandel has been nominated for the Nobel Prize), research into the cellular and molecular basis of learning and memory is, as we have seen, still very much in its infancy.

"Most of what there is to learn about learning," remarked one investigator in the field, "remains to be learned." The research will continue to progress, therefore, and as it progresses, two stories will bear watching.

One is the straight scientific story (if there is such a thing). This is the story of how the research of Kandel, Alkon, Sahley, Gelperin, Walters, and Davis, among others, will turn out and how the models of learning developed in different labs will come to answer the questions that the many different disciplines of biology bring to bear on learning.

Biochemists interested in the biochemistry of learning, for instance, will want to know much more about the phosphorylation of channel proteins and the kinetics of the phosphorylation reaction; from Kandel's model, they will want to know exactly how calcium amplifies the cyclic AMP cascade. Neuroanatomists, on the other hand, will be interested in whether there are anatomical correlates of learning, changes in the structure of nerve cells (a decrease in synaptic terminals, for example) that parallel changes in synaptic effectiveness. Molecular biologists will want to know, as Jimmy Schwartz puts it, what happens to a neuron when it remembers for a long time—Is a new gene expressed, a new molecule made? How are the pairing-specific changes observed by Kandel and Alkon turned into long-term behavioral changes? In Kandel's model, it looks as if *Aplysia*'s short-term memory might be represented by the time in which the level of cyclic AMP is increased—about twenty minutes. But what happens then? It makes sense that long-term memory isn't encoded in a permanent increase in the level of cyclic AMP since that small molecule is important to a number of different cell functions, so the question is how the transient increase in cyclic AMP is translated into some relatively permanent change. One of the possibilities Kandel and Schwartz will examine is that long-term memory involves a specific change in gene expression and that the short-term changes somehow induce the expression of a different gene, resulting in the manufacturing of a new class of regulatory subunits for the protein kinase responsible for phosphorylating potassium channels. The new subunit, they hypothesize, enables the phosphorylating enzyme to now work at normal levels of cyclic AMP. Alkon hasn't really addressed the relation between long-term and short-term memory, but certainly nothing in his model rules out a similar kind of change brought about not by cyclic AMP but by calcium.

Learning psychologists like Chris Sahley will be intrigued by the relation between short-term and long-term learning, but for them, the central questions will be how the models developed by Kandel and Alkon can be made to account for the many known features of associative learning—schedules of reinforcement, interstimulus intervals, extinction, blocking, and so on. The complete answers to these questions are still very far off, but there are hints that Kandel's and Alkon's models will have some provocative things to say. In Kandel's model, for instance, it's possible that the maximum interval between the conditioned and the unconditioned stimuli is a reflection of the amount of time in which the level of free intracellular calcium is increased: if the unconditioned stimulus doesn't arrive during that time, the association won't be made. Alkon's model, on the other hand, is particularly well suited to account for contingency, the fact that the pairing of two events is not enough to produce an association: one event must come to predict another. It is now well known that, during associative training, presentations of an unconditioned stimulus alone degrade the learning. *Hermissenda* provides a very simple answer for why this happens. In these snails, presentations of rotation alone during training act, in effect, as a reset mechanism. Rotation by itself hyperpolarizes the Type B cells, reversing the long-lasting depolarization that results from pairing light and rotation.

At the same time, cognitive psychologists will be interested in the physiological trace left by learning, proof for their long-held assertion that the mind is not just an elaborate web of stimulus / response arcs but, rather, has content, some sort of internal or mental representation of the outside world. And what, in the words of cognitive psychologists, might be the content of the learned association? Jimmy Schwartz's answer for *Aplysia* is probably simplistic, and it sounds downright anticlimactic unless taken in the context of the debate between the behaviorists and the cognitivists and in the context of an entire nervous system with many thousands of cells capable of similar internal representations that act in consort and are, in turn, modified by a complex level of neuromodulation. "Biochemists are now showing that internal representations do exist," Schwartz told me. " A single neuron in *Aplysia* encodes the whole world in its level of cyclic AMP."

The scientific story will also be the story of whether any of the mechanisms found in snails operate in other animals. Vertebrate neurophysiologists will continue to question whether the work in snails has anything to do with human learning, to maintain a certain skeptical distance. At the same time, in Alkon's and Kandel's labs, the search for generality is on. Both Alkon and Kandel have started working with vertebrates (Alkon with rabbits and Kandel with cats) and looking for neurophysiological or biochemical features that would bolster their hopes that the mechanisms they have unearthed will be of general importance. Both are also citing evidence from other animals—vertebrates and invertebrates—to indicate that this might indeed be so. In Kandel's corner is the work on fruit fly learning mutants in which it has been shown that the learning defects of several different learning mutants involve the cyclic AMP cascade, as well as the evidence that activity-dependent neuromodulation operates in the mammalian hippocampus. Moreover, large areas of the mammalian brain seem tailor-made to accommodate Kandel's mechanism. Two types of cell systems in the brain (groups of neurons that use the same neurotransmitter)—the noradrenergic and serotonergic cell systems—

branch widely and diffusely in the cerebral cortex, creating what some have referred to as a cortical sprinkler system. Activation of these systems might alter the attentiveness or retentiveness of large areas of the brain at once, possibly providing a basis for presynaptic facilitation and associative learning in mammals.

Alkon, on his part, has pointed to studies indicating that some cells in the mammalian cortex share important biophysical features with *Hermissenda*'s photoreceptors. Especially important are similarities with some of the cells of the hippocampus. (This structure of the brain came accidentally to be known to be important to memory when William Scoville, a Yale University neurosurgeon, removed it from a patient suffering from epilepsy some thirty years ago. The operation was a success in that the patient, now known as H.M. and said to be the most studied patient in the history of neurobiology, no longer experienced epileptic fits, but it was, overall, a disaster. H.M. recovered with his presurgery memories intact, but he was completely unable to lay down any new memories. He is able to remember the names of the political leaders during World War II but unable to remember a conversation he has had just ten minutes earlier. This type of operation was never repeated, but it forged a still-unclear link, strengthened by subsequent research, between the hippocampus and memory formation.) The features that *Hermissenda*'s photoreceptors share with some hippocampal cells are long afterpotentials and large increases in intracellular calcium following excitation. Not surprisingly, Alkon and some of his colleagues began looking in the hippocampus of rabbits for learning-associated changes.

That was in the spring of 1984. Within a year, Alkon (who is so astonished by his most recent success that, in his forties, he says that he "can retire now") was reported to have found learning-associated changes in hippocampal cells in rabbits and to have determined that the cause of those changes was the reduction of a particular potassium current in those cells. What has Alkon flying over the moon is that this is the same potassium current that changes in *Hermissenda*'s Type B photoreceptors when those snails learn to associate rotation and light. These findings are controversial, and the whole picture is still far from complete, but they give a weight to Alkon's *Hermissenda* model that, just a few years ago, not many scientists would have believed possible.

At the same time, the issue of generality also concerns what generalities can be extracted from this research so far. The differences between Kandel's and Alkon's models are in fact outweighed in significance by the similarities. Both models involve the phosphorylation of potassium channels (albeit different potassium channels) and second-messenger systems (calcium in Alkon's; cyclic AMP in Kandel's), and in both learning occurs in preexisting circuits and close to the input end.

As Jack Davis said, "We didn't know these things before; they might just be true generally."

Chip Quinn noted, "It starts to make sense out of the fact that nerve cells can have up to five different kinds of potassium channels but only one type of sodium channel." It seems apparent now that nerve cells go to such trouble to regulate and modulate their potassium conductance because potassium is very important in regulating a nerve cell's behavior. And if potassium conductances are a key to memory, the existence of up to five different potassium conductances in a cell suggests that there may be several different mechanisms of learning. Perhaps most of these conductances are subject to modification and in a number of different combinations.

What about the fact that in Kandel's model, sensitization is a building block of associative learning, while in Alkon's,

the evidence indicates that sensitization and associative learning may be different phenomena with different underlying
mechanisms? No one really knows what to make of this. Perhaps a fuller understanding of the mechanisms underlying sensitization and associative learning in *Hermissenda* will reveal
a connection, or perhaps among the different kinds of learning
there are some that build on sensitization and some that don't.
Since sensitization is a form of arousal and is related to attention, it's interesting that vertebrate neurobiologists—thanks to
their work with human amnesiacs like H.M.—have evidence
that learning can be classified into two broad types: "fact" or
"declarative" learning, which is involved in the conscious
learning of explicit information like dates, names, and faces,
and "skill" or "procedural" memory, which is concerned with
less-conscious learning, ranging from simple motor skills to
certain types of strategic problem-solving behavior. It's tempting to speculate, therefore, that Kandel's type of learning is of
the declarative type and that in declarative learning a certain
minimal level of sensitization, arousal, or attention is required;
Alkon's learning, on the other hand, might be more procedural
and less dependent on arousal.

Alkon, though, is unwilling even to speculate along these
lines; he continues to laugh at the very idea that sensitization
could have anything to do with learning. "Being sensitized is
the equivalent of taking a cold shower," he says. "What does
a cold shower have to to with learning?" Yet to other investigators, Kandel's findings regarding the relation between associative learning and sensitization ring very true.

"My feeling without any evidence is that sensitization is
the key to associative learning; I've never seen an animal that
doesn't sensitize first before it goes into associative learning,"
Chris Sahley told me. "The first step to forming an association
is becoming more aroused when that stimulus is around. Ani-

mals normally habituate to stimuli, but sensitization prevents them from habituating. It sets the stage so that an animal can learn an association.''

Terry Walters, in fact, calls his mechanism of activity-dependent neuromodulation a mechanism for ''conditioned attention,'' a way in which animals can learn to pay attention to a particular stimulus. Beyond that, he says, it may also be a mechanism useful in forming a conditioned association between a sensory stimulus and a particular motivational state. ''What you have to do to learn most anything,'' says Walters, ''is to pay attention. That act of paying attention is really a form of arousal, and it might involve mechanisms that are similar to the ones that we think explain learning in *Aplysia*. When you pay attention you may have a diffuse release of neuromodulator throughout the brain. When this neuromodulator arrives at the same time as input from a particular sensory source, an association might be formed.''

But while this might explain, for instance, why someone remembers that she was raking leaves when she learned that President Kennedy had been shot—the state of arousal caused by the news has fixed the moment in her mind—it does not begin to explain why you think of raking leaves when you think of the day of President Kennedy's assassination but do not think of President Kennedy every time you rake leaves.

''We have a great mechanism for explaining why something occurs when an animal is aroused and why it doesn't when it is not,'' continued Walters. ''That is a very large step towards explaining associative learning, and under the umbrella of this mechanism, we can begin to study why sequence and timing is important, why one stimulus might block or overshadow another. The model still has a long way to go, though, to fully explain many such aspects of learning as recall or forgetting.''

The scientific story, then, will tell how investigators in different laboratories fill in their currently sketchy models, on the one hand, while continuing to do battle with other investigators in the field over their most basic assumptions, on the other. This scientific free-for-all in which each researcher pushes his or her own piece of the truth and scientific intuitions is hottest at the center of the field. The skirmish lines change as new results become known, but the scuffle will go on long after the work of one investigator or another is generally accepted by other scientists.

And while the direction of research in any lab will be influenced by the issues being tossed about in this scientific melee, it can also be greatly affected by events external to the immediate field, by technical developments that change the ground rules of this research. (For example, scientists are now working on means by which they can measure the voltage changes in many cells at once using voltage sensitive dyes rather than microelectrodes.) Even climatic events can have dramatic effects. Since El Niño, the sudden meteorological change that warmed the waters off California several years ago, *Pleurobranchaea,* the large carnivorous snail that Jack Davis uses in his research, has been extremely difficult to find. It is thought that the snails have taken to deeper and cooler waters and are now out of reach of the trawlers' nets; unless the situation changes soon, Davis's research of the past fifteen years, as well as the work of his many students who have continued working with *Pleurobranchaea* in their own labs, may come to premature halt.

Something else that might affect this research is a shift in what might be called the ruling paradigm of brain science. When Kandel first began his research, radical reductionism and a cellular localizationist view were very much in the ascendancy. Although they remain dominant, there are now signs that the prevailing scientific view of how the brain works is once again changing. Penfield's operation on epileptics, the results of which greatly promoted localizationism in the fifties, are now themselves undergoing reinterpretation. Scientists are beginning to ask such questions as whether the events recalled by Penfield's patients really happened and whether the fact that local stimulation of the brain brings forth these specific recollections means that the memories are actually stored in the cells of those discrete sites. Might not those sites just be important in eliciting memories that are stored much more widely?

Like much of the research on the brain performed in the last twenty-five years, the invertebrate-learning work is founded on a cellular localizationist view, which assumes, among other things, that the properties of nervous systems are the properties of nerve cells, that nervous systems are organized in such a way that information proceeds through them serially—through a chain of transmission. That there is extensive parallel processing of information, especially in vertebrate brains, the cellular localizationists will readily admit, but they make the assumption that even complex processing is at least theoretically subject to analysis on the basis of a complete knowledge of all the cells and circuits involved.

This view led to startling insights into how nervous systems work—Hubel and Wiesel's research on the processing of visual information, for example—but it runs into trouble when taken to its logical conclusion. If serial transmission is the basis of nervous systems, the processing of sensory information takes place when the groups of sensory neurons that are activated by, for instance, the sight of a familiar face in turn activate a smaller and smaller number of central neurons, until they reach the cell or small number of cells that "know." Grandmother cells, they are called, because this theory's implication that there is a cell specifically designed to respond to each and every complex set of stimuli, including the face of one's grandmother. The problem with this theory is that it implies a one-to-one relation between a neuron (or a small set of neurons) and a certain perceptual component—for example, recognition of one's grandmother or remembering a certain melody. However, if you isolated one of these neurons in a dish and stimulated it, would you get perception?

"The answer, of course, is no," says Rodolpho Llinás, one advocate of what he calls a new reductionism. Like cellular reductionism, this approach to the brain assumes that brain mechanisms account for brain functions, but it proposes that the important properties of nervous systems are those that emerge from the activity of large numbers of nerve cells (not the properties of individual cells themselves) and that information reaches the brain not as a result of a chain of transmission but as a pattern of nerve activity created by hundreds of thousands of parallel fibers firing simultaneously. "Even the most eager supporter of 'grandmother neurons,' " continues Llinás, "understands that making the activation of a particular cell necessary and sufficient for the generation of a perception is most unsatisfactory because it leaves the question of the observer (the 'I') not understood."

Llinás and others also criticize the idea that the brain is serially organized, because that would mean that the nervous system is both easy to disrupt and slow. "Yet we know," Llinás once told a scientific symposium, "that the brain can survive diffuse damage, and we know from simple perceptual experiments that it takes about an equal amount of time for us to know whether the person in a photograph is someone we know or don't know. If the nervous system were organized serially, it would take longer to determine that we do not know someone (to get to the end of the file!)." We would, in other words, have to check all of the cells, corresponding to all of the people we know, before we could say that we did not know the person in the photograph. This process, of course, would take longer than finding the right cell—the cell that recognized the person—but we know from experience that it doesn't. It takes about the same length of time for us either to recognize or not to recognize the person in the picture.

"A lot of people still think that we can understand the nervous system by understanding single cells," Llinás explained to me during one of our conversations at Woods Hole, "but there are limitations to the single-cell approach—the fact that you can never fall into the brain and say that is the cell that is me. The question is how is it that I can feel if single cells cannot feel. The answer is probably that the important properties of nervous systems are not the properties of neurons. They are the emergent properties of neurons. So Kandel and Alkon are trying to sell something that can't be sold, and that is that they are working with simple systems. No nervous system is simple. They all must solve basically the same set of problems."

As Jack Davis, who uses a cellular reductionist approach in his research but is skeptical about how far radical reductionism will take us, explains it, "Just as water is an emergent property of the gases hydrogen and oxygen, so personality and other higher-order phenomena of brains are an emergent property of cells. And just as you can never understand water waves by understanding the hydrogen atom, you may never be able to understand personality by looking at single cells. The question is just how far you can take the reductionist approach."

It is hard to say how this emerging appreciation of the limitations of single cells will affect Kandel's and Alkon's field of research, but it will certainly promote a healthy skepticism toward any claims to a full explanation of learning on the basis of the changes that investigators find in a handful of cells in a nervous system whose cells number in the thousands. It also means that we will probably never "have the tools to demonstrate complex ideas and feelings on the cellular level." The point is not that Kandel, Alkon, and others should change their approach—which in the field of learning, as elsewhere, is continuing to turn up valuable new information—but, perhaps, that we should expect that this approach to the brain, like many previous ones, will one day run up against a brick wall in its attempt to fully explain the phenomena of the brain within the context of existing assumptions. At that point, investigators guided by different assumptions about the brain will begin trying to understand the ways of this organ by means of new approaches and new techniques.

Meanwhile, the second story to watch as research into the cellular and molecular basis of learning and memory progresses is intimately tied up with the first. This is the story of the ebb and flow of reputations, of how scientific loyalties form and reform as new investigators come into the field or as postdocs move out from under the wing of their sponsors (out of the magic circle, as Harold Pinsker says) and form labs of their own. This is the story of whether Dan Alkon will get the recognition that he feels he deserves, and, if so, whether he will continue to be as prickly and arrogant; of who will get credit for the mechanism of activity-dependent neuromodulation; and of whether Kandel will indeed win a Nobel Prize. This is also the story of how investigators will handle the scrutiny of their field by an outsider and of how they will continue to cope with the mortality of their research, with the reality that soon after a scientific model comes into being, it is modified and revised by the work of others. Most scientists accept this remodeling as the normal course of things. It is why the French physiologist Claude Bernard said that a "big humility" is needed in science. Even if some investigators might like to resist the shifting sands of science, most do not have the means to do so.

In his preface to *The Double Helix,* James Watson wrote, "That is not to say that all science is done in the manner described here. This is far from the case, for styles of scientific research vary almost as much as human personalities. On the other hand, I do not believe that the way DNA came out constitutes an odd exception to a scientific world complicated by the contradictory pulls of ambition and the sense of fair play."

Here, then, is another episode in science, showing a whole different set of scientific styles. This account is far from complete, but it shows the world of science to be a place quite different from what most people imagine it to be. It is not a bad place (certainly the scientists who people it are as dedicated and hardworking as a group of people can be), but like most human creations it is imperfect, and ideas are judged there not only on their merit but also on the prestige and academic affiliation of the person who proposes them. The world of science is also a lot less ordered and rational than might be expected. Science advances, it seems, less through scientific consensus than by means of a scientific melee, a free-for-all in which every scientist pushes his or her piece of the truth, knowing that only time will tell which piece best fits reality. For neuroscientists, this reality is a particularly elusive one, consisting as it does of billions of tangled nerve cells, a long list of chemical substances synthesized and used by brains, and the many diverse ionic channels that give neurons the ability to make action potentials and the music of synaptic transmission. The equipment and techniques that neuroscientists employ are increasingly sophisticated, but they are still trying to perceive this elusive reality with senses almost as limited as the blind man's four.

Index